THE MOSQUITO BITES

A MYSTERY NOVEL

By James R. Frazee

The Mosquito Bites
A Mystery Novel
Copyright © 2016 by James R. Frazee

All rights reserved. No part of this publication may be reproduced, distributed, or transmitted in any form or by any means, including photocopying, recording, or other electronic or mechanical methods, without the prior written permission of the publisher or author, except in the case of brief quotations embodied in critical reviews and certain other noncommercial uses permitted by copyright law.

FICTION

The Mosquito Bites (2016)

The Mosquito Bites is a work of fiction. Names, characters, locations, and incidents are the result of the author's imagination and used as a fiction. Any resemblance to actual events, locations, or persons, living or dead, is entirely coincidental.

NONFICTION

Beginning Bridge by the Numbers (2014)

Quick and Healthy Recipes from the Store (2014)

Library of Congress Control Number: 2016909860
ISBN-13: Paperback: 9781635246360
          PDF: 9781635246377
          ePub: 9781635246384
          Kindle: 9781635246391
          Hardcover

Printed in the United States of America

LitFire LLC
1-800-511-9787
www.litfirepublishing.com
order@litfirepublishing.com

CONTENTS

Chapter 1 1
Chapter 2 9
Chapter 3 17
Chapter 4 21
Chapter 5 27
Chapter 6 31
Chapter 7 35
Chapter 8 41
Chapter 9 53
Chapter 10 59
Chapter 11 69
Chapter 12 79
Chapter 13 89
Chapter 14 97
Chapter 15 103
Chapter 16 111
Chapter 17 119
Chapter 18 125
Chapter 19 135
Chapter 20 141
Chapter 21 145
Chapter 22 151
Chapter 23 161
Chapter 24 167
Chapter 25 173
Chapter 26 183
Chapter 27 193
Chapter 28 201
Chapter 29 209
Chapter 30 217
Chapter 31 225
Chapter 32 231
Chapter 33 239
Chapter 34 249

I would like to dedicate this book to my partner and friend, Kirk L. Nicholson, who has been by my side through the ups and downs for the past forty years. His wit and outlook have been an inspiration to help make me who I am today.

CHAPTER 1

Alex arrived at the building at 8:45 a.m., thirty minutes before the time instructed in his offer letter, to begin the first day of his first job after college. Here he was, a small-town boy starting work in New York City. Who would have thought? Nothing in Minnesota could equal this city in size and pace. But he was up for the challenge. It was the start of his new life. He didn't want to arrive too early to show anticipation, but he also didn't want to arrive late.

Dress code was business casual. For the past eight years, his wardrobe consisted of jeans and sneakers, so he wasn't exactly sure what business casual meant. Searching the Web, he found his answer.

> *Less formal than traditional business wear, but is still intended to give a professional and businesslike impression. typically includes slacks or khakis, dress shirt, open-collar or polo shirt, optional tie or seasonal sport coat, and loafers or dress shoes that cover all or most of the foot.*

That left a lot of room for him to expand his wardrobe once he got his first check. Right now he was living on what little money he had put away and what his parents had given him for graduation. A big chunk of that had gone to pay for the security deposit and first-month rent on his apartment.

He looked at himself in the mirror that hung on the wall in his bedroom. Wearing a pair of wool slacks, light-blue shirt, and black tie shoes, he was sure he fulfilled the definition of business casual.

He measured a little over six feet tall and had strawberry-blond hair that seemed to always stay in place. When he stood naked in front of a mirror, he was satisfied with everything he saw. His chest was well defined and smooth, and he maintained a flat stomach and muscular legs. A strong square chin, perfect teeth, sky-blue eyes, perfect nose, and long dark eyelashes rounded out his face. In college, everyone told him he should be a model or get into the movies. He certainly had the looks, but that was not the choice he wanted in life.

He had developed confidence in himself through school, and it showed in the way he walked and held himself. Yet inside he remained shy around other people. Even going to college in North Carolina hadn't taken the small-town Minnesota boy out of him.

Picking up his knapsack, he headed out the door to the subway station two blocks away. He had practiced the route several times, so he knew exactly where to go. As he rounded the corner where the small twenty-four-hour grocery store stood, he noticed that most of the people on the sidewalk were walking at the same pace to the subway entrance. As they approached the opening to the subway, everyone converged, disappearing into the hole in the ground, Alex among them. Down the hole they all went, to the platform two stories below the city street. The platform was crowded with people, all looking to the left waiting for the train to arrive.

As soon as the train arrived and the doors opened, people pushed their way into the car, not concerned with anyone around them. The goal was to get on the train. The doors closed, and everyone was packed in the car like sardines in a can.

Thank god there are only two stops, Alex thought. *Doing this every day with more than two stops could really get to you.*

No one said a word. Those fortunate enough to get a seat were reading the morning newspaper or occupied with their Kindle or iPad, some listening to music, headphones making them deaf to the noises of the train. Others simply napped. Those standing gripped on to poles to avoid falling as the train raced down the track to the next stop.

The doors opened at the Times Square subway, which is the second stop. Being a major hub in the transit system, most of the people pushed their way out, Alex one of the crowd. People either moved up the stairs to the street, scattering in all directions as they headed to work, or hastened to catch a connecting train. Alex climbed the stairs with the mob, anxious to see the sky and breathe fresh air again. He walked the four blocks to the large sixty-two-story glass-and-steel building on Park Avenue.

The tall glass-and-steel buildings are New York's signature structure. One building right after the other lined the street as far as he could see, each one trying to outdo the others in style and architecture.

Thousands of people report to work each morning in each building, arriving to work from all directions with varying types of transportation: bikes, train, subway, car, bus, skateboard, roller skates, or walking.

Alex entered the lobby through one of the four revolving doors across the front of the building. The lobby was two stories high with floor-to-ceiling windows across the front and two sides. In front in the center of the lobby was a paneled wall with a large display of the company logo and company name, Sterling Chemicals. On either end of this wall were turnstiles with people reporting to work swiftly passing through before disappearing behind the paneled wall. No one smiled; some carried coffee, and some walked like they were still half asleep, but all moved with a purpose.

Alex walked up to a long reception desk where two young women were sitting, each with a security guard standing behind them. "May I help you?" one of the receptions said with a smile.

"This is my first day, and I was told to report here at nine o'clock," Alex said.

"Welcome to Sterling Chemicals. May I see an ID please?"

Alex pulled out his wallet and handed her his driver's license.

Turning to her computer, she punched some keys. She had short brown hair, steel-rimmed glasses, and too much red lipstick for Alex's taste. Her stiff gray uniform didn't have a wrinkle, nor did it show the curves of her body . . . a robot at work.

"Please stand in front of the camera," she said, pointing to a camera attached to her computer monitor.

Alex moved closer to the counter, looked at the camera, and smiled. She turned to her printer, took the visitor's pass with his picture on it out of the printer tray, and handed it to Alex.

"Welcome, Alex Gregory. Please report to Conference Room 1201 located on the twelfth floor. Enter the turnstile on the left, swipe the badge across the reader, and take the elevators behind this wall. Welcome aboard."

He thanked her, took the visitor's pass, and went through the turnstile. There were eight elevators, each going to a different range of floors. Today he was going to the twelfth floor; he wondered which elevator he would be taking tomorrow when he came to work.

He stood in front of the elevator door for floors 12–25 with a group of other employees. No one said a word. Some carried briefcases, some with coffee, but most looked like they were half asleep. Everyone watched the floor numbers flashing above the door as the elevator descended to pick them up.

Alex looked at everyone else waiting for the elevator. Everyone was dressed in business casual. Most of the men carried briefcases, and the women had large purses hanging from their shoulders. He was the only one with a knapsack and felt out of place. The doors opened; and everyone rushed in, wordlessly, just like at the subway. The doors closed, and he was on his way. Here he was, just another sardine in a can.

The doors opened on the twelfth floor. He had to push his way out, his knapsack hitting the people around him.

"Excuse me, excuse me, excuse me." No one paid any attention. The doors closed behind him. He now stood alone in a wide hallway, the walls covered with dark wood paneling, the same wood that was on the walls in the lobby. Two large wooden doors stood open in front of him. A plaque on the wall next to the door with 1201 in gold letters identified this room, the room where Alex starts his new career. Taking a deep breath, he approached the room, not knowing what to expect.

Here we go, he thought. He checked his shirt and pants to make sure that they looked okay, ran his fingers through his hair, and stepped through the door.

The room was large. One wall was covered in windows from floor to ceiling looking out at a building across the street. The other walls had the same wood paneling as in the hallway. A large wooden table ran the length of the room, with leather chairs on both sides. About half of the chairs were already filled. Everyone was dressed in business casual except one guy who wore a suit and tie and looked out of place.

Guess he didn't check the Web site, Alex thought to himself. The guy had removed his suit coat and hung it over the back of his chair in order to try to fit in, but his tie gave him away.

Some people were checking text messages, some were talking on the phone, but most were just sitting looking around, waiting for the day to begin. A few looked up as Alex entered the room.

Alex scanned the table for an empty chair. His eyes stopped on a woman sitting on the other side of the table looking around the room. She sat straight up, her back not even touching the back of the chair, with her hands in her lap. She glanced his way, and he thought he saw a slight smile as their eyes met. He just stood there and stared back for a moment.

He was sure he had never seen a woman so beautiful and also one who looked so confident at the same time. Just then another person entered the room behind him. Alex quickly moved to the empty chair next to the woman before anyone else sat there, trying to appear nonchalant, even though he was nervous and excited at the same time.

"Is anyone sitting here?" Alex asked.

"No."

He quickly sat down, placing his knapsack on the floor next to his chair.

"Hi, I'm Alex Gregory," he said, extending his hand. "I guess we are both new."

"Good morning, Alex. I'm Leslie Sherwood," she replied, taking his hand softly. "That's unusual . . . two first names."

"That's not the first time I've heard that," he said with a smile so as not to offend.

"Get ready for a long and boring orientation session. I've been through these before. They give you all the rules and regulations and forms to fill out. When the day is over, you will have signed your life away."

"Corporate America, here we come," Alex responded, hoping she didn't hear the quiver in his voice.

She smiled back but didn't say a word. Alex looked away even though he wanted to continue looking at her. But if he did, he would probably drool all over himself. He estimated her age to be in the midtwenties, but he was never good at guessing a person's age. She was dressed in a dark-blue suit with an off-white blouse under the jacket. Her hair was a deep mahogany color that hung to her shoulders and matched the color of her eyes. Her features were flawless, her skin smooth. She had a perfect nose and a smile that would melt any heart. It sure affected him. She sat up straight as if she had been to some kind of finishing school.

"Looks like everyone is early," he said, looking at his watch. "Ten minutes to go yet."

"I'm sure being the first day everyone wants to make a good impression. Isn't that why you are here early?" Leslie asked.

Alex smiled with embarrassment. "Yup" was all he could say. He noticed that she had a paper and a pen placed neatly in front of her. He reached into his knapsack and pulled out a notebook, searched for a pen, and placed them on the table before setting the knapsack back on the floor.

He felt like a schoolboy. *Why do I feel like this?* he thought to himself.

"Boy, these are nice chairs. I wouldn't mind having one in my apartment," he said, trying to continue a conversation. "Think they would miss one."

She gave him a smile.

"Hey, I see that there is coffee in the back. I need a cup badly. Can I get you something?" Alex offered.

"No, thank you, Alex, I already have my tea." It was only then that he noticed a cup sitting in front of her on the table.

"Excuse me while I get a cup of coffee."

"No problem. I'll be here when you get back." Again that smile.

Alex got up and went to the back table to get some coffee. He found himself in line behind two other newbies. He looked to see if there were real cups on the table. He only saw paper cups. He hated drinking out of paper cups. They were always too hot and difficult to hold. He mentally noted "bring coffee mug to work tomorrow."

As he returned to his seat, he noticed that Leslie glanced up at him with that infectious smile.

"So where will you be working?" he asked as he sat down, being careful not to spill the coffee.

"I'm an administrative assistant for one of the VPs. How about you?"

"Wow, VIP status. Congratulations. I'm in the marketing area for new products. I assume this is your first day too." Why did he say that? He had already said that. He felt like a fool.

"We've already established that, like everyone else in this room. And don't let the position influence you. I'll probably be making coffee all day for some big shot or making meeting arrangements and doing some filing. I did that before in my previous job. But I wanted to move to the city, and this gave me the opportunity."

"Hey, don't belittle your position. After all, didn't Nancy Reagan run the country?"

"I don't think I'm in the same league. But it might lead to something else later. And as I said, it got me to the city. So here I am."

Alex tried to think of something to say to keep the conversation going. For some reason, he felt she was way out of his league. "I'm glad it got you here," he said, feeling himself blush.

"Are you from New York, Leslie?" he continued.

"No, I grew up in Connecticut and worked for a bank before coming here. What about you? You don't have an East Coast accent."

"I grew up in Minnesota and went to college in North Carolina. I just graduated. This is my first 'real' job."

"Welcome to the real world, Alex Gregory."

"Quite a view out the window," he said, trying to keep a conversation going so he had a reason to look at her. "Eight million people crowded into such a small space. I wonder how long it will take me to get used to it. The packed subways are something I didn't expect."

"You'll get used to them. Expect lines every place you go . . . grocery stores, movie theaters, post office, museums, everywhere. It is part of living here. But then again, you have so much to choose from in the city. Where else can you order dinner from a restaurant at 3:00 a.m. or go to a movie theater where they have twenty-four screens to choose from? As New Yorkers say, if it isn't here, it doesn't exist."

Just then there was a sound of high heels clicking on the marble floor outside the conference room, getting louder as they approached the entrance. Everyone's attention shifted to the door. Alex looked at his watch. It was exactly 9:00 a.m.

CHAPTER 2

A woman walked into the room, head held high, looking straight ahead, displaying a figure of authority. There was no smile on her face, only a look of self-importance. Her hair was tied tightly in a bun, her clothes screamed "corporate." Her dark-rimmed glasses all but covered her eyes. Too much makeup as if she was trying to look younger than her years. Alex immediately said "tight ass" in his mind to describe her. Everyone watched as she strutted across the room and took her place at the end of the conference table. As she looked around the room, everyone became quiet. Following behind her was a young woman carrying an armload of folders and manuals. The young woman closed the conference room doors and took a seat against a back wall behind Tight Ass.

"Welcome to your first day at Sterling Chemicals. I am Donna Holland, Senior Vice President of Human Resources. I'm the person who sent you the offer letters that brought you here today. We are glad to have you join the company." No emotion in her voice. "Before we start, everyone put your cell phone on silence so we will not be disturbed." It was not a request, it was a demand.

Almost everyone took out their phones and made the adjustment. Alex looked around and counted nineteen people at the conference table, about equal men and women. All eyes were on Tight Ass, afraid that they would miss something if they turned away.

"Again, welcome to Sterling. All of you are new employees. We will spend the morning going over company policies and procedures, completing necessary forms, and watching a short film about the history of the company. After that we will go to lunch as a group. Once you have finished lunch, you should report to your assigned work areas where someone has been assigned to help you through the rest of the day. Tomorrow you will report directly to your work area. Our official office hours are nine to five. You will adhere to these hours unless your specific job requires something different. As a reminder, we are closed on Friday this week for the July 4 holiday weekend, and the office will close early on Thursday, the day before."

Someone at the end of the table let out an audible "woohoo." Tight Ass looked sternly in that direction but said nothing. The guy looked down at the table and slid down a little in his chair.

As if on cue, the young lady behind Donna got up and started passing out a manual to everyone at the table.

"Carol is now handing out the company policy manual. We hope it will answer all your questions about how the company works and what is expected from each of our employees."

Donna waited until Carol finished passing out the manuals before she continued.

As Carol placed a manual in front of Alex, he looked at her and mouthed a "thank you." She smiled back at him with a wink. Alex felt himself blush. Carol finished passing out the material and returned to her chair along the back wall.

"If you look at the table of contents, you will see that it addresses business conduct, regulatory conduct, absences and leaves, compensation and benefits, hours of work, training, performance management, and education.

"You are all expected to read this manual and understand the information. In the back of the manual is a form for you to sign and date, stating that you have read the manual and understand the contents. You must turn in the signed form to the HR representative for your department by the end of this week. You will find the name and location of that person on your office location document which we will be handing out soon. The manual can also be found online on the internal Web site, at www.sterlingchem.org. The URL is printed on the cover of the manual."

Everyone turned to the cover of the manual to see the URL listed.

"Remember, we need the signed document by the end of the week. Since we are closed on Friday, I suggest that you turn it in prior to closure on Thursday. Does anyone have any questions?" Donna stood tall at the end of the table waiting for questions.

Alex leaned over to Leslie. "I wonder how many times she has made that speech."

"I wonder if she was a sergeant in the army before coming here," Leslie responded with a smile.

A hand went up across the table. "What if we don't sign it?"

"Then we may terminate your offer. This is to protect the company and the company assets. However, if you have any concerns about signing, please discuss your concerns with your supervisor or HR representative. They are available to help you through this process."

"What happens if we don't get it back by the end of the week? This is a lot to read by then."

"There is no hard-and-fast rule. We know from experience, however, that if you don't return it as soon as possible, you will forget about it. If your HR representative doesn't receive the signed agreement by the end of the week, he or she will contact you to see if there is an issue or if you just forgot. However, you will not get a paycheck until we have received this signed document. So it is in your best interest to do it as soon as possible."

Ah, blackmail, Alex thought.

"Remember . . . turn the signed form in to your HR representative by the end of day Thursday. We prefer not to have to come looking for you. We have better things to do," Donna said stoically.

Alex flipped through the pages quickly, stopping at the last section to look at the agreement pages. Forty-three pages of rules and regulations. "Are there any other questions?" No one said anything, everyone busy paging through the document. Donna looked around the table and then glanced down at her notes. She waited a few minutes and then continued.

"The company occupies floors 12 through 62 of this building. We are currently on the twelfth floor. The first eleven floors are occupied by rental tenants. In addition to this location, which is the corporate headquarters, there is a research facility in Charleston, West Virginia, production plants in eight different locations and field offices in thirteen states and twenty-seven international offices. All these locations are specified in the manual." She paused a moment so everyone could process this information.

"We will now hand out your individual information. The folder contains your temporary company badge and your office location document." Tight Ass then turned and left the room without looking back. Carol stepped up to the table.

"As I call your name, please come up and get your folder." Carol started calling out the names. As Carol handed the folder to Alex, she gave him a wink again.

"Thank you" was all Alex said.

Alex returned to his seat as Carol continued to call out names. He opened his envelope and pulled out the documents. The first page had his office assignment. He will be on the forty-second floor, office 4218. Not quite the penthouse. The next document was his temporary badge. There was a list of all the people in his department, their titles, office location, and phone numbers, including the name of the HR representative assigned to him. There was also information about the general areas in the building—cafeteria, company gym, security office, as well as some forms to fill out.

Once everyone had their document, Carol returned to her seat against the wall. Everyone in the room was busy looking through their folders. Alex glanced over at Leslie's documents and noticed that she was assigned to the sixty-first floor.

"I see you are in the clouds. I'm only on the forty-second floor," Alex said quietly to Leslie so no one else could hear.

"It's not what you know, but who you know. Gives you something to work towards, Alex," she commented back with a slight laugh.

Just then the conference room door opened, and Tight Ass appeared, taking her place at the head of the table. Everyone became quiet, all eyes on her.

"The temporary badge will only allow you to get into the building and to your assigned area," she said, holding up a badge. "It is only good through this week. You will need to go to security to get your permanent badge. I suggest that you have your permanent security badge made either today or tomorrow. Seek out the person who has been assigned to you today when you get to your assigned location and ask them to take you to security to get your permanent badge."

Donna continued. "Your permanent badge has been preprogrammed for you and must be worn at all times. It gives you access to the areas where you have security clearance. If there are other areas that you need access, you will need to work that out with your supervisor and have your badge updated."

Tight Ass looked at her notes and then looked up. "Are there any questions?"

"What happens if we lose the badge or forget to bring it to work?" someone asked at the end of the room.

"If you lose it, you will need to contact your HR representative immediately so we can cancel the access privileges and issue you a new badge. You would need to go through the same procedures again that you will do today. If you forget to bring your badge to work, you will need to sign in at the front desk and provide some form of identification. You will be given a temporary badge that is good for two days only. However, that will only give you access to the building, your office area, and the common areas. Only a permanent badge will get you to your specific areas."

"Are there any more questions?"

She looked around the room. No response.

"I have two more procedures to discuss. After that we will take a short break. First, you need to complete a W-2 form for payroll purposes. You can fill them out and leave them with Carol today or give them to your HR representative by the end of the week. You will find the W-2 form in the package that you just received. If you have any questions, please contact your HR representative."

Just then two men entered the room, pushing carts carrying three beverage dispensers and baskets of bagels and fruit. They moved silently to the back of the room and started moving the food and dispensers to the table that held the morning coffee. They left as silently as they entered. Their facial expressions indicated a fear of disturbing Tight Ass.

"Secondly, you will find a confidentiality agreement in the package that you need to sign before you leave this meeting today. Basically, the agreement states that you will keep all company information secret and not use company equipment for your personal use without prior authorization. Please take a few minutes to read, sign, and date the document.

"You have all been sitting for a period now. Let's take a break so you can get some coffee or use the restrooms. This would be a good time to read and sign the confidential agreement. We will collect them after the break."

Again it felt like a command, not a request.

"Everyone, please be back here in thirty minutes." Donna turned and left the conference room, Carol at her heels, shutting the door behind her.

As soon as they were out of the room, people slowly got up to refill their coffee cup or to leave to use the restrooms.

"Why do I feel like I am in grade school again and being sent to the principal's office?" Alex said, leaning toward Leslie.

"Wonder how many times she had done this in the past?" Leslie remarked. "There was no emotion or concern in her voice."

Alex followed Leslie to the table. He got his coffee and a bagel. Leslie got a cup of tea and a banana.

"That's too healthy for me this early in the day. I need my caffeine and carbs," Alex said to Leslie's choice of food. "Do you live in the city?" he asked her after they had returned to the table and seated again.

"I live in Brooklyn. I assumed when you said 'the city' you meant Manhattan. Technically I do live in the city, but you get more for your money in Brooklyn. Living in the city would mean I'd have to have a roommate, and that is something I don't want. So I picked a place that gave me both: city and no roommate."

"I can't believe what they get for rent here. Back home I could get an entire house on an acre of property for what I pay for 950 square feet here in the city. Through a friend of a friend, I did find a place on the Upper West Side though. It is a six-floor walk-up but with a nice view of the river. I was lucky to find that. I'm subletting from a guy who is on assignment in Europe for a year. It came furnished, but one of these chairs would add a nice touch. Gives me a year to find a new place."

"Sublets are hard to find in the city. Most buildings don't allow them or have very strict rules." she responded.

"I guess I was lucky then. So how long is your commute from Brooklyn?"

"Twenty to thirty minutes by subway."

"It takes me about the same amount of time door to door. By the time I walk to the subway, wait for the train, and then walk to the office, it is thirty minutes. And I've only traveled four miles. I could probably run it faster. I wonder if I will ever get used to the crowded subways."

"Welcome to the big city," she said, raising her cup in gesture.

"I hear that Brooklyn is the 'new' city."

That brought a smile to her face.

"Good try."

Leslie smiled and put her cup down next to the uneaten banana. "Excuse me, I need to use the restroom," she said then got up and headed out the door.

Alex watched as she left the room, her hips swaying in a provocative way. *Now that is the perfect ass,* he thought as he watched her leave the room.

Alex settled back to read and sign the confidential agreement. He then filled out his W-2 form. Every time he heard the door open, he looked up, hoping to see Leslie enter the room again. It has been a long time since he felt like a schoolboy.

The door opened, and there she was. He couldn't keep his eyes off her as she walked gracefully back to her chair. As she sat down, she tuned and smiled at him. Alex felt his face blush, so he quickly turned back to the papers in front of him.

She began reading her documents and completing the forms. Alex looked over and noticed that Leslie had checked single status on her W-2 form. A warm feeling came over him, and he also felt another twitch in his pants.

Everyone else in the room was busy filling out the forms or looking at the manual. Alex checked his watch. It was now a little after eleven o'clock. He had been here over two hours and had only seen the twelfth floor.

In exactly thirty minutes after she left, Donna reentered the conference room and went to the head of the table. She looked around to make sure that everyone was present. Silence went over the room.

"Thank you for getting back on time. Carol will now collect your confidential agreements. A copy will be sent to you for your files."

As if on cue, Carol walked around the room and collected all the documents.

"I know you are all interested in the health plan and benefits that the company offers. There are manuals in the packet you received. Since these are unique to each situation, it is best you review them on your own and discuss them with your HR representative. Are there any general questions?"

"When does the health plan kick in?" came from across the table.

"Thirty days from today."

Donna waited for other questions and then looked at her notes to make sure that she had covered everything. No one said anything. It was so quiet that you could hear a pin drop.

"If there are no further questions, we have a thirty-minute film about the history of the company and our products. After that you will be escorted to a dining room set up for us. After lunch, you should report to your work area as specified in you documents. Welcome to Sterling Chemicals."

With that, Donna picked up her papers and left the room without looking back.

Carol walked to the back of the room and pushed some button on the wall, and a movie screen appeared from the ceiling. She pushed more buttons, and the drapes closed across the windows, and the lights dimmed. Seconds later, a picture appeared on the screen. Everyone settled back to watch the history of the company. The first time they were able to relax this morning without the glare of Tight Ass looking over them.

CHAPTER 3

The movie started with the company logo and was narrated by some actor. As the commentator talked about the company, pictures of the founders, the products, production facilities, and company locations were displayed on the screen.

"Sterling Chemicals was started over one hundred years ago by two brothers in Ohio. Their first product used a high-pressure catalytic process to synthesize ammonia directly from nitrogen and hydrogen. The process was later used in the synthesis of methanol and hydrogenation of coal to petroleum. Early in the twentieth century, the work on long-chained molecules provided the foundation for plastics and synthetic fibers. Sterling Chemicals took advantage of these new technologies and expanded into other areas."

"I didn't realize we were going to have a chemistry lesson," Alex said, leaning closer to Leslie.

"New divisions of the company developed during the '50s and '60s, including retail divisions that made plastic bags for everyday use, pesticides for agriculture to control insect activities as well as increase plant yield, and a division for the development of batteries. But still at the basis of the company was the production of raw chemicals in bulk quantities to sell to other manufacturing companies. But as the world population grew, it became evident that the development of agricultural endeavors was the future of the company. Although the company still produces raw materials for other industries, its main focus is now on the development of products to increase the world food supply. This includes new compounds to control pests on plants and stored crop, new plant varieties, and ways to increase crop yield."

"The Research and Development facility is in Charleston, West Virginia. Production centers are in West Virginia, Pennsylvania, Ohio, New Jersey, Texas, Oklahoma, North Carolina, and Missouri."

The next segment of the film focused on the corporate headquarters, with pictures of the building as it was being constructed, the changes in the lobby over the years, pictures of offices and conferences rooms, cafeteria, company gym, and IT with all the communication equipment.

"The corporate headquarters moved from Ohio to Manhattan in 1953 to the current location on Park Avenue in 1958. The gross income of the company reached six hundred million dollars last year. The company employs over forty-five thousand people in the United States and Canada and over eighty thousand worldwide."

The final scene was from Charles Sterling III, CEO of the company, from his office on the sixty-second floor welcoming everyone to Sterling Chemicals.

The lights went back on, and some of the people around the table applauded. It was probably because the movie was over.

Carol moved to the head of the table. "Let's head to the dining room for lunch. You can leave your belongings here and pick them up after lunch. At that time, you should go to your assigned work area. Remember to have your company badge with you at all times."

Everyone got up and followed Carol out the door. Alex noticed that her ass was also much nicer to look at than Tight Ass, but not as nice as Leslie's. He never did find out Carol's last name. Alex put his notebook back into his knapsack and set it back on the floor next to his chair and joined the group as they left the conference room.

A special room had been set up for them with a buffet lunch with tables for four placed around the room. Alex found a seat at a table with three other guys, and they spent the time talking about the New York sports teams. He kept glancing over at Leslie who was sitting at a table with three women. A few times their eyes met, and he saw that slight smile. When he noticed that Leslie was getting up to leave, he quickly excused himself and caught up with her at the door.

"It is time to see where we will be working," she said.

"Hope you have your oxygen tank. You are way up there," Alex said, trying to be funny. He was not sure if it worked.

They returned to the conference room to get their belongings. Alex stepped aside, holding the door open.

"Thank you," she said with that alluring smile.

As Alex moved to his chair, he noticed that his knapsack was sitting behind the chair. He was sure that he had placed it on the floor beside the chair. Maybe he moved it back there before he went to lunch. But he didn't remember doing that. Did someone go through his bag while he was at lunch and then left it there by mistake? He quickly checked the contents, but everything seemed to be there. He must have put it there in his hurry to get to lunch.

Several other new employees had entered the room to gather their belongings before heading toward the elevator. None of them seemed to be upset with their belongings. Maybe he did leave it there.

He left the room and crossed to the elevators, looking for the elevator that serviced floors 26–50. He noticed that Leslie was standing in front of the elevator that serviced 51–62.

A man with dark-rimmed glasses who fidgeted was also waiting by the elevator doors. Alex didn't remember seeing him in the room. Alex thought he noticed the guy look at him out of the corner of his eye but showed no expression. He was probably just curious at all the new people. The doors opened, and Alex stepped in. As he entered, he turned and waved to Leslie. "See you around." She waved back.

The elevator moved up, and the door opened on 42. Alex started down the hall in front of him, even numbered offices on one side and odd numbers on the other. In the center area were workstations, most of which were empty. Everyone must be at lunch. He continued down the hall, 4212, 4214, 4216, 4218. He had walked three-quarters of the way down the hall. He stood in the doorway of his office and looked in. He had found his new home.

The office was void of any personal items. The furniture consisted of a desk, a credenza, a bookcase, and two guest chairs that looked used but were better than anything he ever had. Three large windows, floor to ceiling, made up one wall of his office space. He walked over to the window and stood there looking up Park Avenue. What a view from this floor. Far below, the people walking on the sidewalks looked like ants going about their business. He just stood there for a while and took in the view.

Turning around, he moved over to his desk and sat in the desk chair, leaning back. The chair fit his back nicely. He was ready to start work and use his training for real-life situations. A new chapter of his life was starting, one that would last a long time, especially in an office that has this view.

CHAPTER 4

Alex had spent the last four years working toward his doctorate in statistics with a strong minor in chemistry. It had been a struggle, not because of the classes but because of the financial burden. Learning came easy to him. Whereas his fellow classmates used every opportunity to circumvent learning, he embraced it.

His parents were not able to help him very much financially. To help with the cost, he worked three jobs all through his undergraduate years. As a result, there was not much time left for socializing. He did, however, find time to join a fraternity that provided him a limited social life. His education, however, took top priority. He had a long-term plan, and he stuck to it. There would always be time for socializing once he had finished school, got a job, and started his real life.

If he had time for an active social life, he would have had no trouble finding women. He certainly had the looks. But between classes and working, he had little time left over. He did date some, but nothing serious ever came out of it.

His parents had always stressed the importance of education but never lectured him. Both of his older brothers had gone to college and told him how different it was from high school and how much more difficult it was. Both had graduated from the state university, but they didn't have the drive he did.

When it was time for him to go, he was ready. He applied to six different colleges in his senior year of high school and was accepted by all six. He selected the University of North Carolina to start his undergraduate work. He knew it was more expensive than a state school, but he liked their offerings and knew he would somehow make it happen. He also liked the idea of an out-of-state school, where he could get lost in the mass of students and the winters were warmer, and didn't want to go to a school where he would live in the shadows of his brothers.

Alex moved into the freshman dorm his first year. The next three years he lived in the frat house. He worked at a local movie theater three nights a week and in the library on weekends. In his senior year, he got a lab assistant position in organic chemistry, which provided additional income.

Halfway through his sophomore year, he realized that math and chemistry were his favorite classes, and he decided to pursue a double major.

He remembered coming back from class on a Friday one day in the fall of this senior year when a frat brother approached him.

"Alex, you have a registered letter from the Dean's Office. I signed it for you and put it in your mailbox. What have you done wrong now?"

"They're probably warning me about hanging around with characters like you."

Alex rushed to the mail room to get the letter. Sure enough, it was from the Dean's Office, the university logo staring back at him. Why would they be writing him? His mind went through several scenarios as he rushed up to his room to open it in private. It couldn't be his academic standing. After all, he had maintained a 3.92 GPA. He sat on his bed and opened the letter.

Dear Mr. Gregory,

We hope that your four years at the University have been a rewarding experience for you. We pride ourselves on providing the best education possible to our students.

It is important that you contact your counselor at the number below as soon as possible to set up an appointment to discuss an important issue.

Thank you for selecting our institution for your education.

Sincerely

Dean Reynolds

That didn't tell him much. He called the number in the letter and made an appointment to meet with his counselor the following Monday. The secretary had no idea why he was being summoned when he asked.

Monday came, and he headed to the administrative building. He was wearing his best slacks and a long-sleeved white shirt with the sleeves rolled up. On the way over, he thought about the letter. What had he done wrong? Had someone reported him? He searched his mind for any clue but couldn't come up with any. Why did they want him to come in? Why now, just before the holidays?

His palms were sweating as he sat in the hall, outside his counselor's office. He was so nervous that he arrived thirty minutes before the scheduled meeting.

Why would Mr. Michaels want to see him? He barely had any contact with him the past three years. He was surprised Mr. Michaels even knew who he was. He heard footsteps and turned toward the sound and saw Mr. Michaels coming down the hall, his arms full of folders.

As he unlocked his door, he turned to Alex. "Come on in, Alex."

Alex walked into the office and took a seat on the opposite side of the desk. Mr. Michaels put the folders on the desk and sat across from Alex.

The office was dark with no windows and old furniture. It was a mixture of steel and wood furniture. There were bookcases along the wall, no two matching but all overflowing with books and folders. Mixed in with the counseling and "how to" books were mystery novels by Kellerman, Patterson, and Clarke. There were two metal filing cabinets on the back wall and a small table behind the desk with a computer and printer.

Mr. Michaels was a short man, about five feet six inches, twenty pounds overweight, and bald on the top, and he wore steel-rimmed glasses. He combed his hair to try to hide the bald area on top. His clothes were wrinkled, and there was a spot on his necktie. Alex just stared at him, waiting for the ax to drop.

Maybe he was short some credits to graduate. That couldn't be it. He was very careful about his classes and what he needed to meet the requirements for graduating.

"You're probably wondering why I called you."

"Yes, sir, I can't think of any reason why you would want to talk to me this early in the year."

"Don't worry, you aren't in any trouble."

Alex let out a sigh of relief. He hoped that it wasn't loud enough to be heard. He realized that he had been clutching the arms of the chair and now let up on them.

"I have no idea why you want to talk to me, sir."

"I have been reviewing your class progress over the past three years."

Then I must be short of credits to graduate, and Mr. Michaels called me here to let me know, Alex thought to himself.

Mr. Michaels continued. "I see you are in the top 1 percent academically, and your professors have nothing but good things to say about you. You are also active in your fraternity and campus activities while also holding down several part-time jobs. That is quite impressive. I see you are a lab assistant for Professor Barnard in organic chemistry. I took the liberty of calling him personally to ask about you, and he had nothing but praise for you."

"Thank you, sir," Alex responded as a sense of pride came over him.

"Have you thought about what you are going to do after you graduate next year?"

"My intention when I started was to get an education degree and go into teaching. Eventually I would like to get a graduate degree once I can afford to go back to school. But right now I can't financially swing that. But I'm not sure that is the right path for me now. I've been thinking about other options," Alex replied, coming up with an answer off the top of his head. He hadn't really thought about what he really wanted to do and was surprised when the words came out of his mouth.

"Have you considered going on to graduate or medical school?"

"The thought had crossed my mind, but just not a possibility right now. I know my parents couldn't help me financially beyond my undergraduate years, nor would I allow them to, and I don't like the idea of taking out student loans and having to pay them off for the next hundred years. I feel that I need to go to work and save towards graduate school and return when I am financially able to."

"That becomes a problem for lots of students. But with your grades, you should not have any problems getting some type of scholarship or a campus job as a teaching or lab assistant. Not only that, but teaching assistants usually don't have to pay tuition, and they get a salary. Between that and scholarships, you should be okay, especially if you want to consider continuing your education here."

"To tell the truth, I haven't really thought about continuing right away since financially it was not possible," Alex replied.

Mr. Michaels continued. "Not only did I talk to Professor Barnard, but I also talked to some of the professors in the Math Department. Everyone said you would be a good candidate for a teaching assistantship." Mr. Michaels stopped talking to let Alex absorb what he just said.

"As I said, I really haven't thought about it. I do like it here and all the professors and classes I've had."

"I just wanted to talk with you and point out some options that you may not have considered. You should be thinking about what you want to do after you graduate so you can start planning for it now. Statistics show that once a student leaves school, over 60 percent never return even though they had good intentions. I would hate to have you become one of those statistics.

"If you decide to go on to graduate school here or at another institution, you will need to begin the process now. There are many scholarships you can apply for, but you will need to take the GRE exam. Most scholarships are rewarded based on the results of the GRE exam. I just want to let you know that I'm here to help you in whatever decision you make. With your grades and extracurricular activities, you are a prime candidate for graduate school and the kind of student that we would like to have stay with us."

"Thank you, sir, I appreciate that," Alex responded.

"Think about it, and if you want to talk some more or begin the process, please make an appointment. Thanks for coming in."

With that, the meeting was over.

Alex needed to think about his options when he was alone. Right now he had to get to his statistics class.

A month later, Alex was back in Mr. Michaels's office, sitting in the same wooden chair. Mr. Michaels was wearing the same necktie, the stain still visible.

Alex had discussed the options with his parents and his math and chemistry instructors. In the end, however, he knew it had to be his decision. But it was not a hard decision to make.

He felt that Mr. Michaels knew all along that he would be back to begin the process. When Alex walked into his office for his appointment, he noticed three folders on the desk with his name on them. There was his future, a stack of papers in three folders.

Alex had decided that he wanted to continue on with graduate school rather than medical school and would begin preparing for the GRE exam and at the same time submit the forms and requirements for scholarships. Since he was already known in the Math and Chemistry Departments, he had decided to apply for admission to the graduate school at this university.

"I think you made a good choice, Alex. I've put together information on several scholarships for you to review. My recommendation is to apply to several, thus increasing your chances. You will need to get letters of recommendation, but I'm sure your professors will be more than happy to recommend you."

Mr. Michaels picked up one of the folders and pushed it across the metal desk to Alex. Alex opened it and quickly glanced through the pages. There must have been at least two dozen different scholarships available.

"And here are some Web sites and book listings you should review to prepare for the GRE exam." He passed Alex a second folder filled with typed pages of references. "The exam is given in April and September, so you have several months to prepare. I suggest you apply for the April date. That way you will have the results by the time you graduate. I suggest you begin preparing as soon as possible and not wait until the last minute.

"And finally and most importantly, here are the forms you need to complete and submit to get accepted to the graduate school here." A third folder was handed to him across the desk. "You will need six references: three from former professors and three from people not connected to the university. Do you have any questions?"

"Nothing right now, but I'm sure I will when I begin reviewing this information. Thanks for all your help." Alex realized that the meeting was over; so he said his good-byes, shook Mr. Michaels's hand, and left. As he walked away, he realized that he didn't even know Mr. Michaels's first name.

Alex spent the next few months preparing for his GRE exam and filling out all the forms for graduate school, including getting all the references. He also applied for several scholarships, specifying that he would be taking the GRE exam in April.

April came quickly. The GRE was over, and now the waiting period started. He had already received an acceptance to the graduate school provided his GRE score was over 250. Several scholarships also depended on a GRE score of over 300.

Everything was done. All he needed now were the results of the GRE exam. Three months later, he received his results. He took a deep breath and opened the letter. There it was . . . a score of 335. It was time to celebrate.

CHAPTER 5

The next four years went by quickly. Alex concentrated on his studies and ended up majoring in statistics with a minor in chemistry. Math had always been easy for him, so it was natural. Chemistry just fell into place.

The last six months were spent in the library studying for his final oral exam for his degree. This involved a minimum of three hours in front of a committee of four to five professors from areas of statistics, math, and chemistry. The first hour was spent defining and defending his original research. That was the easy part since he was the expert. This was followed by a question-and-answer period from the professors attending. He was expected to answer any questions they asked to show his knowledge of math and chemistry. He had spent hours reading and rereading articles and textbooks.

The day finally came, and he was ushered into a conference room. He wore his best suit and stood in front of the committee, sweating under the collar. In front of him were five scholars staring at him with their notepads and lists of questions. The final stretch of his education was about to begin.

After the presentation of his thesis, the questions started.

"How can you apply quantum theory to everyday life situations?

"Compare and contrast Bertrand's postulate and Sylvester's theorem."

Question after question was thrown at him to evaluate his knowledge of math and chemistry.

The questions and answers went on for over two hours. Once finished, Alex was asked to wait in the hallway. All that was left was the discussion and vote by the five professors in the room. He would either pass or have to do it all over again in six months. The waiting seemed like an eternity. He paced up and down the hallway.

He heard a sound behind him. Turning around, he saw his advisor come out of the conference room alone. He walked toward Alex with no expression on his face.

"Congratulation, Dr. Gregory. It was unanimous" was all he said, holding out his hand. He may have said more, but that is all Alex heard. He had passed. All that was left was graduation and to start the next phase of his life.

The other members of the committee filed out of the conference room, each stopping to congratulate him. They left, going back to their office or classroom. Alex went back to the frat house and immediately called his parents.

"It's over, Dad. I passed" was all he said.

"We knew you could do it, Alex. We are so proud of you. We will be there for graduation in the front row. Mom is here. Let me put her on. She is beaming from ear to ear."

"Oh, Alex, I'm so proud of you. I don't know who to call first to tell."

"Thanks, Mom. I'm sure you will figure it out."

"So now what are your plans?"

"As soon as graduation is over, I will start a new job."

"I know you have several offers sitting there. Have you decided on one?"

"Yes, Mom, I've been thinking about them for a long time. I know you and Dad want me to go to a university and teach. I was leaning that way for a long time. But I think I want to live in New York, and I got a great offer from a company there. Remember, I told you about Sterling Chemicals? I have accepted their offer. It will give me a lot of practical experience, and I can use what I've learned in real-life situations. If that doesn't work out I can always go into teaching at a University or some college."

"I would be afraid to move to a strange place, especially one as large as New York," his mom replied. "But you do what you think is best. You have always made good decisions. And remember, home will always be here."

"Thanks, Mom. You know I like to try new things. And anyway, Sterling wants to help the environment and the world. They produce safe chemicals and new plant varieties that help feed the world. They are also very conscientious of the environment and saving the planet. And you know protecting the environment is something I'm very passionate about. And don't worry about the big-city thing. I can take care of myself. And if it doesn't work out, I can always go back to teaching and doing research at a university."

"But where will you live?"

"You remember Dave Harriman? He was a frat brother. He works in the city here, and we have kept in touch."

"Is he the one with the funny hair?"

"Yes, that's him. He liked to change the color of his hair. Red, green, blue, any color he felt. Now that he is working, he is back to his normal color. Anyway, he has a brother who lives in New Jersey, across the Hudson River from New York. His brother offered to put me up until I find a place. I don't have a lot of stuff to move. Basically I just have my clothes and a few boxes of books, so the move will be easy. Once I get there, I'll start looking for a place. I'm sure I can find something right away."

"You do what you need to do. You have always made good decisions. I'm so proud of you, Alex. I can't wait to tell everyone. We will see you at graduation. Your dad wants to talk you. Love you, Alex."

"Love you, Mom."

"Hey, son, do I have to call you doctor now?"

"No, I'll let you call me what you always have."

"We are proud of you, son."

"Thanks, Dad. I'll let Mom tell you the details, but I've accepted a job in New York. I'll be moving there shortly after graduation. I'll be home for a week before then, and we can spend time together."

"Do you need anything?"

"No, I'm fine. I'm just going to finish up the rest of my classes and then graduation. I'll see you in a couple of weeks."

"Okay, son. I'm proud of you, son. Bye, Alex."

The phone went dead. His father was not much of a phone talker. This was probably the most he had ever talked to his dad by phone. He hung up the phone and sat back on his bed, his books and papers scattered all around him from his weeks of studying. It started to sink in. It is done, finished. School is now behind him. Like someone has taken a weight off his shoulders.

The phone rang.

"Hello?"

"Hey, buddy. Do I call you Doc or just ol' Alex?"

"Hi, Dave, you have to call me Doc. Everyone else can call me Alex."

"I guess that means that you passed."

"Yup, I passed. It is all over. Now I just have to wait for graduation. Again, thanks for putting me in touch with your brother. It will be nice to have a place to stay until I find my own place and also someone to hang with while I look."

"No problem, buddy. You two will get along fine. Rod is nothing like me," he stated with a snicker. "Anyway, how about going out tonight and celebrating. Several of us want to go out and whoop it up. And Sarah will be there. You know she has a thing for you. Eight p.m. at Player's Retreat."

"Any excuse to go drinking . . . right? It sounds great to me. I'll be there."

"Again, congrats, buddy. We'll see you tonight."

Alex sat back and finally relaxed for the first time in months. It is all over. Everything has fallen into place. He closed his eyes, and before long he was asleep, totally relaxed. Something his body needed after months of long days and late nights.

CHAPTER 6

Graduation had come and gone. Alex spent a week at home and then packed his books and clothes and shipped them off. The rest of his clothes he packed in his suitcases. Dave drove him to the airport, and he was on his way to the East Coast. The move to New Jersey was easy. Dave's brother lived alone in a two-bedroom apartment on the Hudson and offered him a place to stay while searching for an apartment in New York. His start date for work was July 1, so he had two weeks to find his own place in the city. He was determined to live in Manhattan, not in one of the boroughs. He thought that would be plenty of time to find something.

Each morning as he got out of bed, he could see the skyline of the city across the river from his bedroom window. He couldn't wait to live there and experience real big-city living. He could even see the area where the Sterling Chemicals' building was located. It was right in the center of Manhattan.

He had just finished another long day of searching for an apartment with no prospects. He was stretched out on the sofa contemplating his next move if he didn't find anything quickly. It was a week until he had to report for work, and he was hoping to have the apartment search behind him by now. Maybe he would be forced to find someplace here in New Jersey and commute to work like thousands of others did every day. Every apartment he looked at was just too expensive. Even a small studio was out of his price range.

Rod, whom everyone called Butch, had gone to the kitchen to get a couple of beers. Returning, he handed one to Alex and then sat in the old brown leather chair, his legs spread far apart.

"Boy, it is tough finding a place to live here. I can't believe they are getting $3,000 a month for two hundred square feet of living. I thought I would just have to look in the newspaper for vacancies, find a few I liked, and check them out. I thought I could do that in one to two days and be out of your hair."

"New York is not your typical city. Why do you think I live here? Don't worry so much. You can stay here as long as you need. I'm not around that much, and when I am, it is good to have company."

"Thanks. But I want my own place, and I'm sure you would like me out your hair. And I don't want this daily commute."

Butch stood over six feet tall, brown curly hair like his brother that was cut short. He was tan from working outside in construction, and his body was well toned. His eyes were set deep, and he had a slightly crooked smile.

"Let's finish and head to the garage. I want to show you my latest baby."

"Bottoms up and we're out of here."

Just then Butch's cell phone rang. "He's sitting right here. I'll let you talk to him." Butch handed the phone to Alex. "The brother of a buddy of mine recently got an international position. He wants to sublet his apartment while he is out of the country. I told him you were looking for an apartment, so he's calling to see if you are interested. His name is Marc."

Alex took the phone. "Hello, Marc, this is Alex Gregory. I understand you have an apartment to sublet."

There was a long silence on his end of the phone as Alex listened.

"That sounds great. Yes, I'm interested." Butch sat there listening to the one-sided conversation as he finished his beer. He motioned to Alex. "I'm getting another. Want one?"

Alex nodded.

"Yes, I can meet tomorrow. Just give me the address and time. I'll be there." Alex wrote down the information and hung up.

"That sounded good," Butch said, handing Alex a beer.

"It sounds very promising. I'm going to check it out tomorrow. Now let's go see your latest purchase."

They left the apartment and walked two blocks to a row of garages where Butch was renting two of them. He pulled out a garage door opener and pressed a button, and the door opened.

"There she is." Butch pointed to a car in the garage.

"Hot pink!" Alex said, laughing.

"It's a 1957 Oldsmobile, a classic. And it is not hot pink, it is fuchsia."

"You may think so. But I bet if you ask ten people, nine of them would say it was hot pink. You drive that down the street and everyone will know it's you."

"It is fuchsia, not hot pink."

"Keep telling yourself that . . . but it is hot pink," Alex remarked.

"I got a good deal that I couldn't pass up. It belonged to the grandfather of a guy I did some work for a while back. It has been in his garage for years. After his death, it was given to his grandson who offered it me. He knew I'm into fixing up classics."

"What condition is it in?"

"Perfect. Just a few scratches I need to buff out and a little work on the engine and only sixty thousand miles. I got it for $2,500, and I can fix it up and can easily sell it for $30,000 to $35,000 at a car show. Check out the inside."

Alex opened the door and got in the passenger side.

"Almost still has the smell of new leather. Look at this glove box. It is in the center of the dashboard and all that chrome. The leather is in good shape. Not faded at all. At least the inside is not hot pink too."

"Fuchsia!"

"You're right, this is in good shape for a hot-pink car. How's the engine?"

"The keys are in the ignition. Start it up and see."

Alex moved over and turned on the ignition. It started right up.

"Boy, this is quiet for an old car."

"The engine is in good shape. I just need to clean it up and put in some new plugs and tubing, and it will be as good as new. It will take a couple of weeks of work, but it will be worth it."

"I have to admit that it looks like you got yourself a gem here, even if it is hot pink. Did you get the title papers?"

"There are no title papers. As far as anyone knows, this car no longer exists."

"Is there a market for old cars like this?"

"I've already restored three and sold them all. Since it's just a hobby of mine, I do one car at a time. I've always come out ahead. So far, I've had no lemons . . . knock on wood. Let's go grab some dinner and hit the bars. We need to celebrate my new baby here and your new home."

"Let's not put the cart before the horse. Let's go, but not late. I have to be in the city early tomorrow to check out that apartment. Maybe we should take the hot-pink car to the bar."

"It's not hot pink. The color is fuchsia."

"Hot pink . . . ," he repeated, slapping Butch on the arm. "Let's get some dinner."

CHAPTER 7

Alex woke up early the next day in anticipation of seeing the apartment. He hoped that this would be the end of his search. He had looked for almost two weeks now and had seen so many places, but nothing he could afford. He'd spent hours searching ads online and in local newspapers. In the end, he had hired an agent to help him find something. Every place he looked at was way over his budget or located in an area he didn't want to live. The rents were running from four to six dollars a square foot per month depending on the part of the city. And on top of that, he would have to pay for electricity and gas. His budget for rent was a maximum of $2,000 a month. He thought that would have been enough.

He hoped that this newest lead would work out since he would be starting his new job next week, and he didn't want to have to commute every day from New Jersey. That would be an hour or more each way and would only leave weekends for him to search for a place to live. He had heard that commuting was the norm for a lot of people, but he didn't want to be one of them. If you are going to work in New York, you need to live there. Butch was probably tired of him hanging around too.

Alex showed up fifteen minutes early for this appointment. He didn't want to miss the guy and was anxious to see the apartment. It was easy to find. This location would make his commute to work about twenty to thirty minutes door to door. It was less than half the time it would take to commute in from New Jersey.

He sat on the front steps of the building waiting for Marc. The building was right across the street from a park that ran along the Hudson River. From the steps, he could see people jogging along the river in shorts, mothers pushing strollers, people walking dogs, or people just walking about enjoying the day. He could feel the breeze off the river on his face. The street had little traffic, so it was very quiet.

Alex saw a man come around the corner of the building heading toward him.

"You must be Alex. I think you are here to see me. Hope you didn't wait long."

"I haven't been here long. And I'm enjoying the view. It is so quiet and peaceful." Alex put out his hand and shook hands with Marc.

"It is a nice view. I often come out here at night and just sit on the steps and watch people go by. You will be surprised how many familiar faces you see while sitting here. This area has a very neighborhood feeling, and I've gotten to know many people that live in the area just by sitting here. People who are going to the park to walk their dogs or just out for an evening walk often stop and sit with you. And in the summer, gals in shorts and halter top come by walking their dogs. Now that is a sight to see. But you are here to see the apartment. The view is better from up there. Let's go up so you can see it for yourself."

Alex followed Marc into the building and up the stairs. "Hope you don't mind, but you have to walk up six flights," Marc said as he opened the door to the stairwell. "Good for the leg muscles though. It's the top floor, so you don't have anyone living over you. You also have access to the roof deck from that floor. The roof is for everyone to use, but not that many use it since it is a walk up. So it is almost your own private oasis."

At the sixth floor, they turned right and then entered the apartment at the end of the hall. The view of the river was the first thing that Alex noticed. There were three large windows across the front. He immediately walked over to the windows to take in the view. He could see the river, and across from it was New Jersey.

"Wow, you are right. This is some view."

"I told you it was better from up here. If you look to the right, you can see the George Washington Bridge, and to the left, down the west side of Manhattan. There are four apartments per floor. Two are facing the front, and two are facing a courtyard."

Alex immediately looked to the right and then to the left. "This is fantastic."

"Let me show you around. Then we can talk."

Alex turned and followed Marc.

"This is what they call a convertible two bedroom. It only has one bedroom, but the dining room could be converted to a second bedroom if needed. It is about 950 square feet and has lots of light, as you can see. There are windows on two sides."

Alex immediately started calculation. At five dollars a square foot, that is $4,750 a month. Way over his budget. He started to feel depressed.

"The kitchen is a small area off the dining room but has everything you need. I don't cook much, but if you do, you will find it adequate. There are no laundry facilities in the unit, but there are washers and dryers in the basement for the tenants."

Marc turned and led Alex into the bedroom. As they walked to the bedroom, they passed the bathroom. Alex looked in and saw it was a typical bathroom. Tub with shower. But more important, there was a large frosted window in the bathroom that let in lots of light. Something you don't see in New York apartment bathrooms. Across the hall from the bathroom was a storage closet.

"That closet is large, and I have put all my personal items there and locked it. The rest of my personal items will go in a storage unit I have in the basement. That way you will have room for your stuff."

Alex could put all his possessions in a small closet.

"The bedroom is small, but it holds a queen-size bed nicely and has a walk-in closet. What more do you need?"

A large window faced north, and Alex could see the George Washington Bridge in the distance.

"Let's go back to the living room and talk."

They returned to the living room, and Alex sat on the sofa, and Marc sat in a rocking chair.

"So, Alex, how do you know Butch?"

"He is the brother of one of my frat buddies from college. When Butch heard from his brother that I was moving to New York, he offered me a place to stay while I was looking for a place of my own."

"In this city, it's who you know that counts. So what questions do you have for me?"

"How can you leave this place? More important, how can you afford it? This place is phenomenal."

"I'm not really giving it up. I own this place. I couldn't afford it if I was buying it today. It was left to my brother and me years ago. He didn't want to live in the city, so I bought his half."

"You are one of the lucky ones who can own a place in Manhattan. He is probably kicking himself now for giving it up."

"He is married and has two kids. New York is not the ideal place to raise a family. He is happy in the burbs."

"You're right, I couldn't imagine raising a family here."

"Anyway, I've taken an international job for the next year so will be coming back. I just want to sublet this place while I am gone. I don't want to sublet it to a stranger, but rather to someone who I know will take care of it. My brother told me that Butch gave you the thumbs-up. He said you needed a place to live, and I need someone to live here."

"I really like the place. Does the furniture stay?"

"What you see is what you get. I've moved all family pieces and items important to me to storage. Not much furniture in this room but enough for you. I've already moved out of here and living with my girlfriend until I have to leave."

"This place fits my needs perfectly. I'm afraid that it is out of my price range though."

"My company is covering my maintenance while I'm gone. So I'm just looking to cover my mortgage and taxes. They are also paying for my lodging for a year at my new location. I want someone to live here and take good care of it while I'm gone. That comes to $1,500 a month. Of course you will need to pay the utilities on top of that."

Alex could hardly believe what he heard and tried not to show his excitement. "That sounds fair to me. I would like to sublet it from you then. I'm so tired of looking around, and I have to start my job next week. What do you need from me? References, security deposit?"

"Butch recommended you highly. That is all I need in regard to references. I would like a copy of your job offer letter so I know that you are employed. As far as security, just half of a month's rent."

Alex took his checkbook out of his pocket. He wanted to make sure he had this apartment.

"So that comes to $2,250 for the security deposit and first month's rent if my math is correct." Alex quickly wrote the check and handed it to Marc.

"As I said, I've already moved out, so you can move in as soon as you want. I can have a lease written up in a couple of days and send it to you, or we can arrange to meet."

"I don't have much to move," Alex said. "Basically I just have my clothes. I'd like to move in this weekend if that is okay with you."

"That's fine with me. I thought you might take the place so brought a set of keys for you."

Alex took the keys that Marc offered.

"There is a key to the front door downstairs, a key to the apartment, a key to the mailbox, and a key to the bike room if you want to store a bike. I'll drop off the lease this weekend."

"Thanks, Marc, I'll take good care of it, I promise." Alex put out his hand for a handshake.

He had a place to live. He looked around the apartment. He couldn't believe this was his new home.

"I have to get back to work. I'll leave you here to look around and scout out the neighborhood." With that, Marc was out the door, and Alex was alone in his new home. Another weight had been taken off his shoulders. He was now a New Yorker.

CHAPTER 8

The door opened on the sixty-first floor, and Leslie stepped out into the reception area. A plush oriental carpet covered the high-glossed wood floor, and a large vase of fresh flowers sat on the reception desk in front of her. Her feet sunk into the softness of the carpet as she walked to the reception desk.

"May I help you?" the woman at the desk asked.

"I am Leslie Sherwood. I was told to report here."

"Oh yes, we have been expecting you. Welcome to Sterling Chemicals. I'm Barb Marshall. Mr. Clark is out of the office today. He will be in tomorrow. Let me call someone to show you to your workstation and help you get settled."

Barb picked up the phone and dialed four numbers. "Brianna, Ms. Sherwood is here." There was no emotion in her voice. Barb hung up and turned to Leslie. "Brianna Welch will be right out. So how has your first day been going? No . . . let me guess. You had an orientation meeting with Donna Holland. You went over a lot forms and then saw a movie about the company. During the entire time, Donna Holland didn't smile once. Am I close to what you just went through?"

"Sounds like either you have been through it, or you were sitting in the room with the rest of us."

"We've all been there one time or the other. Her orientation sessions are infamous." Just then the phone rang.

"Excuse me, I need to take this call. Please have a seat." She gestured to a sitting area behind her desk while she took the call. As she moved to the chair, Barb answered the phone in a pleasant yet businesslike manner.

Leslie sat quietly in a large leather chair behind the reception area. She was calm on the outside, but inside she was excited with anticipation of what lay ahead. She looked around to see where she would be working.

Behind her was a glass wall separating the reception area from the rest of the floor. Two glass doors with a security keypad to the right were in the center of the glass wall. Behind the wall, she could see another sitting area and a large open area with three workstations.

Just then a woman got up from one of the workstations and walked toward the glass wall. As she approached the glass doors, they slid open automatically. Leslie recognized her from the interview but didn't remember her last name . . . This was Brianna. She had the same authoritative walk and no expression on her face she had then. She reminded Leslie of Donna Holland in her movements. Maybe they both went to the same finishing school for corporate America employees.

"Welcome to Sterling Chemicals and the executive floor. I'm Brianna Welch. We met at your interview. If you follow me, I'll get you settled." There was still no emotion in her voice. In fact, Leslie had the feeling that Brianna felt it was an imposition on her to have to do this task.

"Good to see you again too, Brianna."

Brianna placed her badge on the security panel and punched in four numbers, and the glass doors slid open. Leslie quickly followed her, trying to keep up with her pace. Not a word was said.

Brianna wore an expensive tailored blue suit and designer shoes. Her hair was tied in a bun on the back of her head, and she wore little or no makeup. A pair of designer glasses rested on her nose. Leslie found it surprising that a person who had expensive well-tailored clothes didn't display the same care in her hair and makeup. Maybe she was hiding something or wanted to blend in.

If Brianna would spend time on her grooming, she would be an attractive woman. But like this, she gave the appearance of a stereotypical powerful woman who was all business.

"How is your first day going?"

"Fine, thank you. I just finished the orientation program."

"Oh yes. I suppose Mrs. Holland was there. She does all these new employee orientations."

"Yes, she did, and we got a good overview of the company." Leslie thought she saw Brianna roll her eyes at that comment. They headed to the three workstations that Leslie had seen through the glass partition.

Brianna walked over to one of the workstations. The man working there looked up from his computer. He was wearing a blue shirt with a striped tie, gray flannel slacks, and highly polished shoes. His hair was cut short. He was very good looking, the type you would not be afraid to take home and introduce to your parents.

"Rob, this is Leslie Sherwood. She is the new administrative assistant to Mr. Clark. Leslie, this is Rob Schimel. Rob is the administrative assistant for Mr. Milton. Mr. Milton is the senior vice president of Operations and R&D."

Rob and Leslie exchanged pleasantries, and then Brianna quickly moved to a vacant workstation.

"This is your station, Leslie. I sit over there," she said, pointing to a third work area. "I'm the senior administrative assistant to Mr. Gianti, Senior Vice President of Finance and IT." She emphasized the word "senior" in both instances. She wanted to make sure that Leslie knew the pecking order around here. Brianna was all business and direct to the point with no smile or pleasantries included.

"Give me a few minutes to return some phone calls and I'll show you around. Make yourself at home."

With that, Brianna turned briskly on her heels and walked to her workstation, picked up the phone, and started dialing. She didn't look back to see if Leslie was comfortable in her new location or if she needed anything. Leslie did notice that Brianna's workstation was larger than hers or Rob's and was situated farther away from the other two, and the privacy walls around it were higher. Guess the "senior" title has its privileges.

Leslie sat down at her workstation and placed the company manual and all the papers from the meeting on the desk. The chair was very comfortable, as if it was made for her. There was a computer at the desk, and she noticed a company phone book and a computer manual. She picked up the phone book and saw that her name was already in the book. She looked up Alex's name, and sure enough, he was in the book as well. That brought a smile to her face. She stood up to look around the area to see the layout of the floor.

The workstations were large and each separated from the others so that any conversation could not be heard by anyone else if they talked softly. Across from each workstation was a large office. A large glass conference room took up most of the entire back wall, and to the left of the conference room was an elevator. Leslie's workstation was directly across from Mr. Clark's office, her boss. She could see his name on the door, and a security pad to the right of the door. The door was closed and the lights off.

"It won't take long for you to find your way around."

Leslie turned to see Rob standing behind there.

"Thanks, Rob. New jobs are always tough the first couple of days. They want you to start right away, and you have no idea what you are supposed to do."

Rob stood there leaning on Leslie's cubicle wall, legs crossed and arms folded across his chest like you see models stand in magazines. With his "all-American boy-next-door looks," he could easily be one of those men you see in the fashion magazines. Leslie couldn't help notice his perfect shape. He has to be an athlete, or he works out on a regular basis, or maybe both.

"I remember when I started. You're expected to get everything by osmosis. These bigwigs don't have time to spend with you. But you'll catch on, just takes time."

"I hope so. I hate sitting around waiting for something to do."

"If you have any questions, feel free to ask me or Barb. Between you and me, I'd stay clear of Brianna with day-to-day questions. She is all business and all Brianna." He leaned in as he said that last statement to make sure he wasn't overheard. "She doesn't get close to anyone. I've been here a while and have never witnessed anything but business." As he pulled back, he winked at Leslie and gave her a big smile, showing his perfect white teeth.

"Thanks for the tip."

"I better get back to my area. I see Her Majesty heading this way. Welcome to the penthouse." With that, Rob returned to his station, turning around and giving a small wave. Leslie watched as he walked back to his cube, her eyes on his perfectly shaped butt.

Why would he be working here? she thought. *With those looks, he should be in movies.*

"Okay, Leslie, let me give you a quick tour of this area."

Leslie turned to see Brianna standing there watching her. *I hope she didn't see me staring at Rob*, she thought.

"You will need to discuss your duties with Mr. Clark. He is out of the office today. I'm not sure if he will be back tomorrow. Barb can give you that information. She has been filling in until you got here."

"Barb already mentioned that Mr. Clark will be here tomorrow." Brianna showed no reaction.

"There are three offices on this floor. Mr. Gianti's is the largest," Brianna said with authority and pride in her voice. "Each office has a private conference room that can be entered from both the office and this area.

"We can go into Mr. Gianti's office since he is at a lunch meeting. You should never go into any of the offices without permission, and always knock before entering if someone is in there," Brianna said, looking straight at Leslie as if giving her a warning. "Mr. Gianti, however, has given me permission to enter his office when needed." She placed emphasis on the word "me."

Brianna placed her badge over the card reader to the right of the door and then punched in a four-digit code. Leslie heard a click, and Brianna opened the door. Leslie followed Brianna into the room and looked around the office.

Why does Brianna feel she needs to show me her boss's office? Leslie thought. *Maybe it is to again emphasize her importance on the floor. Probably best to just go along with it.*

"The furniture in each office is different. Each VP has his own style."

The office was very large with a huge mahogany desk and a leather executive chair. A credenza was behind the desk with several pictures of what Leslie guessed were family members. One picture, larger than the others, showed a dog. Nothing else was on the credenza.

"Nice-looking family," Leslie stated, trying to get some type of conversation going.

"I wouldn't know. I've never met them."

Leslie found it surprising that there was not a scrap of paper in sight. On the other side of the room, there were two leather sofas facing each other with a large marble coffee table between them, covered with assorted business magazines. On the wall were artworks that she surmised to be originals. Brianna led the way through an open door to the right of the sitting area. They entered a large private conference room with eight leather chairs around a mahogany table. There were three other doors in the conference room.

"That door leads to the hallway, that one to a private bathroom, and there is one that leads to the area behind the wall that contains all the audio-video equipment," Brianna stated, pointing to each door in succession.

"Each office up here has the same layout. This one of course is the largest." Again she was trying to impress Leslie with her position.

One entire wall of the office and conference room was glass windows looking out over the city. Brianna turned and quickly escorted her out, and Leslie heard the door lock behind her.

"That elevator goes from the first floor to this floor and to the sixty-second floor." She pointed to the elevator on the back wall. "The CEO,

Mr. Sterling, is on the floor above. The boardroom is also up there. This elevator is for the senior VPs' and CEO's use only. I have access as well, so I don't have to take the common elevator bank." Again she placed emphasis on the word "I." "It will be up to Mr. Clark to decide if he will give you access."

Leslie thought, *This woman really thinks she's the cat's meow.*

Brianna headed toward the outer reception area. As they got close to the glass wall, the doors opened automatically.

"Barb, please take Leslie to security so she can get her permanent badge. Then spend some time with her and show her around. I'll have Rob take over the front desk." It was more like a command than asking a favor.

Barb nodded and replied with a simple "okay." The expression on her face was one of either fear or annoyance. Leslie wasn't sure which.

"Welcome to Sterling Chemicals." With that, Brianna turned on her heels and disappeared to the inner sanctum.

"Thank you," Leslie replied, not sure if Brianna even heard her. "She is all business, isn't she?"

"Oh yes! Don't get on her wrong side, and don't say anything bad or negative about the company or any of the VPs on this floor."

"Thanks for the heads-up."

"There are only seven people who occupy this floor full time: the three VPs, their assistants, and me. You are now one of us. Only these seven people have access to the codes needed to get through that glass wall. Anyone else you see on this floor is temporary and has to be escorted through the wall by one of the seven. Rules rules rules."

Just then Rob appeared.

"Thanks, Rob, for watching the desk while I take Leslie to security."

"Did I have choice? When the queen commands, the peasants jump."

Another confirmation of who ruled the area.

"Do you have your badge with you?" Barb asked.

"No, I left it in my purse at my desk. Let me go get it."

"I'll need to go open the door for you." Barb walked with Leslie to the glass doors and placed her badge on the card reader and punched in the code. "Don't worry about getting out. Sensors will open the door when you get close to them. We monitor who goes in, but anyone can escape. Some days I feel I let more people in than come out. I often wonder what happens to them," Barb said with a smile.

Leslie quickly returned to her desk and pulled her badge from her purse. She noticed Brianna on the phone. Brianna saw her and turned away, putting her hand over the mouthpiece as she continued talking.

With badge in hand, Leslie put her purse in her desk drawer and then returned to the front desk as quickly as possible. "Sorry I didn't have it with me."

"Remember you must have your badge with you at all times. That is why I wear it around my neck, so it is always with me. Not the fanciest piece of jewelry I have, but it goes with everything. Let's go get your permanent badge, and then I'll show you around."

They entered the elevator, and Barb pressed the button for the fifteenth floor. As the door closed, Rob waved to them from behind the reception desk. No one else was in the elevator. As they headed down, the elevator stopped on several floors to pick up and let people off. No one spoke once they got on the elevator. They exited at the fifteenth floor, turned left, and walked down a hall. About halfway down the hall was a window similar to a bank teller's window. Barb stepped up to the window and pushed a buzzer on the wall.

"There is so much security in this building. You spend half your time unlocking and locking doors or waiting for someone to let you in," Barb told Leslie. "Did you notice that no one talked in the elevators?"

"Yes, I found that strange."

"It is company policy not to talk business in the elevators, in the restrooms, or any common area where there might be people not part of the company. You never know who is listening near you. Company secrets, you know. You will read about that in the company manual."

A young man with stringy hair down to his shoulders appeared at the glass window. "We are here to get a permanent badge for a new employee," Barb said to the attendant.

"Go to the first door on the left."

Barb led the way. Leslie was hoping to see some of the other new employees from the orientation meeting, maybe Alex. As they got near the door, they heard a buzz, and Barb pushed the door open. No one else was in the room. The stringy-hair man was standing there.

"Give me your temporary badge."

Leslie handed the badge to the man. He walked over to a computer and punched in some numbers.

"State your name and the last four digits of your social security number?"

"Leslie Sherwood 3615."

The man looked at the screen to verify the information. "Stand behind the white line in front of that screen." He pointed to a white screen that hung on a wall. No emotions in his voice.

Leslie positioned herself behind the white line and tried to give her best smile. The flash from the camera went off. The attendant punched some keys on the computer again, and they waited. A few seconds later, a printer started. The man handed Leslie her badge with her picture and employee number already laminated. He also gave her a plastic bag with different attachments to hold the badge.

"You're all set," he said as he put her temporary badge through a shredder. "Keep the badge with you at all times," he said in a monotone voice then went back to his desk and picked up a newspaper. "Welcome to Sterling."

"Thank you." Leslie looked in the bag, pulled out a lanyard, and attached it to the badge and placed it over her head.

"Now I have my piece of jewelry."

They returned to the elevator and the sixty-first floor.

"Keep your badge with you at all times. It is programmed to open certain areas based on your needs. Security will stop you in the hall if they don't see your badge." The same lecture she had already heard several times.

"Okay, now that you are official, let's start the tour of this floor. I'll have you use your badge to open all the doors to make sure it works.

"Rob, can you watch my desk a little longer so I can show Leslie around?"

"No problem, I can work here just as well as at my desk. Have computer, will travel."

They went to the glass wall behind Barb's desk. Leslie placed her badge on the card reader.

"Now enter the code 6605. The code is changed every six months." The glass doors slid open. Leslie repeated the code several times in her mind so she wouldn't forget it.

"Most areas don't have codes. You just need to swipe your card. Each VP has a unique code for his office if he wants. Mr. Clark has used the same code for his office for the past ten years. He says he doesn't have time to change and remember all the codes."

They were now in the sitting area inside the glass wall before getting to the office area. There were two doors on across from each other. One was open, and the other was closed.

They first entered the open door on their right. This room was almost as large as Leslie's apartment. The room contained a sink, a large refrigerator, a dishwasher, and a large commercial stove. A storage pantry took up one wall. Four glass tables, each with four chairs, were scattered around the room. Along the back wall were two doors, one marked MEN and the other WOMEN. A commercial espresso machine sat on one of the counters. Everything was neat and in order.

"As you probably guessed, this is our break room as well as a place to prepare food for conference meetings or to get your morning cup of coffee. It is used only for meetings held on this floor."

They left the kitchen and moved across the common area to the closed door. Leslie noticed that it only had a card reader.

"Open this door, Leslie, to make sure your badge works."

Leslie placed her card over the reader. She heard a click and pushed the door open. As they entered the room, the lights automatically came on. The door closed behind them, and she heard a click as it locked.

"This is the only door on this floor that you need your badge and a special code to get out," she said, pointing to the keypad. "So never come in here without your badge. There is an emergency phone next to the door that is connected directly to security in case you do get locked in."

"I noticed there aren't any security cameras in this room. I see them every place else but none in this room."

"I guess they figure that if someone gets in, he will be caught because he won't know the code to get out."

"Here is another code to remember," Leslie said.

"I know, but you will get used to them. The code to get out is 6570. Don't worry, I'll write them all down for you."

Along the wall were file cabinets and shelves. The shelves were filled with books and piles of paper. The file cabinets were labeled by year. In the corner was a table with a computer.

"This room is where all the confidential papers are stored. The computer is used to search the documents and tell you in which cabinet they are stored. Over time you will learn where things are so you don't need to look them up."

"I hope that it's sooner rather than later. Seems like a lot of trouble to get to a document."

"These are the really confidential documents. These documents represent the heart and soul of this company, as well as all the trademarks and new product information. Some people feel they are more secure here than stored on a computer. With all the hackers out there, you can't be too careful."

"You have a point there."

"Those three file cabinets in the corner have special security." Barb pointed to an area in the far corner. "Each VP has his own filing cabinet. In order to get into those files, you will need a special code. Each of the vice presidents has his own code for their filing cabinet. You just enter the code into the computer in this field, and the file cabinet for your boss will unlock," Barb said, pointing to the input field on the computer screen. "Once you open and then close the drawer, it automatically locks again. Mr. Clark never gave me his code. There was no need for me to get into his file cabinet since I was only temporary. It will be up to him if he wants to give you his security code."

More security.

More codes.

After letting themselves out using the badge and code, they headed back to the front area where Rob was working on the computer.

"Can I have a few more minutes, Rob, and then you can go back to your area?"

"I'd rather stay up here with the princess than back there with the queen," he said sarcastically.

"Why, thank you, Rob. Nicest thing I've heard today. Remind me to name my firstborn after you," Barb replied as they headed down the hallway.

"I thought you already have," he yelled to her as they walked away.

Barb turned and gave him a flirtatious smile as they headed down the hall.

"The common restrooms are down these halls. Women's restroom is here and men's down the other hall." She pointed to a door on the left as they continued down the hall.

They passed several empty offices and conference rooms. "These are used for visitors while they are in town." The hallway wall was glass, so you would see the interior of the office as you walked down the hall. Each office had a carved wooden desk, leather chairs, and a computer. They passed an office that was occupied by a woman on the phone. "That's Dr. Phillips from our research facilities in West Virginia. She is head of the R&D labs and is here to meet with Mr. Milton," Barb said.

Dr. Phillips didn't even look up as they passed the office. She seemed to be in a heated discussion with someone on the other end of the phone.

They could hear the loud talking through the closed door but couldn't make out what was being said.

They had reached the end of the hall and turned back to the reception area. "Let's get a cup of coffee, and then we can sit down and talk in more detail about procedures and answer any questions you might have.

"Just a few minutes more, Rob, and you can go back," Barb said as she passed the reception desk. Rob just gave a quick wave and okay sign.

They entered the kitchen. Barb opened a cabinet and got out two mugs. Leslie noticed that they were bone china with the company logo on them. "I'm having tea," Barb said, opening another cabinet and taking out a wooden box with all types of teas.

"I prefer tea also," Leslie stated.

"This espresso machine makes all types of coffees. Let me show you how it works. Just place your cup under the spout and select whatever you want by pushing the button of your choice. There is one button for hot water. Mr. Clark likes his coffee extra strong with no sugar or cream," Barb said, pointing a button on the machine.

Leslie placed her cup with the tea bag under the spout and pushed "hot water."

"Sugar and spoons are in the drawer, and cream is in the fridge. Let's go back to one of the conference rooms to talk. The chairs are more comfortable in there."

"Let me drop this bag of clips I got from security at my desk on our way." Leslie quickly headed to her desk so as not to keep Barb waiting. She noticed that the drawer that held her purse was slightly open. She was sure she closed the drawer before she left. But maybe this time she forgot in all the excitement. Or maybe someone else opened the drawer?

Leslie headed to the front where Barb was talking to Rob. But she couldn't get the purse in the drawer off her mind.

They headed to an empty conference room to talk, with tea in hand. "Where do we start, Leslie?"

"How about we start by you telling me about you and how you got here and the other people on this floor," Leslie replied.

CHAPTER 9

Leslie was finally going to live in New York, something she had dreamed about for a long time. She liked her current job, but working for her father was not all that exciting. And all the other employees whispered that she got the job because of the relationship. She was leaving now so the accusations would stop. Now everyone wanted to be her friend, hoping she would put in a good word for them as her replacement.

Leslie was raised in Connecticut in an upper-middle-class family. She was the middle of three children, and the only girl, so was the apple of her father's eye. Her older brother lived in Concord, New Hampshire, where he managed several stores for a major grocery chain. Her younger brother recently moved to Minneapolis to take a job with a baking company in the finance department. Her father was president of the largest bank in Hartford and had controlling interest in several small banks throughout Connecticut. They didn't see much of their father growing up because of all his travels, yet their home was always full of cheer and love.

Her mother stayed home to raise the children and was very active in the school programs and community affairs. As the children got older, she started volunteering at the local historical society museum; and after the kids went to college, she took on the full-time job of managing and running the museum. It wasn't a large museum, but she loved the work, and the community appreciated her tenacity.

Like her brothers, Leslie went to the University of Connecticut and graduated with a degree in sociology. Not much call for that major in the workforce, especially with only a BA degree. Her father pulled some strings and got her a position in a branch of a major loan company. After three years, she was a senior VP loan officer. An executive position in her father's bank brought her back home.

Leslie hoped she wasn't boring Barb with her life story. "One day while searching the Internet, I saw the listing for this position. I told my father about it, and he said to go for it. I'm sure he secretly hoped I wouldn't get the job."

"What did your father think when you told him you did get it?"

"Of course he wasn't happy, but he knew I would win any argument in the end. So here I am. I'm just not sure why I got the job since this is out of my area of expertise. I'm sure there were a lot more qualified candidates."

"They must have seen something in you during the interview or you wouldn't be here. Don't sell yourself short."

"I just wonder if my father had something to do with it."

"Don't look a gift horse in the mouth. Even if your father got you the job, it is up to you to keep it. And you know Brianna will be watching you. Just do your best, which is all any of us can do."

"Thanks for showing me around. I know it took you away from your regular duties," Leslie responded as she sat back in the chair. She was starting to relax.

"Don't worry about that. Rob loves to come up front. He says it gets him out of his cage for a while."

"I really appreciate it."

"Let's start by me telling you what my responsibilities are and take it from there," Barb started. "In general, I'm responsible for everything that happens on this floor that involves equipment and supplies. I make all travel arrangements for everyone on this floor and also Mr. Sterling on the floor above. I make sure all conference rooms are clean and have all the supplies and any food necessary for meetings. I also assign conference rooms and offices to visitors and make sure they have everything they need and serve as their assistant while they are on this floor, which takes up a good part of my time . . . kind of like a gatekeeper and gofer for the floor. I'm sure you've noticed the pecking order around here from the little time you've been here," she said with a wink.

"That came across loud and clear," Leslie added.

Barb continued. "I'm also responsible for the kitchen and all the supplies. Therefore, I would appreciate it if you help by cleaning up after yourself and putting your cups and spoons in the dishwasher when you are finished, rather than just in the sink. Some people just leave the dirty cups in the sink for me to clean."

"No problem. Anything I can do to help. And make sure you tell me if I am doing something wrong." Leslie bet that Brianna was one of those who left dirty cups around as a way to show off her seniority.

"I'm also responsible for keeping the room stocked with supplies and everything in working order. There is a supply cabinet in the kitchen if you need paper or pencils or whatever. Not that we use a lot of paper around here. Everything is computerized. But once in a while someone wants a pen. So if you see anything missing or running short, please let me know. I'd appreciate it if you let me know by an e-mail rather than just a phone call, or passing in the hall. That way I have a record and don't forget."

Leslie nodded, showing her understanding.

"I also help with any overflow work that you, Rob, or Brianna might have. So don't be afraid to ask for my help. I am glad to have you here," Barb stated. "I have been doing my job and your job for the past several months. I can now get back to what I am supposed to be doing. So what questions can I answer for you?"

"First of all, thank you for spending time with me today. A new job can be both exciting and frightening . . . You are out of your comfort zone. I'm sure I will be coming to you with questions the next couple of weeks. But I'll try not to bother you so much."

"Don't worry about that. That is why I'm here, and it does get kind of lonely up there. Oh, by the way, don't forget to read and sign the manual by the end of the week and fill out any other forms that were given to you this morning. Just give them to me, and I'll make sure they get to the right people."

"Thank you. First, can you tell me about the people on this floor? How long have you been with the company, where did they come from, and any other information you want to share? And anything you want to share about your personal life or special quirks."

"You mean the Magnificent Seven, as we refer to ourselves? Let's see, I've been with the company for six years, three years on this floor. I started out in HR and then moved to an assistant in Marketing and eventually came here. I'm originally from New Jersey but now live in Carroll Gardens in Brooklyn with my husband, a daughter, and a dog. My husband works for an advertising agency in Times Square. That is my life in four sentences. Kind of boring, right," she said with a smile.

"Sounds like a typical American family. What about Rob and Brianna?"

"Let's start with Rob Schimel. He has been on this floor for two years. I'm not sure how long he has actually been with the company. He just showed up one day out of nowhere. I assume he is single since he doesn't wear a wedding ring. He is a very private person but gets along with everyone. Other than that, I know nothing about his private life. Oh yes, he does like to go camping. I've seen some of his vacation pictures. He seems to be the rugged outdoor type, if you know what I mean."

"Some people just like to keep their personal life separate from their work life."

"And he is very nice to look at," she said with a wink. "He will also help you in any way you want. Don't be afraid to ask him. I've never heard him complain about anything around here."

"He does seem very nice and helpful. And he is very nice to look at. I just wonder why he is working here when he could be in the movies or modeling someplace."

"I've asked myself that questions several times, but I'm glad he is here so we do have someone to drool over."

"What about Brianna?"

"Brianna Welch has been here forever. No idea where she came from, how long she has been here, and nothing about her personal life. Not sure she has a personal life. All work, nothing else. Usually the first one here in the morning and last to leave at night."

"I talked to Brianna once during my interview, and she came across very stoic and all business. She never smiled. Seemed liked she felt she had more important things to do than interview me."

"That's Brianna."

"Can you tell me why the person before me left? No one seemed to know or would tell me," Leslie asked.

"Dawn Manning was here before I was. I don't know much about her. One day she just never showed up for work. No one had any idea what happened or where she went. I really liked her. She was very competent and loved learning about the company. Once I found her in the file room just reading some of the new product documents. When I asked her why she was reading them, she just shrugged and said she just wanted to learn about the company and how it works. Then one day she just didn't show up for work. It was like she vanished from the face of the earth. Her e-mails came back, and her cell phone was disconnected." Barb ended that conversation with a questioning look on her face.

That look registered in Leslie's mind. Was there more than Barb was letting on, or did she have doubts about what she had been led to believe about Dawn's leaving?

"So let me tell you about your boss, Mr. Clark. Since I have been filling in for you for the past ten weeks, I've gotten to know him a little better," Barb stated.

"I only met him shortly at my interview. While Brianna was talking to me, he stopped by. He only asked one question: 'How did you find out about this position?' I guess I made a good impression. The rest of the time he talked about the company and their goals. After about fifteen minutes, he said he was done and left the room and said 'good luck' as he exited."

"He gets the information he needs and makes his decisions quickly. He is a master at that."

"What can you tell me about Mr. Clark's work ethics?"

"Mr. Clark is a tireless worker. He is usually here early in the morning and the last to leave at night when he is town. He does travel a lot. But he is fair. He will be a good mentor to you and help you get settled. He is a company man though. He depends a lot on his assistant. You will need to be on your toes at all times. His mind processes like a computer, never stopping. Just pay attention to him and try to anticipate what he needs. And don't be afraid to make suggestions if you see something that doesn't seem right. He will listen and accept it or reject it. But I have never seen him criticize a person for a suggestion. Don't try to second-guess him though. If you don't understand something, don't be afraid to ask. You will learn a lot from him. Believe me, he will keep you on your toes."

"I guess the learning begins when he returns tomorrow. I hope he gives me more than the fifteen minutes he gave me at the interview."

"Don't worry, you will be okay. And I'm here to help you. Unless you have any more questions, I need to get back so Rob can get back to his desk. Brianna gets upset when she sees he has been gone for a long period of time. You can go back to your station and get settled."

Looking at her watched, Barb continued. "It is four thirty, and I have a few things I need to finish before I head out. Word of caution, don't leave early unless Brianna is aware of it ahead of time. She has no say over you since you don't report to her, but she considers herself to be in charge."

"Thanks for the advice."

They got up, put their cups in the dishwasher, and headed to Brianna's cube.

"Brianna, here is Leslie. She has her badge, and I've given her the tour of the floor and answered all her questions. I'm going up front, and I'll send Rob back."

"Bye, Leslie. If you have any other questions, you know where I am." Barb turned and headed back to the front.

"Thanks, Barb."

Leslie looked at Brianna to see if she needed to spend any more time with her. Brianna had turned back to her computer with her back to Leslie. Leslie returned to her work area. She opened the company employee manual and started to read it. She signed and dated the document when she was done and then walked over to the copy machine and made a copy for herself. She would give the original to Barb tomorrow. Her first day was over, and she made it through with no visible scars.

CHAPTER 10

"Welcome to Sterling Chemicals, Dr. Gregory."
Alex looked up from his desk and saw a woman standing in the doorway. "Thanks," he replied. "I'm just trying to get settled and find everything. I did see the coffee machine as I got off the elevator," he said with a snicker in his voice.

"I'm Jeanette Braun, Mr. Mathews's assistant. He asked me to take you around and introduce you to the other people in the department and see if there is anything I could do to help you get settled."

"Thank you. That would be nice."

They stopped at an empty cube right outside Alex's office. "This is where Lindsey Meyer sits. She has been assigned to you. She must be at lunch now. We can stop by later and introduce you.

"After I introduce you to others in the department, I'll take you through the procedures to order supplies and then take you to security to get your permanent badge. I'm sure you've heard how important that badge is. Your computer and cell phone are here, but you will need to work with the IT department to determine what additional software you might need. Okay, let's go see who isn't at lunch."

Alex followed Jeanette around the department as she introduced him to one person after another. He tried to remember everyone's name by repeating them in his head after the introduction, but it was a losing battle after the fifth person.

They passed three conference rooms and stopped in front of a locked door. "This room contains all the marketing and R&D information about the products. It is locked at all times, and only certain people have access to it. You just place your card on the card reader, and the door will unlock. Because of your security level, you will have access to this room."

"Why does this room have so much security?"

"We have lots of people who don't work here that stop by for business. We have to protect the company assets from wandering eyes. This is our way of protecting the company's secrets."

Alex put his badge over the reader, and the door didn't open.

"It will be on your permanent badge. We can test that later."

They continued into an open area full of cubicles and stopped at a cubicle with the name Janet Ekblad on the nameplate.

"Janet, this is Dr. Gregory. He is starting today. Alex, this is Janet Ekblad. She is the HR representative for our department. Besides HR work, she assists several of the principals on this floor on day-to-day activities."

"Welcome to Sterling Chemicals, Dr. Gregory. I have already received a copy of your file from Corporate HR and am looking forward to working with you. I know you attended the orientation meeting this morning. Let me know if you have any questions. I'm the person you need to turn in your forms to once you have completed them. Remember we need the signed acceptance form from the company manual by the end of day Thursday. I'll get you a copy of all the documents that you have already signed."

"Thank you, Janet. I look forward to working with you, and I'll have everything to you by Thursday if not before."

"Welcome to Sterling, Alex." Just then her phone rang, and Janet looked at the extension calling and gave an indication that she needed to take the call.

Jeanette turned and started down the hall. Alex gave a wave and followed Jeanette. As he walked away, he heard Janet answer the phone. "Janet Ekblad, how may I help you? Oh, hi, Donna. Yes, he is here right now."

They arrived at the corner office.

"This is Mr. Mathew's office. He asked me to drop you off after showing you around."

Jeanette knocked on the door. The man behind the big desk looked up and motioned for them to come in. Jeanette stepped in, and Alex followed. Mr. Mathew walked around the large mahogany desk with his arm extended. It was a larger office, with floor-to-ceiling windows on the outside wall, and an oriental carpet on the wooden floor. On the shelves were pictures of kids next to a couple of golf trophies, and a plaque of some sort. Papers were scattered all over the desk, and a computer was buzzing away on the corner of the desk, the keyboard tucked away in a tray below the desk.

"Welcome, Dr. Gregory, or can I call you Alex?"

"Alex is fine. Actually I prefer it. I haven't gotten used to the title yet. Good to see you again, sir."

Gene Mathews was head of the department and had interviewed Alex for the position. Alex found him very personable and knew he would enjoy having him as a boss.

"Let's sit and chat a few minutes. Thanks, Jeanette. I'll bring him back when we're done, and you can finish the tour." They moved to a sitting area with leather chairs in the corner of the office next to the windows.

"So how is the first day going? I'm sure you have been through the typical orientation BS all new employees go through on their first day. At least that is behind you."

"Yes, I have. Lots of forms to complete, but I guess that is necessary to protect the company and their assets and get me documented," Alex responded.

Gene was about fifty-five and balding in the back. His glasses were pushed up and rested on the top of his head. His clothes were wrinkled and shoes unpolished. Although he was overweight, he carried it well. The image of a Santa figure came into Alex's mind.

"Your credentials are impressive, and I am pleased that you decided to choose my team. I'm sure you had several other offers, but you will enjoy working here and will soon realize you made a good decision."

"Thank you, sir, I look forward to being part of the team."

"So are you settled in the city? Are you living in the city or commuting in like most of us? Not an easy city to find an affordable place to live."

"I was lucky to find a sublet on the Upper West Side for a year. Easy commute to work. But I'm all moved in and settled. Thanks for asking."

"That's good. Finding a place can be rather stressful. Okay, let's talk a little about the team and our charter. First of all, take the rest of the day to get settled in your office and finish any paperwork. I also see that you still have your temporary badge. Make sure Jeanette takes you down to get your permanent badge before you leave today."

"Yes, she said she would do that later today."

"I'm sure you are interested in your responsibilities here. Starting a new job is like entering a tunnel blindfolded. For a while you are wandering around aimlessly. Eventually you get oriented and find your way around."

"I got a little information during my interview, and I'm sure I will catch on quickly and meet your expectations," Alex said.

"Over the past several years, the company has shifted its direction from making commercial chemicals to products that help the consumer, especially in the area of increasing food supply. The company is still highly involved in the commercial chemicals business, the core of our business, but we have decided to diversify. There are seven billion people in the world, and they are increasing currently at 1.4 percent a year. This growth rate is declining, but it will always be around 1 percent. Also, people are living longer. Each year there is less land to produce food to feed all these people. Our mission is to help increase the yield and quality of food products to keep up with this population growth."

"That is quite a challenge," Alex replied.

"With this new philosophy, the company established this division. That is where we come in. Farmers and commercial growers are constantly at war with bugs and crop diseases. About 15 percent of global crop production is lost to pests. This includes insects, fungi, bacteria, and virus that destroy the crops in the field as well as stored food products. The diversity of crop pests continues to grow, and mutations and new strains are constantly evolving. Imagine what we could do if we reduced that to only 10 percent."

"I didn't know it was that high."

"Our direction is to find ways to decrease the lost due to these destructive pests without hurting those insects that are beneficial to us. It wouldn't do us any good if we destroyed the pests but at the same time harmed bees that are necessary for pollination. And if we can get an increase in crop yield at the same time we control the pests, we have a winner. Each year there are fewer acres to raise food crops. So you can see how important our charter is."

"Yes, I do. I hope that the products that we produce are also eco-friendly. The company's philosophy in regard to the environment is one of the reasons I wanted to work here."

"We are very aware of the environmental concerns and don't want to infect our earth in any way with chemicals. We want to keep the naturalists on our side. So creating products that are effective, increase yield, and are eco-friendly, and at the same time are profitable to the company and its shareholders, is our charge."

Alex was glad to hear the philosophy of the company again. It fits right into his beliefs.

"So where do you come in? Some of this I'm sure we discussed at your interview, but let's go over it again."

"I'd appreciate that, sir," Alex said.

"Our Research and Development facility in Charleston, West Virginia, has a host of top chemists who are coming up with new products every month that are potential products. Once the chemists come up with a new formula, they are tested in the greenhouse under controlled conditions to see if they have any potential. More than 99 percent of the new products have no merit. A few of them, however, pass the rigid screening process and are ready to take to field trials.

"We have three research farms where we test our products, Florida, North Carolina, and Texas. There is a farm manager at each location that reports to me and takes his direction from this department. You will be the key person for setting up the testing protocol at the research farms as well as analyzing the data that they send to you. You will also help R&D analyze any data they send you."

"That sounds very interesting, and I'm up for the challenges," Alex interjected.

"Another way we get information on our test products is through our grant programs. We have good relationships with many universities across the country. We provide them with grant money to set up field tests on our products, collect the data, analyze the information, and submit a report back to us. This is usually done on university property where they have an Agriculture Department. Where they don't have property for testing, we will lease land for them to use. That way we can test all types of field crops and maximize the crop and climate interactions across the country. There is a field force of people who report to this division that are responsible for working with the universities."

"How many universities are involved?" Alex asked.

"We work with universities and colleges in all fifty states. We test and retest products in the field for two to three years before we make a decision whether or not to move to the next step."

"What happens then?" Alex asked.

"Once we see we have a potential new product, manufacturing starts working on a cost-effective way to make the product. Finance and marketing start shortly after that. No sense having a product if you can't make it. Also, we prefer to use the current production facilities to keep costs down rather than having to build a new facility."

"How many products are in each phase of the testing cycle?" Alex asked.

"R&D comes up with twenty to thirty new products each month. Most of these fail the greenhouse tests."

"Will I get involved in the greenhouse testing?"

"No, that is under control of a different group. But you will be working with them as a consultant as they see fit, so you will need to get to know those people."

"How many products actually get to the field tests?"

"We usually have two to four compounds good enough to be taken to the field trials each year. Many of those are eliminated because of bad test results or can be scrubbed because there is no cost-effective manufacturing process. Hopefully we get one new product every two to three years to move to market."

"Sounds like a lot of trial and error," Alex remarked.

"Well, that is what it takes. But if we get a good product, it can bring hundreds of millions of dollars to the company, especially if we can take it worldwide."

Gene continued on. "You will be responsible for making sure our field testing is done correctly and helping analyze the data to make sure we make the right decision on which products move forward and which ones we scrap. Each new product goes through a rigorous set of tests to make sure it meets the charter and direction of the company. We must always keep that in mind. We owe this to our shareholders. You are part of the team that will make the decision on the future of our products and direction of the company."

Gene added, "Once a product is identified and we meet FDA approval, we start finalizing production and marketing strategies. The production side is not your concern. You just need to identify potential products and help get it to market.

"Tomorrow you will be meeting with the head of R&D who will take you through the process from their end. She is in town for a couple of days, and I've arranged for you to spend some time with her."

Gene took a breath, leaned back in the chair, and looked at Alex with a serious face. "So is this what you expected when you signed on?"

"Yes, it is. But I'm sure the rest of this week will open my eyes more. You covered a lot of this during our interview, and I've had time to think about it before I accepted the job. It sounds exciting, and I feel my decision to join the company was the right one. It is a big responsibility and one I'll take seriously."

"Good, then we made the right decision too. Do you have any other questions?"

"What happened to the person who held this job before me? Did he leave the company or get promoted? I would like to talk to him to get some kind of perspective if he is available."

There was silence for several seconds before Gene started to talk, and there was a strange look on his face that Alex couldn't interpret.

"Um, Dr. Hudson went on vacation with his family to Montreal several months back, and while there, he had a heart attack."

"That's tough. I'm sorry to hear that," Alex responded.

Gene quickly changed the conversation. "Let me call Jeanette so she can take you to security." It was as if he didn't want to talk any more about Dr. Hudson and what happened to him.

Gene dialed four numbers, and almost immediately Jeanette appeared in the door. "Jeanette, take Alex down to security so he can get his permanent badge. Also, make sure he knows what areas he has access to with his badge.

"I'll see you tomorrow, Alex," Gene said, moving back to his desk, and picked up his phone. He didn't even acknowledge that Alex was still in the room.

"Thank you, sir."

Alex followed Jeanette back to his office.

On their way back, they stopped by the cube that was outside Alex's office. A young woman was working at her computer. She was about thirty years old, slim with short dark hair and dark eyes.

"Lindsey, this is Dr. Gregory. He is the new marketing analyst." Lindsey stopped what she was doing and stood up, offering her hand to Alex. "Alex, this is Lindsey Meyer. She is your administrative assistant. She will help you get settled, answer any questions you have, take care of your travel arrangements, order supplies, and anything else you need done. She is assigned to three other people in this area as well."

"Welcome, Dr. Gregory, just let me know if there is anything you need."

"Thanks, Lindsey, and call me Alex."

Just then Alex heard Jeanette speak softly. "He went on vacation to Montreal with his family and had a heart attack. I still can't believe it."

Alex turned and saw Jeanette staring into his office, talking to no one in general.

"Dr. Hudson?" Alex asked.

"Yes. He was an active person and ran in the last two city marathons. He was a wonderful person." She didn't look at Alex. She just continued to look into the office, with a sad look on her face.

"I'm sorry to hear that," Alex replied, not knowing what else to say.

Jeanette continued as if she was talking to herself. "He had a wife who was devoted to him. She used to come to the office and meet him for lunch. She is a very pleasant person. I haven't seen her since the funeral. He was only thirty-four years old. It is just so hard to believe. He was always a happy guy, smiling, and made sure he said hello to everyone he met. I still can't believe it."

Alex noticed that her eyes were wet, and she wiped back a tear just about to run down her cheek.

She turned to Alex. "Something must have been bothering him. The last couple of weeks he changed. He wasn't his happy self and seemed to be secretive about something." She turned back and looked into the office. "I can still see him sitting there. The furniture belonged to him. It's just so hard to believe," she repeated.

Jeanette looked back at Alex, and he noticed that her eyes were teary. She turned and headed back to her area.

Dr. Hudson's death sure had an effect on Jeanette, Alex thought to himself. He walked quietly behind her, not knowing what to say. When she got to her cube, she pulled out the company manual from the shelf over her desk, the same one that Alex had received that morning. She opened the book to an area she had marked with a sticker.

"Section 4 explains the procedures on how to order your supplies. It is an internal Web site. Just put in your request, and the items will be delivered in morning if there is inventory. If not, they will be ordered for you. Any item over fifty dollars will need approval from Mr. Matthews. Just tell Lindsey, and she will get the necessary signatures and order the items for you.

"Let's go to security and get your permanent badge, and then I'll take you to IT to get your phone and computer." She was back to her composed self. They headed to the elevator and to the fifteenth floor.

Alex went through the standard procedures of getting his permanent company badge. He attached it to the lanyard and put it over his head. He followed Jeanette as she headed to the next stop. He had to almost run to keep up with her.

"The badge will allow you access to the building during and after business hours. During the day, you just need to swipe it at the turnstiles or hold it up to the card reader. After business hours, you will need to show your badge to the guard as well as sign in. Your badge will also give you access to all the common areas like the cafeteria, conference rooms on the twelfth floor, and employee gym. You will now have access to the marketing file room we saw earlier. I'm not sure what other areas you have access to. Mr. Mathews has taken care of that. I don't know why he asked me to tell you. You will need to talk to him about the other areas."

"Thank you, Janette. I appreciate all your help today. I know you have other things to do."

They headed to the IT department on the eighteenth floor, Alex again having to rush to keep up with her. Jeanette introduced him around, and they gave him his company cell phone and wanted to talk to them about the software he needed added to his computer.

"You may be here for a while, so I'll leave you to get things worked out. I have some things I need to finish. You can find your way back. If you have any other questions, Lindsey can help you. Welcome to Sterling Chemicals. We are happy to have you join us." She turned on her heels and headed back to the bank of elevators.

Alex yelled out a "thank you" as the elevator door opened but wasn't sure if she heard him. He then spent the next hour with the people in the IT department discussing his requirements. His computer would be delivered the next day.

Alex headed back to his office and settled in his desk chair. He swiveled around and looked out the large window at the skyscrapers lining the street as far as he could see. Here he was in New York City in his office on the forty-second floor overlooking Park Avenue. He made it through the first day. A small-town boy arrives in the big city, ready to take it on.

CHAPTER 11

Alex looked at his watch and noticed that he still had almost an hour before the end of the day. He didn't want to leave early and have everyone notice. Through his office door, he saw people working away in their cubes and a small group standing and talking in the hallway. He opened the employee manual and started reading, wanting to get that out of the way and the form signed. He was almost through it when his phone rang.

"Alex Gregory, Analytics."

"Oh, I must have dialed the wrong number. I wanted to get hold of Janet Ekblad. Can you transfer me?"

"I'm sorry, this is my first day, and I don't know how to transfer a phone call."

"What number did I call?"

"3432." Alex read the number off his phone.

There was silence on the phone.

"That was my husband's number."

It took a while for it to register that this was the wife of the former occupant of his office, the man who died while on vacation, Dr. Hudson.

"I'm sorry to hear about your husband. I understand that he was well liked here. I hope I can live up to his reputation."

"Thank you. This is Cindy Hudson. And who are you?"

"Alex Gregory. This is my first day," he responded, forgetting that he had already said that.

Again, there was silence on the phone.

"My husband really enjoyed his job at first. He liked the idea that he was helping the people with more and better food."

"That is good to hear. That is one reason I took this job. I want to make a difference too."

"However, the last couple of months he changed. He wasn't the same happy person. Like something was bothering him." It was as if she was talking to herself.

Again, there was silence. Alex didn't know what to say, so he just replied, "I'm sorry."

"He was so happy at first."

Again silence.

"Alex, you don't know who I am, but if it is okay, can we meet sometime for coffee and just talk? It would make me feel better. And I want you to know who my husband was. I don't know anyone else at the company to talk to. So maybe talking about my husband to a complete stranger would help me have some closure."

"Sure, if it will help."

"I think it would help me. Here is my number. Call me after you have thought about it, and we can set something up. If you decide not to, that is okay too. If you decide to call, however, make sure you do it when you are away from the office and on your personal phone." With that, she hung up.

Alex sat there with the phone in his hand, wondering why she wanted to talk to him. What a strange request. He looked at the phone number and noticed that it was a 212 prefix area code. She therefore lived in Manhattan. He put her phone number in his wallet. He sat down and continued to read the employee manual. But nothing registered. All he could think about was the strange request he just got. Her call never did get transferred. And she described her husband's personality change prior to his death, just as Jeanette had stated. Did she intend to call his number, or was it really a mistake? And why the request to make sure he calls from an outside phone?

He heard noises in the hall. Looking up, he saw people leaving or getting ready to leave. It was after five. He could finish the manual tomorrow and turn in the signed sheet then. Right now he couldn't concentrate. He got up, grabbed his knapsack, and headed to the elevator with everyone else.

Nineteen floors above, Leslie had just finished the employee manual.

"Well, how was your first day?"

Leslie looked up and saw Rob standing there, leaning on the wall of the cubicle. Again, the magazine model pose.

"It was okay. First days are always the worst. You don't know what you are doing, and you don't know anyone. Basically you just find things to do to pass the time."

"Cherish these moments. Soon you will be so busy you will be wishing for a day like this."

"Make sure you remind me when I start complaining about not having enough hours in the day to get my work done."

"Locked in my memory bank," he said, pointing to his head. They both laughed. "I have a few more things to do before I can go. I just wanted to make sure we didn't scare you and that you will be coming back tomorrow."

"Don't worry, I'll be here. Thanks, Rob, for helping me today."

"It was my pleasure." With that, he turned and headed back to his work area.

She looked at her watch and noticed it was 4:55 p.m. It was too late to start anything else.

At 5:00 p.m., she took her purse out of the drawer and got up ready to head home, knowing that tomorrow would be a busy day. She walked over to Rob and said good night.

"Good night, Leslie. Glad to have you on board. See you tomorrow."

She was going to stop at Brianna's cube and say good night, but she heard her on the phone.

"Hope she works out. We don't want to have to find a replacement for her too."

Leslie continued to the door without stopping to say good night so as not to interrupt. What did Brianna mean "have to find a replacement for her too"? She's probably talking about someone else. Don't read anything into that statement.

Leslie passed through the glass wall and headed to the elevator. Barb had already gone, home to the typical American family. She pushed the button for the elevator and waited. The door opened, and she got on. She was the only person on the elevator. As it descended, more people got on, and she was pressed against the back wall. It took forever to get to the main floor. At the main lobby, she exited with everyone else and headed to the front door.

"Leslie, hey, Leslie . . . Wait up."

She turned to see Alex dodging everyone and walking at a fast pace toward her. "I thought I recognized you getting off the elevator. So how was your first day?"

"Hi, Alex. Everyone but me had something to do, so it was a long day. Hopefully tomorrow will be better. I see you still have your badge hanging around your neck," Leslie stated.

"Yup, I got it. Hey, I'll show you my picture if you show me yours. See who took the worse picture. But I'm sure you never take a bad picture." They both laughed.

"I've already put that away for the day. Sorry, you will have to see it another time." She took hold of his badge and turned it over to look at his picture.

"That's a good picture of you. I'll take a dozen."

"How about going out for a drink to celebrate our first day? I think we both need it. There's a little place around the corner. Join me?"

"Why not? Let's go."

The bar was already crowded. There were all types of people celebrating the day's end—bankers with coats and tie, young entrepreneurs in jeans and shorts, blue-collared guys, some still wearing their tool belts. You almost had to yell to hear yourself talk. They saw two empty barstools at the end of the bar open up and walked quickly to get them.

"Not sure why I feel like sitting when that is all I have been doing all day," Alex said.

"Tell me about it."

One wall of the bar was covered with mirrors to give the illusion that the place was bigger and more crowded than it actually was. The ceiling was old copper that was polished regularly based on its shine. A young bartender came over and placed a napkin in front of them. "What can I get you?"

"I'll have a margarita on the rocks with salt. What's your poison, Leslie?"

"I would like a glass of the house white wine please."

The crowd got louder as more people entered the bar. Over in the corner, someone yelled, "Happy birthday!" Their drinks came, and Alex toasted, "To our first day." They clicked glasses.

Alex continued. "Today sure was long. I didn't think it would ever end. I can't wait to get something to do."

"I agree. I'm used to being busy all day. This sitting around is not my thing. My boss was out of the office today, so I just had a tour and sat around. Hopefully that will change tomorrow when he's here. But I did read the manual from cover to cover."

The noise got louder, everyone screaming to hear each other.

"It is so hard to talk here with all this noise. I have an idea. Let's finish our drinks and let me take you dinner. There is an Italian restaurant down the street that I've been to. Food is good, and we can talk without screaming. Let's get something to eat to really celebrate our first day," Alex asked.

"It sounds good to me, but only if we split the check."

"You got it." He raised his glass in a toast.

"But I can't stay late. I need to get home."

"Bottoms up and we are out of here."

They finished their drinks. Alex laid some bills on the counter, and they got up to leave. He noticed a guy leaning against the wall close to the door looking in his direction. He was just standing there, not a drink in his hand, and didn't seem to be with anyone. He looked familiar, but he couldn't place him. Where had he seen him before? As they walked toward the entrance, Alex glanced again at the guy. He seemed to be watching them.

"I'm glad to be away from that noise," Alex remarked. "My days of crowded noisy bars are over. I guess I'm an adult now or have entered a new life stage. I'd be deaf if I stayed there any longer."

They merged in with people on the street heading out for dinner, to a bar, to the subway to get home, or to the trains to head to the suburbs. At the corner, they turned left and entered a restaurant called Gaetana's. A waiter escorted them to a table with an open wall to the outside.

"This is much better, and I'm hungry." Alex picked up the menu to look at the options. "The pumpkin ravioli is great. I've had it."

"I'm kind of thinking I'll just have a salad. Baby spinach looks good," Leslie said.

The waiter came. Alex ordered a glass of wine for each of them and gave the waiter the food order.

"So that being done, now can you tell me about the penthouse?"

"It was a typical first day. More forms to complete, a tour of the area, and meeting people on the floor. My boss wasn't in today, so I had nothing really to do. How about you? Apparently you survived the day too."

"It was about the same as yours. Take the new guy around and show him off. I'm trying to remember all the names and functions, but it is a losing battle."

The waiter arrived with the drinks.

"Again, to our first day," he said, raising his glass.

"So tell me about the sixty-first floor. What is it like? I'll probably never get up there."

"If you are good, I might give you a tour sometime."

"I'm going to hold you to that."

"There are only seven of us up there: three VPs, three assistants, and one receptionist. I understand they call us the Magnificent Seven. Not a lot of people to talk to. You won't believe the security though. I've never seen so much. We are behind a glass wall that you need both a badge and key code to enter. And they change the code every six months. Apparently we are the only people who have the codes to enter. And all the offices and rooms need codes to get in, and one room needs a code to get in and out. It is probably easier to get into Fort Knox. And security cameras everyplace."

"I guess with all the technologies people have these days, company secrets need to be secure, unless there are skeletons in the closet they are trying to hide," Alex replied in a sinister voice.

"There were only three other people there today. Rob, the assistant, and Barb, the receptionist, were very friendly. They showed me around and helped me get my badge and talked about their duties."

"You said there were three there. Who was the third?" Alex asked.

"That would be Brianna. But she's a different story. Like the queen bee of the floor. She is all business and also an assistant to a VP. I don't think she smiled once the entire time I was there. I think the others are afraid of her and just keep their distance."

"Guess you will just have to put her in her place and become the new queen bee. Good to be goal oriented," Alex said.

"I doubt it. That's not my style. Just let me do my job. I'm meeting with my boss tomorrow, so I'll get a better idea of a normal day, if there is one."

"I'll check back with you in a month and see who the queen is."

"I hope I don't have to wait that long to hear from you," she replied with that infectious smile.

Just then the waiter brought their food.

"So tell me about your first day. Did you make it through the new-kid-on-the-block routine?" Leslie asked.

"Yup, like you, I was introduced around and then sat with my boss for about an hour. Got the song-and-dance routine about the company and what they are trying to do. Pretty much the same as we heard this morning. I also have an assistant assigned to me. I've never had an assistant. Not sure why I need one. Tomorrow I'm meeting with someone from R&D to talk about new products."

"So, Alex, what exactly will you be doing here?"

"Well, as you know from our orientation today, one division of the company is in the business of developing pesticides to kill bugs that attack crops. The company has three research farms that test the products. They spray the crops and to see if the product killed the bugs, and they also take yield samples. Hopefully the plants sprayed have fewer bugs than those not sprayed. My job will be to analyze the data they collect and determine which products actually work. I'm part of a team that will select which products we market and which we drop. I will then help in the marketing of any of the new products. It takes several years of field testing before marketing kicks in. I'll find out more tomorrow exactly how the process works and who is involved. So that is what I understand I will be doing."

"Wow, sounds important and lots of responsibility."

"Nah, I'm just a number cruncher. But it is a chance to put my training in statistics and chemistry to the test."

"Are there other people doing this with you?"

"Nope, I'm it. I'm replacing a guy who had the job before me."

"What happened to him? Did he get promoted or leave the company?"

"Neither, he died."

"Oh, I'm sorry. Had he been sick?"

"That's the strange thing. Apparently he was on vacation with his family and had a heart attack. I was told he was an active runner and even ran in several New York marathons. Everyone seemed surprised when he had that heart attack. I guess you never know."

"That's too bad. It must have been a shock to his family."

"In regard to that, something strange happened today."

"What was that?"

"Right before I was getting ready to leave work today, I got a call from his wife."

"His wife?" Leslie asked.

"Yes, she said she was trying to call HR but dialed my number by mistake. Apparently it was her husband's number, and she just dialed it without thinking. But before hanging up, she said she wants to meet with me some time to talk about her husband. Apparently she wants me to know what type of person he was."

"That's a strange request," Leslie remarked.

"But I sensed there is something more that she wants to tell me, but no idea what it could be. She gave me her number and hung up. Not sure if she ever did talk to HR or if she even wanted to talk to them. Or was she using that as an excuse to talk to me?"

"Are you going to call?"

"I don't know. But it seems odd. She calls and wants to talk about her husband with a total stranger. And on top of that, she told me to make sure if I do call, to call her from my private phone, not on a company phone. Why was she so specific on how I should call?"

"Sounds like what happened to a person in my area."

"What do you mean? What happened?"

"The person before me, Dawn Manning, just didn't come to work one day. Barb said she just didn't show up one day. Barb has been sending e-mails and calling. The e-mails keep coming back, and her phone is disconnected. Barb says she has been trying to contact her for weeks but no response. It's like she dropped off the face of the earth."

"Sometimes people just get tired of what they are doing and just want to sever all ties," Alex said.

"What was so strange about it is that she was totally interested in the company and how it works. Barb said she caught her once in the file room reading about new products just to learn about the company."

"Good for her," Alex said.

"But then to leave the company like that and go as far as to change your phone number and e-mail address? That is extreme."

"Everyone is different. When some people leave a company, they want to totally disconnect themselves with everyone and everything about it."

"Then when I was leaving, I overheard Brianna on the phone say, 'We don't want to have to find a replacement for her too.' No idea who she was talking to, but it left a creepy feeling with me. Probably nothing though. I tend to overanalyze things."

"I guess we are both lucky in one way—we got a job out of someone else's misfortune. So when do I get to see what it looks like upstairs?" Alex asked, changing the subject.

"You will have to wait until I find my way around more and find out what the rules are. Don't want to ruffle any feathers yet, especially the queen bees. I'll give you a tour sometime, I promise."

"I'll hold you to that. Well, sounds like we both had interesting first days. What will we uncover tomorrow?"

"And with that, let's get the check. I need to get home. I'm a working girl now," Leslie said with smile.

Alex motioned for the check. When it came, he tried to pay.

"Remember our deal. We split the check fifty-fifty."
"Okay, I'll agree this time. But next time, I'm buying dinner."
"Okay, next time."
They both put their money on the table and headed out the door.
They walked the four blocks to the subway.
"Thanks for the dinner, Alex. I enjoyed it."
"It was fun and a good way to end the first day."

Leslie turned and disappeared down the stairs to the subway to Brooklyn. Alex turned and headed in the opposite direction to his subway entrance. He really enjoyed being with Leslie. She was so easy to talk with, unlike any other woman he had ever met. Strange, he thought of her as a woman, not a girl like all his prior relationships. He continued to think about her, and as he did, he felt his body react. As he pushed his way into the subway car, he hoped no one noticed. The train was crowded, and he had to stand. As the subway pulled out of the station, he looked out the window, and he saw the same guy he noticed at the bar as he was leaving. The guy was staring at him through the window of the subway, the same way he looked at him at the bar. Was it a coincidence, or was it deliberate?

CHAPTER 12

Alex woke up ten minutes before the alarm went off and reached over to turn it off. He hated to wake up to a loud ringing. He usually never used an alarm clock, but this being his first real day at work, he wanted to make sure he didn't oversleep. He got out of bed and pulled up the shades to see what type of day it was. Not a cloud in the sky. It was going to be a good day.

This apartment was perfect for him. The right size, the right location, and the right price. He gave another sigh of relief that he no longer had to look for a place. It had enough furniture for him for now. But he needed to go out and get a TV. Sometimes he just wanted to relax and enjoy an evening at home alone. One of those conference room chairs would be nice too.

He made his way to the kitchen, put on the coffee, and headed back to shave and shower. By the time he got out of the shower, the coffee was ready. He toasted a bagel, and breakfast was ready. Putting on a pair of slacks, one of several pairs that he owned, and an open-collared blue shirt with sleeves rolled up and he was ready for the day. He would have to go shopping soon for some more "business casual." Grabbing his knapsack, he headed out.

He stood on the underground subway platform with everyone else, waiting for the train. The temperature in the tunnel must have been close to one hundred degrees. When the train arrived and the doors opened, he pushed his way in, pushing the people in front of him, while the people behind him pushed him in. Although the train car was air-conditioned, the heat of all the bodies quickly took over. He was glad when he got off at the second stop so he could get aboveground to fresh air.

He arrived at the office ten minutes before starting time and took the elevator to the forty-second floor.

"Good morning, Dr. Gregory."

He turned to see Jeanette getting off the elevator behind him.

"Good morning," he said with a smile. "I didn't see you standing there. I apologize."

"That's okay. Most of us aren't awake yet. Don't hesitate to contact me if you have any questions."

"Thank you again for your help yesterday," he said as he watched her head to her work location.

Alex entered his office, took off his knapsack, and sat at his desk. There was a sealed envelope on his desk with his name on it. Opening it, he saw that it was a letter from IT telling him that his computer was all set. The letter also contained his temporary password and instructions on logging on to the company Web site and setting up his passwords. He heard some commotion outside his door and looked up to see Lindsey settling in for the day.

"Good morning, Lindsey," he yelled from his desk.

"Good morning, Dr. Gregory."

First things first. Alex reached into his knapsack, pulled out a coffee mug, and headed to the coffee room. There were several people there for the same reason. Everyone said hello, and he tried to remember who they were. But until he had his coffee, he was a zombie, and no names came to mind.

Just as he got back to his office, his phone rang.

"Good morning, Alex Gregory." He had rehearsed several phone openers while he lay in bed last night and decided this was the one for him.

"Good morning, Alex. How is your day going?" Gene Matthews's name appeared on his phone readout pad.

"Good morning, sir. I have my coffee and am ready to go."

"Bring your coffee and stop by. I have someone I want you to meet."

The phone went dead. He picked up his coffee mug and headed to his boss's office. When he got there, he stood outside the door and waited to be invited in. There was a woman sitting in a chair across from Gene.

"Come in, Alex. This is Dr. Rachael Phillips."

Dr. Phillips, Dr. Alex Gregory."

She extended her hand to Alex without rising from her chair. "It is good to meet you, Alex. Please call me Rachael."

"Thank you, Rachael, it is nice to meet you too. Call me Alex."

"Rachael is the director of New Product Development from our research center in Charleston, West Virginia. She is in town for a few days, and I thought that you two needed to meet. You will be working together and sharing results and ideas."

"Gene has been filling me in on your credentials and background. They are quite impressive. I'm leaving tomorrow, but I hope we can find some time today to talk. I'd like to review our testing procedures with you. I've also brought some data I'd like to have you start analyzing and give me your feedback. We have been at a lost without Peter Hudson these past months."

"I'm available all day today."

"I'll bring her by when we get done here, Alex."

Alex took that as an indication for him to leave. "I'll see you later. Just come by." His coffee cup still in hand, he returned to his office.

On his way back, he stopped by Lindsey's cube.

"Can you tell me where to get some pens and paper?"

"I'll get it for you unless you want to tag along in case you see something else you need. Then I'll show you how to order things on the company Web site. Your company charge card arrived this morning." She reached in her desk and handed it to him. "This is to be used for all your travel expenses and any other authorized expenses."

Alex put the card in his wallet as they headed to the supply room. By the time he got done picking things, his arms were full. He returned to his office and started putting everything away.

"Lindsey, could you come in and show me how to use the phone and basic log-on procedures for the Web site?"

Lindsey was right there as he was putting things away.

"Thanks, Lindsey. It is so much faster to have someone show me than reading the manuals."

"You should be set now, Dr. Gregory," she said after going through the basics with him.

"Thanks, Lindsey. But let's do away with the formalities. You can call me Alex. Just use Dr. Gregory when we are around other people, or follow the same rules you had with Dr. Hudson."

"Let me know if you need any more help," she responded as she left.

He glanced at his computer and noticed he had several e-mails in his in-box. Most of them were welcoming him to the company. But there was one from Leslie. She thanked him for dinner last night. Her last sentence: "How about meeting for lunch today in the cafeteria at about 12:15? You are the only one that I know so you win the lottery to have lunch with me."

A good feeling went through his body as he read her message a second time. Of course he would meet her for lunch. After all, he didn't know that many people here either. And he wanted to see her again anyway.

Looking at the icons on his computer screen, he noticed he had everything he requested. He was ready to go to work. Just then he heard a knock on his door. Looking up, he saw Rachael standing there.

"Come on in." He stood up and motioned her to one of the chairs across his desk.

"I hope I'm not interrupting anything. My day is filled with meetings, but I told Gene I needed to spend time with you."

She sat down, opened her briefcase, and took out a stack of folders and placed them on his desk.

"So how is the second day going? I'm sure yesterday was full of the normal introduction to the company lectures."

"Slow so far. I have nothing really to do right now, so I am checking out the statistical software on my computer."

"That will change now. I brought some data that I need to have you review and give us your analysis and thoughts by the end of the month."

Alex looked at the three folders she placed on his desk. They were each about two inches thick.

"But first, let me tell you about our research program in West Virginia and where you fit in."

She was a short woman, barely five feet tall, and overweight for her size. She filled out the chair as she sat back. Her short black hair was molded around her round face. The shape of her head reminded Alex of a bowling ball. Her business suit was too tight, as if she was trying to hide her weight by wearing something tighter than she should.

"Our research facilities are in Charleston, West Virginia. We have six PhD chemists there who are responsible for developing potentially new pesticides for the market. They come up with sixty to eighty new compounds each month. This is usually done by taking prior compounds, changing the structure to see if it changes the effectiveness of the product. Sometimes they develop an entirely new class of compounds. But that usually takes longer and is more expensive. We also prefer to find products that can use our current production facilities. That helps keep production costs down."

"Eighty new products a month! That's some accomplishment," Alex responded.

"Ninety-nine percent don't pass the first greenhouse screening so are discarded.

"At the same time we have to find products that do not affect the environment in any way. The company prides itself on providing eco-friendly products. We only have one earth, and we have to keep it healthy."

The speech is exactly the same I heard from Gene, Alex thought.

"Our manufacturing plants are also located in West Virginia because of the tax laws. So it makes sense that R&D be there also."

Alex was trying to take notes as fast as he could, especially the names of people involved.

Rachael continued. "These eighty products are then given to Tony Sossatt who is in charge of our greenhouses. His team tests these potential new products in a controlled environment. They apply the new products on corn, soybeans, cotton, and wheat to see if there is any damage to the plants. At the same time, they test the product for control of mosquitoes, aphids, corn worms, and potato beetles to see if they kill any of these bugs and for how long it is effective. Less than 1 percent of the products we give to the greenhouse people pass this first screening. The few that do pass are put through a secondary screening of different plants and insects. Also, at this point we test the products on beneficial bugs like bees and lady bugs to make sure they are not affected. More are discarded after this round. Those that pass both screenings move to field testing. From the potential thousand products developed each year, only two or three make it to field test. That is where you come in."

This was what Alex was waiting for, where he fits in from her point of view.

"Testing in the greenhouse doesn't give us the effect of wind, sun, and rain on the lasting effects of the products. Also, we can't test for changes in crop yield as a result of the product. We could have a great product for killing bugs or mold, but if it causes the plant to decrease yield, it is of no benefit to us. Any new product has to be as good as or better than anything already in the market and have some advantage over existing products," she said.

"It takes five to six years to get a new product to market once it leaves the chemist's lab. During these years, manufacturing gets involved to see if they can find a cost-effective production method using current plant equipment. It may be a great product, but if we can't make it in large quantities that are cost effective, we put it aside."

"That is a lot of trial and error just to get a new product," Alex stated.

"Maybe one, and if we are lucky, two products make it to market every two years. By that time, we have spent millions of dollars. But a new product could potentially bring hundreds of millions of dollars to the company, so the development costs are worth it."

"I hope I have the opportunity to visit the facilities in Charleston sometime," Alex said.

"I'm sure that Gene will want you to make a trip to West Virginia at some point so you can see the whole process firsthand and also meet people responsible for each phase of development. They are a wealth of information when it comes to development and marketing of new products."

"I look forward to meeting them and learning from them," Alex stated.

"The company has three research farms where we test the new products in a natural environment. Each farm is run by a manager who reports to Gene. We have total control over how the testing is done. This gives us good data on how the chemicals react under field conditions. We also get yield results here."

"Gene already discussed the farms with me and my role there," Alex added.

"At the same time, we give grants to universities to test the products for us. We can't cover all areas of the country and all crops and environment conditions by our own farms, so letting the universities help is a great aid to us. They run the tests, analyze the data, and send us the results. Either they have their own farms to use in testing or we lease land for them."

"Gene gave me an overview of that function too, but I'd like to hear what you have to say to get another perspective of the program and how it works."

"Gene has a field force of PhDs who identify and work with the universities to set up these testing programs. They are responsible for making sure the universities are following our protocol and also providing them with whatever they need to run the tests. These field people get the final reports, and they will be sending them on to you to review to see if the research is sound and if the results are supported by the data. If the university does good work, we will renew their grant. The universities look forward to working with us and our competitors. This is one way they get grant money for research projects."

"Do we have standards and criteria that we use to determine the good universities from the bad?"

"We do, but they are outdated, and that is something we want you to review and update. They are only a guideline for setting up protocol for the research methodology and evaluation. You can't tell the universities how to run the test. Basically we give them the money, the product, and the guidelines of what we would like accomplished. From that point, they are on their own. As long as the tests are sound and we get accurate results, good or bad, we are happy."

"Sounds like a good way to get information on new products from all parts of the country," Alex added.

"All of these field people have their PhD in some agricultural field, so they get the respect of the universities. And they speak the same language. I tease Gene about this all the time. He is among the few people in his department that doesn't have a PhD."

"Do you have a big turnover in university participation?"

"The universities like to partner with us. They get the grant money which helps the school and also provides fellowships for graduate students. So they want to remain part of our program. And we get someone to do all the testing for us on our products. It is a win-win situation for everyone. I hope this gives you an idea of our process and where you fit it."

"Now I am starting to see where I fit in and looking forward to being part of the team."

"In this position, you will be wearing many hats and interacting with many different areas of the company," Rachael added.

"What type of interaction and with whom?" Alex asked.

"You will be interacting with R&D, field testing, production, finance, and marketing. You will provide input to R&D where there are new opportunities for products. You will help marketing decide on which products should be deleted from the program and which to carry to the next phase. You will work with the field group to make sure the tests are accurate and data supports the conclusions and also work with the research farms and our farms to make sure test procedures are followed. And last, but probably not least, you will have input to the financial group on the potential profitability of the products tested."

"That is a lot of areas, but I'm sure I can do it. Where do you suggest that I start to get acclimated to the culture?"

"First I suggest you should visit one of our research farms. You will see our setup and get a firsthand look at our procedures and the new products we are currently testing in the field. After all, the farms will be sending you the data they collect to analyze. That will give you a chance to get out of the office and meet some of the people with whom you will be interacting. So that covers my input on your role," Rachael concluded.

"I knew I would be involved in analyzing the data. I didn't realize how involved the process was and that I would be wearing a lot of hats. I'm looking forward to the opportunity to make a contribution to the company."

"You should also spot-check some of the testing done by the universities. Generally their recommendations are right on and supported by the data. But there are those who are only interested in the grant money, and we need to identify them and either cancel their program or work with them on setting up correct testing protocols. You won't have time to check all the reports, however. The field force can also help you identify potential slackers."

"So what do I do if I find university data that looks suspicious?"

"You just report that back to Gene. It is his responsibility at that time. He will work with the universities then or with the field team. He is not a scientist nor a statistician, so he won't be any help to you in the analysis area. He is the first to admit that. But he is a good manager and negotiator. And he will get you what you need to do your job."

"That's good to hear. After I analyze all this data, what do I do with it?"

"You will be part of a team that meets monthly to discuss the progress of these products and make recommendations to senior management. The team consists of me, Tony, Marie Rosa from Finance, Gene, and Pat Saunders from Marketing. Sometimes Mr. Milton sits in on the meetings. He is senior VP of Operations."

Rachael consulted her watch. "I brought some data that I would like to have you review and see if the testing looks sound and how you would interpret the results. There are three products we are currently testing in the field. Two are new this year, and one is in its third year of testing and will go to market in the spring. Write up your thoughts and send it to me by the end of the month. In the meantime, I suggest that you arrange to make a trip to at least one of our research farms as soon as possible. Gene has already approved the trip. Just work with Lindsey, and she will make the arrangements."

"I'll get on this right away," Alex said, pointing to the folders.

She again consulted her watch. "With that, I have to get going upstairs to meet with Mr. Milton. If you have any further questions, you can e-mail me or call me. I prefer an e-mail so I have a record of our conversations."

With that, Rachael stood up. Alex jumped to his feet. "Welcome to Sterling Chemicals, Alex. I look forward to working with you."

"Before you go, can you shed any more light on what happened to Dr. Hudson? I heard he had a heart attack while on vacation."

"We were sorry for what happened. He was a good guy. But in the past several months before his vacation, he became distant." With that, she turned and left his office without any further information.

He had his first assignment. Evaluate three new products by the end of the month. He looked at the folders she left behind. They were labeled with numbers: 57126, 62541, and 67689. He assumed they were in order from oldest to newest in discovery. He needed more coffee. He grabbed his cup and headed to the coffee machine. On the way, he stopped at Lindsey's cube.

"Lindsey, I need to make a trip to one of the research farms. I'm going to get some coffee. When I get back, we will make the arrangements to visit one of them next week. Can I get you something?"

"No, thank you, I have my tea."

Alex turned and headed to the coffee room.

When Alex got back, there was a piece of paper on his desk with the location of the three research farms and the name of the managers for each farm. Alex walked to his door. "Lindsey, can you come in when you have time to talk about this trip." Lindsey stopped what she was doing and followed Alex into his office.

"Let's see," Alex said, picking up the piece of paper. "There is one in Texas, Florida, and North Carolina. Do you have any recommendations?"

"Dr. Hudson liked to go to North Carolina. He said the weather was better, and the farm manager was easy to work with. It is also close to Raleigh, so easy in and out."

"Then North Carolina it is. I have a fraternity brother who lives close by. Maybe I'll look him up if I have time."

"When would you like to travel?"

"Well, this is the short week due to the holiday. So let's make it Monday morning."

"The farm is about thirty-five miles from the Raleigh airport. How long would you like to be there?" Rachael asked.

"Find a flight that leaves Raleigh Wednesday afternoon so I will be back here Thursday morning. That gives me about two days at the farm."

"I'll make the hotel and car reservations and also get a car service to pick you up at your apartment."

"Can you make sure the rental car has a GPS?"

Lindsey left to make the arrangements.

He sat back and pulled the first folder toward him. But all he could think about was Rachael's last statement. Was Peter hiding something?

Did he find out something about the company or one of the products? That couldn't be it. If it was, Alex was sure it would have been addressed and he would have been told. Why did Jeanette, Gene, and now Rachael avoid further discussion of Dr. Hudson's death?

CHAPTER 13

Leslie arrived at work right on time. Brianna, Barb, and Rob were already there. Barb and Rob gave her a "good morning." She said "good morning" to Brianna as she passed her desk but just got a look in return. As she settled at her desk, she noticed that Mr. Clark's office door was open, and he was behind his desk. She got up from her desk and went to his office and knocked on his door.

"Good morning, Mr. Clark."

"Good morning, Leslie. I heard you started yesterday. Good to have you on board. Give me a few minutes, and then we can talk."

"Can I get you some fresh coffee?"

"I'm way ahead of you. Get what you want and get settled. I'll get back to you in a few minutes," he said as he picked up his phone.

Leslie got her coffee and returned to her desk. She turned on her computer and checked her e-mail. There was nothing there. She sent Alex an e-mail asking if he wanted to meet for lunch. That put a smile on her face. She really did like him. She hoped he was available.

"You can come in now, Leslie."

She picked up a notebook and joined Mr. Clark in his office. He was still on the phone when he entered. "We'll talk about that when I'm there next week. Put it on the agenda. It sounds like we might have a winner, as long as we don't encounter any other issues." He hung up and turned to Leslie. "Take a seat, no need to stand there. Welcome to Sterling."

"Thank you, sir," she replied as she sat in a chair across from him.

He leaned back in his chair, his shirtsleeves rolled up to his elbows. He appeared shorter when sitting than she remembered and looked like he had trouble pushing away from the dessert table. His stomach rolled over his belt. There was a half-eaten candy bar on the desk next to him. He had a full head of hair that was a mixture of black and gray. Leslie estimated his age to be midfifties.

"So I assume you are settled in and ready to go. Did Brianna fill you in?"

"Everyone showed me around yesterday but didn't tell me too much about my responsibilities as related to your needs."

"Let's start with a few things that need to be done right away. And then we will add to that as we go along. First, you will need to complete my expense report after each trip. Since you will also be making my reservations, you will be familiar with my itinerary. I'll give you all the receipts and paperwork, and you fill out the forms. I'll then sign it, and you take it down to accounting."

He gave Leslie a folder. "Here are the receipts for the trip I was on last week and yesterday. Barb can get you the forms and get you started. I like my expense reports hand carried to accounting rather than sent through interoffice mail. When you go to accounting, give them to Carren Steffin on the twentieth floor. Here is my company credit card. Write down the numbers so you have them when you need it."

Leslie was busy writing as he talked. She wrote down the numbers from the credit card and handed it back to him.

"I also want you to make all my plane and hotel reservations. You can have Barb do it if you want, but I will go through you when I want them made."

"Second, I will answer all my phone calls. However, if I am out of the office or on the phone, you take the call and relay any issues you feel I need to know. You can call me on my cell phone if it is urgent and I'm out of town. However, if it doesn't need an answer right away, you can wait until I call in or until I get back into town."

"Third, the important company documents are stored in the file room. I'm sure that you have been shown where that is." He picked up his phone and turned it over. Leslie noticed a piece of paper with numbers written on it attached to the bottom. "The code for that room is 4055. I suggest you spend some time in there getting familiar with the system. Barb can help you.

"I also keep some currents documents in my office," he said, pointing to a cabinet in the corner.

"Do you also want me to file documents there?"

"Those are my personal documents. The file is locked at all times. There is no need for you to have access to that cabinet."

"I keep my office door locked when I'm not here. The code to get in is 3802."

Leslie quickly wrote down the numbers.

"I have some documents here"—he pointed to a pile on the credenza—"that I need copied and filed. After you copy them for me, file the originals in the file room. Barb can show you my filing system. I need to fly to Charleston tomorrow morning. Work with Barb and get the flights and hotel to me by the end of day today. I need to come back Thursday morning."

Just then his phone rang. He looked at the caller ID. "I need to take this. We'll talk later. Please shut the door on your way out. Oh yes, you can use the elevator by the conference room if you want when you come and go. The code there is the same as the glass doors."

Leslie picked up the pile of folders and left.

"So what is the issue now with that product?" she heard him say as she shut the door.

Leslie went back to her desk and started to go through the receipts and files to get a sense of what they were before she went to Barb with her questions.

Alex had finished reviewing the first set of documents when he looked at his watch and realized it was time to leave to meet Leslie for lunch. He picked up the documents to put them in his desk drawer. As he pulled the desk drawer open, he heard a "snap" sound. He pulled the drawer all the way open and looked inside; it was empty. He put the folders into the drawer and closed it. But it didn't close all the way. He tried again, but it still wouldn't close, as if it was catching on something. Finally out of frustration, he bent down and pulled the drawer out. Reaching back, he felt around and found a tightly folded piece of paper taped to the top of the drawer causing it not to close. He pulled the paper out and threw it on his desk then put the drawer back in.

Glancing at this watch, he noticed he would be late meeting Leslie if he didn't leave right away. He walked quickly to the elevator, taking it to the cafeteria.

Just as he stepped out of the elevator, another elevator door opened, and Leslie stepped out.

"Now, that's good timing. Let's go check this place out. I'm hungry."

There were different food sections in the cafeteria: a salad area, cold sandwiches, hamburgers, hot entrees, and a dessert bar. Leslie went to the salad bar, and he went to the cold sandwiches. Leslie found a table and signaled to Alex when she saw him looking around.

"Quite a selection," he said, putting his tray down, his change still in his hand. He opened his wallet to stuff his bills away. As he did, a piece of paper fell out. He picked it up and noticed it was Cindy Hudson's number. He stuffed it back into his wallet.

As Alex sat across from her, Leslie looked past his head and noticed a guy looking at them. He was sitting alone at a table with just a cup of coffee. That was not much of a lunch. She had the strange sense that she had seen him before but couldn't place him. Maybe one of the many people she passed in the hall.

"You are only having a salad for lunch? That won't put meat on your bones. So how is your second day?"

"I met my boss today, and he gave me some things to do, but nothing really exciting. I hope it gets better. How was your day?"

"I'm sure your days will get better and exciting. You just have to give it time. I actually got some real work to do. They gave me some data to analyze. One of the new products is showing good field results. It's called 571 something. I can't remember the rest of the numbers. And on Monday I'm traveling to the research farm in North Carolina. They want me to check it out and evaluate the testing procedures. I'm also going to try to see an old college buddy who lives close by if time permits."

"That sounds exciting. It is good to keep in touch with people who have been part of our lives."

"I know. We had some good times together during my undergraduate years. After graduation, I keep in touch with him."

"Again, thank you for dinner last night. It was fun." She glanced over Alex's shoulder and saw that the guy was still looking their way.

"It was my pleasure. I had a good time too. We need to do it again."

"I'd like that, especially when I don't have to do any cooking."

"Remember me telling you that I got a phone call from the wife of the person who had my office before me? She gave me her phone number and told me to call her sometime when I'm away from the office."

"Yes . . . and?"

"What do you think about that? Should I call her?"

"Do you have any idea why she wants to talk to you?"

"She said she wanted to let me know what a wonderful man her husband was. But I think there is something more she wants to tell me. But for some reason, she didn't want to talk about it on the phone. It was just a feeling I had. And she made a point that I should call her when I'm away from the office. She said she wanted to meet too. Why would anyone want to meet someone they don't know to talk about their spouse?"

"What do you have to lose if you meet with her? Maybe it will help her, and who knows, maybe it will help you too. Give you some insight about the job and the people you are working with. If you don't call, it will probably nag at you."

"You're probably right. I'll always wonder if I don't call. Okay, I'll call her. You see, already I can't let it go."

"So are you doing anything special for the holiday weekend?" she asked.

"I'm in New York. I'm going to go watch the fireworks. Doesn't everyone? After all, it is the Fourth of July."

"I've lived most of my life in this area and have never seen them, except on TV."

"Why don't you join me? It would be fun to watch them with someone."

"You know, it just might be fun. I'd like that very much." The rest of the lunch was spent talking about job expectations and things to do in New York City.

Alex looked at his watch. "Well, lunch is over, and I need to get back and finish looking at some numbers. And you probably need to get back to the penthouse."

They picked up their trays, put them in the drop-off station, and headed back to the elevator. As they left the cafeteria, Leslie looked back and saw that the man was still looking at them. Why was he watching them? And where had she seen him before?

Alex's elevator arrived first. As he got on, he turned and waved to Leslie as she stood waiting for her elevator to arrive.

He headed to his office to start reviewing data. As he sat down at his desk, he noticed the folded paper that he had found taped to the top of his desk drawer. He unfolded it. He had no idea what he was looking at, but it must have meant something to someone. On it were two chemical structures with a large question mark.

He didn't recognize the chemical structures. He kept looking at the structures, but nothing came to mind. Must have been something Peter Hudson was working on and put in the drawer, and it got caught there. No, it couldn't have gotten caught; it was taped to the top of the drawer as if he was hiding it from someone. What did it all mean? He would try to figure that out later. Right now he had some data to analyze. He wanted to get some more done before he left for the day. He folded the paper and put it back in the desk drawer. Grabbing the folder with the data, he turned back to his computer.

Leslie exited the elevator and returned to her desk. She picked up a folder and started toward the copy machine. She heard loud talking in Mr. Gianti's office. She picked up a file and headed to the copy machine. Just then she heard the door open in the glass partition. She looked in that direction. Coming through the glass door was the man that she had seen in the cafeteria staring at her. He walked over to Mr. Gianti's office door and knocked. Someone opened it, and he entered. When he passed Leslie's area, he didn't even look at her. Did he do that on purpose, or did he not see her? He must have been someone important because he knew the code to get through the glass security door.

"Who is that?" Leslie asked no one in particular. Rob was nowhere in sight, and Brianna was sitting at her desk staring at the closed door with an angry look on her face.

"He's from security," she blurted out.

Just then the door opened; and Rob stepped out of Mr. Gianti's office, closed the door behind him, and returned to his desk.

Brianna watched Rob return to his desk, and she had that same angry look on her face.

Several questions went through Leslie's mind as she watched the parade of people.

What was Rob doing in Mr. Gianti's office with the door closed?
Why was Rob there and not Brianna?
Was he the person Mr. Gianti was talking loud to?
Why is the security guard there?
Why does the security guy know the codes for the glass door?

Leslie keep looking back and forth at Rob and Brianna and then back at the closed door. She could not hear anything. Just then the door opened, and the security guy came out, shutting the door behind him. As he passed through the work area, he didn't look at anyone. The glass door opened, and he was gone.

Leslie realized she had been standing the entire time holding the folder and watching the parade of people.

She returned to her desk, picked up a pile of documents, and headed to the file room. She put her badge on the card reader and heard the click of the door. As the door closed behind her, she wondered if any of this was about her. But how could it be? She had only been here a few days. Yet the guy was the same guy who was there at lunch, and she was sure she had seen him before. But where had she seen him?

Then it hit her. She had seen him in the bar after work yesterday. The same night that Alex had taken her to dinner. He was standing against the wall as she left with Alex. Was he watching her? And if so, why? A shiver ran through her as she opened the drawer of the file cabinet.

CHAPTER 14

For as long as he could remember, the view from the kitchen window was his favorite from the old farmhouse. It was here that he could see everyone approaching down the long driveway from the county road. He watched the dust kick up from the wheels as the vehicle moved closer and closer to the house until it finally came into view. He watched and waited with anticipation to see who was coming to visit. As a child, he had to stand on a chair to see the cloud of dust. As he got older, he no longer had to stretch to see, but the excitement and anticipation was still there. It was his window to the world as a child.

No cars were coming down the road now, but Mark stood looking out the window. He saw the fields of corn and soybeans and the two neighboring farms. Even the large willow tree that was in the front yard didn't block the view. To its right, the old barn was visible. He remembered it being a bright red, getting a new coat of paint every few years. Now it stood faded after years of weather abuse. As a child, he used to play in the hayloft on the second floor, making forts from the stored hay bales. He and his friends would spend hours living in a fantasy world. Now it stood empty.

"Mark, how many sandwiches do you want?"

He turned to see Diane standing at the round kitchen table in the center of the room, a butter knife in her hand and a questioning look on her face. His mom was sitting in a chair at the table folding napkins.

"Two."

"Sure, you always say that, and then you complain that I didn't make you enough. I'll better make three," she responded softly, turning back to the table and pulling out two more slices of bread. Even though he had a good appetite, there wasn't an ounce of fat on him. He often wondered where he got his six feet height since his mother was only five feet six and his father stretched to reach five feet ten. His father would tease him as a child, telling him that he was left on the doorstep by gypsies. But that was impossible. His facial features were just like his dad's.

In college, he would wear his hair long, the front hanging over his blue eyes. Now his hair was short, cut close to the scalp. He had a nose just like his father and grandfather, and the same crooked smile. There was no doubt that he was a member of this family.

It was Sunday, the weather was perfect, and he had promised to take the family on a picnic to the far pasture. It was a patch of land that his dad had left unfarmed, with trees and grass for just such purposes. As a child, the family would go there on warm Sundays after church. His father had built him a treehouse where he would play while his parents relaxed below. As he got older, he would join them sitting on the old blanket, the one set aside just for these occasions. They would sit and talk about the events of the week, or he would just close his eyes and think about the future.

In those days, his thoughts were about leaving the small town and the farm and moving to the city where there was excitement and adventure. There must be something special about the "big city" that lured people there. So after high school, he headed to the city and entered the university. Five years later, he was back, realizing how great this simple life really was.

His dad had lived on this farm all his life, as did his grandfather who was also a farmer. The four hundred and sixty acres provided a good livelihood for the generations of families. Now Mark had come home with his wife and daughter. They had moved into a small extended wing of the main house that he and his dad had built, with a covered porch between the two houses. But it seemed as if they spent most of their time in the old farmhouse with his parents. His parents adored Diane and worshipped his daughter. It was a good life.

As Mark turned back to the window, he noticed movement in the field beyond the shed that housed the farm equipment.

"Gretchen is ready, Daddy."

Mark looked down to see his five-year-old daughter standing there holding her favorite doll. He reached down, picked her up, and gave her a kiss on the cheek. Lisa held her doll tightly as he gave her a hug.

"We will be ready as soon as Mommy and Grandma get everything packed. You go play with Gretchen, and I'll call you when we are ready. Tell Gretchen she just has to wait like everyone else."

He gave his daughter another kiss on the cheek and put her down, watching her run into the living room and sit on the floor in front of her grandfather. As usual, his dad was sitting there reading the newspaper.

"We have to wait until Mommy gets the food ready," she stated with a stern face to her doll. "Then we will go on the picnic. You just have to wait."

Mark watched Lisa for a while, and a smile came over his face as he looked at his only child. Lisa got her red hair and sparkling eyes from her mother. He hoped that someday she would have a little brother or a sister. Being an only child himself, he always wanted a sibling. But right now she was enough. Mark turned back to the window and watched the movement in the field to the left. There were people there walking up and down the rows of crops swinging nets. Mark had seen them there for a few weeks now but didn't pay much attention to what they were doing. One of the workers was standing at the edge of the field that bordered their driveway.

"I'm going for a walk. Call me when you are ready."

"As usual, leave all the work to the women," Diane responded with a smile

"That's because you are so much better at it than I could ever be."

Mark gave her a kiss on the cheek, grabbed his baseball hat from the hook by the door, and headed out. He pushed the screen door open and heard the familiar squeak as it slammed shut, then headed toward the field.

The field where he saw the movements belonged to Joe G. No one used Joe's last name, everyone just calling him Joe G. He had never married and worked the farm by himself all his life. It had belonged to his parents, and upon their retirement, he just stayed on and continued farming. He always said he was born to be a farmer. Joe G. was now in his sixties and still lived in the farmhouse, leasing out the land.

Mark watched the two people in the field moving up and down the crop rows. The field ran along one side of the gravel driveway that divided Joe G.'s property from his dad's. The two were swinging nets across the plants, stopping periodically to look inside before continuing down the row, repeating the sequence of events.

Mark continued to walk toward the field, stopping at the edge of the driveway. It was then that he noticed that one was a female. The other person, a man, was standing on the edge of the field. He looked up, and Mark gave him a wave. The guy stopped what he was doing and waved back.

"Isn't it kind of hot to be out in the field without a hat? Also, don't you know that today is Sunday? You should be home resting."

"I'm used to the heat by now. Anyway, I like the sun, and it is good for my tan. Gals like it too." The guy was shirtless and had a golden tan. Mark guessed he was in his early twenties.

"I've seen you out here from time to time and am just wondering what you are doing."

"We are collecting bug samples."

"For what reason?" Mark asked.

"This land is leased by a company that makes insecticides and plant growth products. This is how they test new products. We spray the plants; and then twice a week, we take one hundred swings of the net in five locations, count the number and types of bugs we find, and measure the height of the plants. Then at the end of the season, we measure the yield."

"But today is Sunday. You should have the day off."

"We were scheduled to work on Friday, but being the fourth, we got the day off. We will only be here a couple of hours, so no big deal. We still have plenty of time to get home and enjoy the day."

Mark's curiosity got to him. "So have you found anything interesting?" A mosquito landed on his arm, and he swatted it before it had a chance to bite him. "Damn mosquitoes. Too much rain this spring, I guess. Got something for them?"

"I wish. I've been swatting them ever since I started here a couple of months ago. I've never understood the need for these critters."

Just as he said that, Mark swatted another mosquito on his arm.

"Well, a couple of the products seem to be okay. One is in its third year of testing and looks damn good. It seems to kill almost every bug on the crops we have planted here, and we have also seen an increase in yield and rate of growth. If you look across the field, you can see the rows that have been treated with this product. They really stand out. Plants seem to be taller and thicker. But apparently it doesn't kill mosquitoes," he said as he swatted another one.

Mark looked across the field. "You're right, I can see differences. What is it called?"

"I don't know. We just know it by 57126. Rumor has it that it will hit the market soon, ready for next spring. They probably have a name for it, but I don't know what it is. It should make the company a butt load of money though."

"Do all of you work for the company?" Mark asked, gesturing toward all the other people working in the field.

"None of us are full-time employees of the company. Most of us are students doing this for a summer job. This is my third year at it. I must be getting old though, because by the end of the day, I'm out of breath and worn out. Never used to be like that," he said as he swatted another mosquito.

"What's the name of the company?"

"Sterling Chemicals."

Where have I heard that name recently? Mark asked himself.

"The company provides grants to universities to lease land for testing of products. They just fund the research, and the colleges do the work and send in their results. That is how we all got these jobs. Two of us are graduate students, and we do this as part of our research. Kill two birds with one stone: get our data and get paid for it. And it helps with my tan too. There are three others that are here from time to time. But they are just students looking for summer jobs while in college.

"I would like to be more involved with the manufacturing and distribution of the new products," he continued, "but they don't tell us worker bees shit, except get out in the field and swing those nets."

"I wouldn't complain if I were you. As you said, you get paid, and you get the gals," Mark responded with a smile, as he swatted at a mosquito buzzing around his head.

"Damn bugs, it is as if I'm wearing a sign that says, 'Bite me'," Mark said.

"Well, I better get back to swinging this damn net so I can get out of here. Nice talking to you." The guy turned and went back to his work.

Mark stood and watched the rhythm of all the workers. Just then Mark heard the squeaky screen door open, and Diane yelled to him, "Mark, come on. We're almost ready to go."

"The boss calls. You see, everyone has a boss," Mark said and turned toward the house as he waved good-bye.

Mark picked up his pace as he returned to the house. He knew his mom didn't like to wait when she was ready to go. Patience was not one of her strong suits.

Diane stood in the doorway, her red hair pulled back away from her face.

Sterling Chemicals . . . Mark couldn't get that name out of his mind. Where had he heard it recently? Then it came to him. It was in an invitation letter he received from his college fraternity about a reunion after the homecoming game in October. It listed all the fraternity brothers by year of graduation, their current location, and their e-mail addresses. Mark remembered going through the list to see where all the guys ended up. He remembered seeing the company name on the invitation letter he had received in regard to the fraternity reunion. But who was working there?

"I'll be right back. I have to check something," he said to anyone listening and headed to the living room. In the corner was an old rolltop desk that belonged to his grandfather. He opened it and pulled out the invitation and scanned the list. There it was, Sterling Chemicals, Alex Gregory. They had been good friends in college even though they were a year apart in school. Alex went on to graduate school as he finished his ungraduated work. They kept in touch for a while but slowly lost contact. He had gone back to the farm, and Alex had moved on. What a small world.

CHAPTER 15

Mark stood there holding the letter. Memories poured into his head as he watched Diane and his mom finish packing the picnic basket. Lisa was trying to pull her granddad out of his chair to get him into the kitchen so they could all go on the picnic.

"They aren't ready yet, Lisa. You sit and play with Gretchen. Grandma will call you when we are ready to go on the picnic." Lisa sat down on the old rug with Gretchen, and his dad went back to his newspaper reading. A big smile came over Mark's face. Life couldn't be more perfect than this.

Mark thought back to the time when he first saw Diane. He was standing in the hallway of a sorority house waiting for his date, a girl he had met a week earlier at a party. Now several years later, he couldn't even remember her name.

The front door of the sorority opened, and in walked two young women, one of them the most beautiful woman he had ever seen. She had long red hair that hung down to her shoulders and green eyes that sparkled. As she walked by him, she looked up from her conversation and caught his eye. A smile appeared on her face, and their eyes met and held there for what seemed like an eternity. She then climbed the stairs and disappeared somewhere on the second floor of the sorority house. He continued to look up the stairs even after she had disappeared, hoping that she would reappear again.

"What are you looking at?" Mark turned to see his date standing and looking at him.

"Oh, nothing . . . ready to go?" he responded as he stood there hoping she didn't see him staring at another girl. He took his date's arm and headed toward the door, glancing one last time over his shoulder to see if the goddess would by chance be standing there. But the stair landing was empty.

Mark remembered very little about that date. His mind kept thinking about the girl who smiled at him in the hallway. He was out with one woman but thought about another the entire evening. That was the last time he ever went out with that girl, whatever her name was. But to this day, he thanked her for being available that night.

For weeks after that, he found himself going out of his way to walk past the sorority house to see if he could run into the goddess. But he never saw her.

Then one day he walked into the reading room of the library; and there she was, sitting at a table, her head buried in her books. His palms became sweaty as he sat down at the other end of the same table on the opposite side. He had a good view of her as she leaned over her books. They were the only two people at the table. He started to spread out his books and notebooks, making as much noise as he dared in the library, in the hopes she would look up. But she never did. He continued to stare at her. He was afraid that if he stood up, his knees would buckle under him or she would see the bulge in his pants. He was like a schoolboy with his first crush. In all his nervousness, he knocked one of his books off the table. The noise of it hitting the floor echoed through the library. She looked up briefly, and he saw a hint of a smile on her face before she went back to her studying. Mark felt his face turn a bright shade of red.

He sat there and tried to study, but he kept looking up to see if she was looking his way. This went on for almost an hour. Then she suddenly started putting her books together to get ready to leave. Mark hastily did the same so he could leave at the same time and try to start up a conversation. As they came to the front door, Mark stepped ahead and held the door open. As she passed through the door, she turned back, smiled, and said, "Thank you," with that twinkle in her eye.

"Aren't you a Sigma Chi?" Mark blurted out.

"Yes, how do you know?"

"I saw you one night when I was at your sorority house." Before she could ask any more questions about why he was there, Mark changed the topic. "I'm Mark, Mark Lundquist. Do you have time to stop at the Student Union for a cup of coffee? I'm sorry if I came on too strong, but I've wanted to meet you ever since I saw you at the sorority house that night."

"Hi, Mark, I'm Diane Winston," she responded, looking into his eyes. "Yes, coffee would be nice," she said with that same twinkle in her eyes that he remembered.

He desperately wanted to grab her hand as they walked from the library to the Student Union.

She had the most beautiful long red hair. She stood about five feet eight inches, just four inches shorter than Mark, and had that envied hourglass figure. She wore a yellow dress that stopped right above her knees. The color made her red hair stand out. She seemed sure of herself and had a smile that could melt ice.

Over coffee, he found out that she was a year behind him in school and had also grown up in a small town. She had two brothers, and her father was a pharmacist in the only drugstore in town. She had come to the university because her older brothers had both gone there. One was a senior like Mark, and the other had already graduated. She was the little sister with the big brothers to help her adjust to the city.

They talked for several hours over several cups of coffee and even shared a piece of pie. It seemed like only a few minutes had passed when they realized how late it was.

"I need to get back to the sorority house. I have an early class tomorrow."

"May I walk back with you? I want to make sure you get home safe."

When they reached the front of the house, she turned to him. There was that twinkle again.

"Thanks for the coffee and the conversation. I had a wonderful time"

"No, I should be thanking you. Um, if you are free on Friday, how about a movie?"

"I'd like that very much," she answered with a smile.

"How does six thirty sound? We can stop and get something to eat first."

"That will be fine. Thanks, Mark, and I'll see you on Friday," she said and then turned to go into the house.

Mark opened the front door for her. After she entered, she turned around and gave him a small wave with that big smile. He watched through the glass as she climbed the stairs and disappeared on the second floor. He stood there for a few minutes just reliving the great feeling.

Mark couldn't get Diane out of his mind. He didn't think that Friday would ever come. As he sat in his classes or tried to study in the library, his mind kept going back to the vision of Diane turning and smiling back to him. He wondered if she had the same feeling toward him.

His classes on Friday were finally over, and he was back in his room getting ready. He put on a sport jacket over a blue shirt and climbed into his best jeans and black shoes. He stood in front of the bathroom mirror, ran his fingers through his hair, and took a deep breath. He was ready for the night and whatever it might bring.

He didn't remember walking to the sorority house, but he found himself standing in the foyer waiting for Diane to appear. One of her sorority sisters had gone up to get her. He wasn't the only one standing there. Several other guys were waiting for their dates as well. He wondered if they were as nervous as he was. One after another their dates came down the stairs, and they left. Soon there were only Mark and another football-type guy waiting.

Then there she was, coming down the stairs smiling, more beautiful than he had remembered, wearing a green skirt and a yellow and green matching top, her hair flowing over her shoulders.

"Hi, Mark, here I am, ready to go."

"Hi, you look nice," Mark responded then thought, *What a stupid remark.*

"Thank you. Shall we go?" She sounded so confident.

They headed to the front door. Mark held the door open while she walked out, and they were at the start of their first date.

Mark had suggested a local Italian restaurant that was close to campus and frequented by the college crowd.

"That's a nice place, one of my favorites," she responded.

On the way to the restaurant, they talked about school and the upcoming football game on Saturday. Like Mark, she wanted to try living in a large city so went to the state university where her brothers had also attended. She was majoring in math and wanted to be a high school teacher. Since he was an economics major, they had something in common to talk about.

When they got to the restaurant, they found an empty table by the window and grabbed it before someone else did. The table was dark wood and looked like it was made out of old ship planks. In the center was a small vase with a single flower and a candle. The waitress came over and gave them the menu.

"Have you been here before?" Mark asked after they were seated, forgetting that she had already said she had been there before.

"Yes, several times with my sorority sisters. The food is good, and I like Italian food. Why don't we just share a pizza tonight?"

"That sounds good to me. Do you have a favorite?"

"You pick."

"How about we order half Hawaiian and half mushrooms?"

"Perfect."

"Would you like something to drink?

"Yes, a Diet Coke. Thank you."

Just then the waitress came over, and Mark gave her their order.

Over pizza, they talked about classes and found out that they had some of the same professors.

"Did you ever have Dr. Baumgartner? His accent was so thick I had trouble understanding anything he said. Good thing it was a math class. Numbers don't have accents." They both laughed at that.

"So what are your plans after graduation?" Diane asked.

"I'm hoping to get into the financial department of some company here in the city. I've got my feelers out now and will just have to see what happens. But to be honest, I haven't done a lot of thinking about it. My counselor says I need to start working on getting my resume out, especially if I want to stay in the city."

She just finalized his decision to stay in the city close to the university so he could be close to her.

"What about you? Any thoughts where you want to teach?"

"Originally I was thinking about the city, but I kind of miss the simple life of a small town. Some place where everyone knows each other and takes care of each other. Funny, when I lived there, I couldn't wait to leave. I guess I've grown up. But then again, I don't have to make that decision yet."

Mark knew exactly what she was talking about. Mark was so happy to be here that he didn't care if the food was good or not. He hardly remembered even eating. All he knew was that he was enjoying himself and didn't want the evening to end.

After dinner, they headed to the movie theater, getting the typical box of popcorn to share. Since it was Friday night, the theater was crowded, mostly with college students.

During the movie, Mark debated: should he or should he not take her hand, and how would she respond? A rejection would have killed him. But he decided to chance it, and at the right moment, he grabbed her hand.

She accepted it and didn't let go for the rest of the movie. He remembered laughing at the funny parts of the movie but couldn't remember any of it afterward. All he remembered was the feel of her hand in his.

After the movie, they walked to a local coffee club around the corner from the theater. Although the club was full, he felt he was all alone with no one around. They talked till about eleven thirty and then walked up and down the street, stopping to look in the store windows. They held hands the entire time. At twelve thirty, they headed back to the sorority house. Mark didn't want the evening to end. There was no one else at the front door of the sorority house when they arrived. She turned to look at him.

"Thank you for a wonderful evening. I had a great time."

"Thank you for going out with me."

"It was a perfect evening," she replied with a smile and that twinkle.

"Would it be okay if I called you?" he said, holding his breath.

"I hope you do." She reached into her purse and pulled out a piece of paper and a pen and wrote down her direct phone number and handed it to him.

Mark slowly leaned in, and she leaned to meet him, for the first of many good-night kisses. Mark felt sparks go off in his head. It was the best kiss he had ever had. She pulled away and looked up at him.

"Thank you again. I really enjoyed myself."

She turned to go in, and he opened the door for her, and she was gone. He stood there for a few moments clutching the piece of paper she had given him, watching her disappear up the stairs to the second floor. He walked back to his frat house with a smile on his face, trying to relive every moment and every feeling from that evening.

Mark and Diane continued to date the remainder of the year. Every date was a new adventure.

After graduation, Mark got a job in a small accounting firm close to campus so he could be near Diane. She moved out of the sorority house her senior year and moved in with him in the small one-bedroom apartment five blocks from campus. Neither parents were happy about them living together, but his parents adored her and overlooked the living arrangements. He was never sure how her parents felt.

Diane's senior year seemed to last forever. She had to study at night when Mark wanted to go out. But being in the same room with her while she studied was all he needed. The thought of being married to this woman was constantly on his mind, and he couldn't wait for it to happen. He proposed to her on graduation day after she received her diploma. Both sets of parents were there and were very happy. They planned an October wedding.

A month before the wedding, Mark received a phone call from his mom while at work that would change his life's direction.

"Hi, Mark. I've got some disheartening news to tell you. Your father had a heart attack this afternoon, and he is in the hospital."

"How bad is it?"

"The doctors said that it was a mild one; but it was a warning that he needs to slow down, watch his diet, and get his cholesterol level down. What the doctor doesn't understand is that you don't tell a farmer to slow down."

"Mom, do you want me to come home?"

"No, he is okay and will be home tomorrow. They are going to keep him in the hospital overnight as a precaution."

"We can postpone the wedding. I want Dad there, and we don't want to put any strain on him."

"No, your father said he will be okay. He wants to be in the front row at the wedding. He said nothing could keep him away. In fact, he didn't want me to call you. He knew you would want to postpone your plans and come home."

"All right, keep me informed. How are you doing? Are you sure you don't want me there? I can take some time off work."

"I'm fine, Mark. I really am. Once I get your dad home, we will have more information."

"Call me tomorrow and let me know how he is. Give him my love."

With that, she hung up, leaving Mark there holding the phone.

That night at dinner, Diane looked up at him with a serious face.

"Mark, I know you are worried about your dad. He shouldn't be working alone at the farm."

"I know. What would happen if he had a heart attack again and it was a major one? But I don't know what to do. You've heard me talk to him about giving up farming and just leasing out the land like Joe G."

"Mark, he has farmed all his life. You can't expect him to just stop. It's not in his blood."

"But what can we do?"

"What do you think about moving back to help out?"

"You mean leave the city? We have jobs here."

"I know, but I kind of miss that simple life. A place where everyone knows everyone would be nice. We've lived in this apartment now for over a year, and I don't even know the people next door."

"Yeah, I know what you mean. I kind of miss the farm too."

"And when we have children, I'd like to have them live in a place where we wouldn't have to worry about them every time they went outside."

"I'm sure Mom and Dad would let us live with them until we had a place of our own. I could help on the farm, and I'm sure you could find a teaching job there. The money wouldn't be as great though."

"Money isn't everything, and it is cheaper to live there than here."

"Well, let's not make any decisions now, but think about it and keep it as an option."

Mark looked across the table at Diane and knew that the decision had already been made in both of their minds. They both missed the small town and the simpler life, and Diane wanted to start a family. Mark knew his parents would be glad to have him back home again, not only to help out. Also, they adored Diane.

Mark resigned from his job, and they moved back to the farm. They had their October wedding as planned. In January, Diane surprised Mark with the fact that she was pregnant, and nine months later, Lisa was born. Back to basics and the simple life, the life Mark wanted to leave behind five years earlier.

CHAPTER 16

"Everything is packed and ready to go," Diane announced.

"Come on, Lisa, get Gretchen and let's go!" Mark yelled into the other room.

Lisa jumped up, grabbed her doll, and ran into the kitchen. Oliver, Mark's father, put down his newspaper and slowly pushed himself out of his chair, walked into the kitchen, and grabbed his hat and announced, "Let's get this show on the road," as if he had done all the preparations. Mark and Diane grabbed the food, and Lisa ran out the door in front of her grandmother, dragging Gretchen behind her.

The old red pickup truck had seen better days. But his dad kept it in tip-top shape. Oliver and Elizabeth, Mark's mother, climbed into the front of the truck.

"You can ride in the back with us," Mark said as he picked up Lisa and sat her next to Diane. Mark climbed into the back, reached up, and knocked on the roof of the pickup to signal that everyone was ready to go. "Let's go, Pop."

Oliver took off along the road behind the barn on their way to the far grove of trees. Mark put his arms around his wife and daughter, leaned back, and closed his eyes, listening to the wheels of truck against the gravel as they headed across the field.

"This was such a good idea," Diane said as she stroked Mark's arm. "It has been a long time since we've had a picnic. I like it when the family spends time together."

"Pop was smart to leave that area in the middle of the field with grass and trees. As a boy, we used to come here a couple of times a month for a picnic. Sometimes my friends would join us, and we would play while Mom and Pop just sat and watched. Those were good times. I want Lisa to have the same memories."

"How old were you when Dad built the tree house?"

"I must have been eight or nine. I remember seeing the movie *Swiss Family Robinson* and wanted a tree house like that. I was dreaming big."

"Yes, you were," Diane responded, grabbing and holding on to his arm.

"Pop just built a platform with railings and a ladder. But it was good enough for me. It is only about twelve feet up, but I felt I was on top of world looking down on everyone. Good thing there was a big old oak tree there."

The truck continued across the field, heading to the "back forty," as it was called. Mark looked around the cabin of the truck as they got nearer and saw the tree house just waiting there.

The truck came to a stop at the edge of the grove. Mark jumped out of the back and helped Lisa and Diane down. Lisa ran to the grassy area, dragging her doll behind her. Diane spread out the blanket, and Oliver and Elizabeth slowly sat down. The same blanket that was used for picnics when Mark was Lisa's age.

"Damn," Mark said as he slapped a mosquito on his neck, then another, and another. "What is this, the year of the mosquito? Here I thought we would have a nice relaxing afternoon, and already the mosquitoes have found me. You better put something on Lisa or she will be bitten up."

Diana and Elizabeth started unpacking the food and placing the containers on the blanket. They brought a pile of sandwiches, individually wrapped; a container of pickles; a thermos of lemonade; and bags of celery, carrots, and cucumbers. "A picnic for a king," Mark stated. "You two outdid yourself again." He planted a kiss on the cheeks of his mom and then Diane.

"Damn mosquitoes," Oliver said. "They are going to ruin our picnic. We just had too much rain this spring."

"You complain if we get too much rain, and you complain if you don't get enough rain," Mark said jokingly.

"Put on some spray. It seems to help," Elizabeth said, spraying her arms and then on her palms to rub the spray over her face.

"Have a sandwich. That will take your mind off the bugs." Elizabeth handed Oliver a chicken sandwich and poured him a glass of lemonade. "Here, put on some bug spray."

"I don't need any of that grease on me. I'll just keep swatting them."

"No, put some on, Pop, or we will have to listen to you grumble all afternoon."

"Lisa, come get something to eat."

Lisa came running over with Gretchen in her arms and sat down on the blanket. Immediately a mosquito started to buzz around her head.

"Mommy, the bugs are biting me."

"Close your eyes and let me spray those nasty bugs away."

Lisa closed her eyes tight as Diane sprayed her arms and then rubbed the spray using her hand over Lisa's forehead, cheeks, and neck. "All better now." Lisa moved over and sat next to her dad to eat her sandwich.

"This has been a good year for the crops. We got in the field early, and we had good early rains. Maybe a little too much," Oliver said as he swatted in the air at another bug.

"I'm sure glad you left this area like this for picnics and a place for Lisa to play. It sure brings back some good memories."

"I can't believe how fast she is growing," Diane said to no one in particular. "It seems like just yesterday that we brought her home from the hospital. She will be in school before we know it."

"Times goes by so fast. I remember Dad telling me that all the time while I was growing up. One day you will look back and say, 'Where has all the time gone?' It's is hard to believe that he has been farming this area for almost forty years," Mark commented.

"It has been a good life," his dad said. "I brought your mother here when she was a bride. Never thought she would take to farming as she did. After all, she was raised in town and had all the comforts of townsfolk. That first year was hard. I thought she was going to give up several times," Oliver said.

"Remember what we promised?" Elizabeth said.

"Yes, we promised for better or for worse. It was so bad then that I knew it could only get better," his dad responded as he planted a kiss on his wife's cheek.

"It has all been good, Oliver. It has been a good life. We didn't have running water in the kitchen when your dad brought me here. We had a pump at the end of the sink that you had to prime every time you wanted to get water. We kept a bucket of water under the sink to prime that old pump," Elizabeth added with a smile on her face. "I almost hated to see it go. But there were some trying times that first year. We were young and had no money. Now we are old and still have no money. But we have each other. We don't need anything else."

Oliver swatted at two mosquitoes that landed on his arm.

"I can vaguely remember that pump," Mark added.

Lisa picked up a sandwich and headed to the tree house. She put the sandwich in her mouth, and up the ladder she went.

"She is a real tomboy," Diane said, watching her climb up. "She keeps swatting at the mosquitoes. I wonder if the spray is working."

"Just wait, she will grow up to be as beautiful as her mother, and the boys will be buzzing around her like these damn mosquitoes are buzzing around my head," Mark added, watching Lisa.

Mark lay back on the blanket and closed his eyes. He heard the buzz of a mosquito around his head, but it didn't land. He swiped at it anyway. His stomach was full, and he was content. Where has all the time gone? he thought to himself, turning his head toward the tree house to see Lisa sitting there eating her sandwich, Gretchen by her side, swatting mosquitoes on her leg.

"Mommy, the bugs are biting me all over!" Lisa yelled from her perch.

"As much as I love being here, I think we should pack up and leave. These bugs are too much, and the spray doesn't seem to help all that much," Diane responded. "No one's going to have a good time, and I don't want Lisa all bitten up."

"I think you're right. Let's go back and finish the picnic on the back porch," Mark stated as he sat up and started to pack the food into the basket.

"Damn bugs," Mark heard his father mumble.

"Come, Lisa, we are going back home to finish the picnic. We'll come back when there are no bugs."

Once everything was packed up, they all climbed back into the truck and headed back to the farmhouse to finish their picnic away from the pesky bugs.

"I was so looking forward to this picnic to be outside with the family," Diane said.

"There will be other times. And we will be together on the screened porch to keep the mosquitoes out," Mark replied.

"I don't feel good, Mommy. My tummy hurts."

Diane put her hand on Lisa's cheek and forehead. "Mark, Lisa is running a fever. Look at her arms and legs. They are full of red bumps from the mosquito bites."

"We will get you home, sweetie, and into bed and make you feel better." Diane placed her arm around Lisa and held her close.

They pulled up in front of the farmhouse, and Mark carried Lisa into their house and put her in bed with Diane right behind. Oliver and Elizabeth carried in the picnic baskets.

"Mark, she is burning up. Get me a cold cloth and the thermometer. It's in the bathroom medicine cabinet."

Mark got a washcloth from the bathroom, ran it under the cold water, rung it out, and took it to Diane. "This will make you feel better. Open your mouth, baby, so I can take your temperature.

"It's one hundred and one, Mark, and she is breathing heavily. I don't like that. She was doing okay an hour ago. What could have happened so quickly?"

"Let's call Dr. Stein and see what he suggests. You stay here, and I'll go make the call."

Mark returned to the kitchen to make the call. He was just about to pick up his cell phone when it rang. It was his mom calling from the other house.

"Mark, how is Lisa doing?"

"She has a high fever, a stomachache, and breathing heavily. I was about to call Dr. Stein when you called."

"Oliver isn't doing well either. He's complaining about a stomachache and nausea and has a fever. What's going on, Mark? Are you and Diane feeling okay?"

"We feel fine, Mom. I'm calling Dr. Stein."

"No, let's take them to the emergency room to be absolutely sure."

"I'll get the car. Get Dad ready, and come on out."

Mark grabbed his car keys and yelled to Diane, "Get Lisa ready! We are going to the emergency room. Dad is not feeling well either."

Diane wrapped Lisa in a blanket and headed to the car. By the time she got there, Mark had the engine going and his mom and dad in the car. "Diane, call Dr. Stein on his cell and tell him we are heading to the emergency room and bring him up to date."

Diane called and relayed the situation to him. "He said he would meet us there."

"Great. How is Lisa doing?"

"She is burning up and nauseous. Can you go faster?"

"We'll be there in ten minutes. Keep her calm. How are you doing, Dad?"

"I'm hang'n' in there but feel like crap."

Mark drove as fast as he felt comfortable driving and finally got to the ER. He carried Lisa while Diane helped his dad. As he opened the door, he saw Dr. Stein standing there talking to a nurse on duty.

"Let's go in here." Dr. Stein led the way to an empty examining room. "So tell me what is going on."

Mark gave him as much information as he had and answered all his questions. Dr. Stein turned his attention to the patients. He started to examine them. After a few minutes, he turned to Mark. "I can't tell you anything right now. I would like to run some tests to see if we can find out what is going on. I might want to keep them overnight in the hospital so we can monitor them. If it only happened to one of them, I wouldn't be as concerned."

"Do you have any idea?"

"One of things that come to mind is some type of poison in the systems. Poisons tend to act similarly on elderly people and children. The fever, shortness of breath, and nausea are classic symptoms of poisons. I'd like to do some blood tests right away and then get them settled. We will know more once the lab results are available. There is a quick test we can do to rule poison out. Then again it could just be a virus. But I want to be sure."

Dr. Stein got on the phone, and almost immediately, a technician entered the room to take the blood. A second nurse entered the room and said they had their beds ready. Once the blood was taken, the two were taken to separate rooms. Mark and Diane went with Lisa. She seemed to be getting worse and vomiting more. They tried to keep her calm, but all she could say was "I want to go home, Mommy."

"We will be going home soon, baby. Just lay there. Mommy and Daddy are here."

After about thirty minutes, Dr. Stein returned and hooked Lisa up to an IV. Mark and Diane looked puzzled as to what was going on. Diane grabbed Mark's hand.

"Let's go outside and talk. The nurse will stay here with Lisa."

Mark and Diane followed Dr. Stein into the hallway.

"The first quick test of their system shows that both Lisa and Oliver have some type of poison in their system. We are giving them something to counteract it while we search for precisely what it is. It is at a very low level, so they should be okay. I just want to keep them here at least overnight to see how they react. We've also given them something so they will sleep."

"Poison, how could they get poisoned?" Diane cried out, looking at Mark.

"Can you think of any way they both could have been exposed to some poison in the last twenty-four hours?" "No, we were all together all day and just had a picnic. We have everything locked up in the home and the barn so she can't get into anything. Can we stay with her tonight? We don't want her to be alone."

"I understand. I'll tell the nurse." Dr. Stein walked away to talk to the nurse.

"Mark, how could this have happened?"

"I don't know. I'm just as curious as you are. But right now we have to concentrate on Lisa and Dad. I want to go check on Dad."

Mark turned and headed down the hall to his dad's room. Elizabeth was sitting next to the bed, holding Oliver's hand.

"How's he doing, Mom?"

"He seems to be doing a little better. His breathing is better."

"Do you need anything?"

"I'm fine. How's Lisa?

"She's resting. Diane is with her. I wanted to see how you and Dad were doing."

"We are doing fine. You go back to Lisa. You need to be there. I'll take care of Dad."

"I'll be back in a few minutes, and I'm right down the hall." He leaned over and kissed his mom on the cheek and headed back to Lisa's room.

What is going on? How did they get poison? Why is this happening? Mark kept asking these questions over and over in his mind but couldn't come up with any answers.

CHAPTER 17

Mark sat next to his daughter's bed, comforting her as she lay there. She was feeling better, but they wanted to keep her one more day to make sure everything was okay. Diane had spent the night in the hospital sleeping in a chair next to the bed. She refused to leave Lisa's side. Mark went home but couldn't sleep and was back at the hospital early in the morning with a change of clothes for Diane.

Lisa was sleeping, her breathing and temperature back to normal. Mark was glad yesterday was over, and everyone was okay. It had been a long and trying day.

His dad had a rougher time, but he was doing better too. It seemed to take him longer to get back to normal. The doctors said they both would probably be able to go home tomorrow. He wanted to keep them another night just to be sure.

Both Mark and his mom had been going back and forth between the two rooms to check on their two patients. He tried to get Mom to go home and get some rest, but she refused. She said she didn't need a lot of sleep and was able to get some rest in the hospital. He knew it was a losing battle. But she did go home to get a change of clothes but came right back.

What could have caused this? Why did they get sick and no one else? And why did it happen all of a sudden? These questions kept going over and over in his mind. He tried to think where they might have gotten some poison as he looked at his daughter lying there so peaceful. He couldn't keep his eyes off Lisa sleeping like an angel. He was afraid to even look away, even for a second, in case she woke up.

"Excuse me, Mr. Lundquist?"

Mark looked up to see a uniformed policeman standing behind him. Next to him was Dr. Stein.

"Can we go someplace and talk in private?"

"I really don't want to leave my daughter."

"I think it might be better to find a more private area."

"What's this all about?"

"I'll explain in a second. Just follow me, sir." He continued down the hall to a conference room that was empty. "Have a seat, sir."

Mark took a seat and again asked, "What is this all about?"

"How are your daughter and father doing?"

"They are doing fine and will be going home tomorrow," he said, looking at Dr. Stein for confirmation. "I really need to get back in case Lisa wakes up."

"This won't take long. The doctor called us when they got the results back from the toxicology test on your daughter and father. The results show that they both tested positive for pyrethrum poisoning. Can you tell us how they both could have gotten that in their system?"

"What!" Mark exclaimed with a questioning raised voice, looking at Dr. Stein. "Pyrethrum poison?"

"Mark, the results for both your dad and Lisa came in, and they both seem to be poisoned by one of the pyrethrum compounds. When the test results came in, I was required by law to contact the authorities. I insisted on being here. I've known your family too long to think it was anything but an accident."

"Do you have any idea how they could have accidentally gotten into some chemicals?" the policeman asked again.

"I have no idea. I keep everything locked up, and I don't think I even have any pyrethrum poison on the farm."

"We can understand an accident for your daughter, but when your father also showed the same symptoms, we got suspicious."

"As I said, I don't have any of these chemicals on the farm. There must be a mistake. I have to get back to my daughter," Mark said as he got up to leave.

"Mark, we tested the blood samples twice and both time the same results," Dr. Stein added.

"I'm sorry, sir, just a few more questions."

Mark sat back down.

"Do you have any idea how they both could have gotten something like this?"

Mark searched his brain for an answer but couldn't find any. "As I said, I don't know."

"What about your wife or mother? Would they have any idea? Or can you think of anyone that might have a grudge against you or your family?"

"I'm sure that Diane and my mom would give you the same answer. And I can't think of anyone who would do this to us."

"I understand that the two of them got ill at the same time, right after eating?"

"Yes, we were on a picnic in a grove of trees on the farm at noon today. They both got sick right after that."

"Who prepared the food for the picnic?"

"It was made by my wife and my mom."

"Do you still have any of the food left or stored away?"

"I'm sure what we didn't eat is in the refrigerator." Mark paused a second. "Wait, you don't think one of them had any part of this? You are crazy if you do."

"Sorry, sir. I'm just covering all bases. Would it be okay with you if we checked the food just to be sure and also looked around the farm to see if we can find the source of the problem?"

"Search all you want. You won't find anything."

"I'll let you go back to your daughter. If you think of anything, I'd appreciate if you would contact us. Anything, no matter how insignificant you think it is." The policeman handed Mark his card.

"I need to get back," Mark said and got up and started to leave.

"As you agreed, I'd like to check out your farm right away to see if we can find anything that you might have forgotten."

"Yes, go ahead, look all you want. You won't find anything. I want to know too how they could have gotten this."

Mark headed to the door. As he got to the door, a thought came into his head. He turned to the policeman.

"There is a research farm right next to our farm run by some big chemical company. Maybe something they are doing caused this," he said, looking straight at the policeman.

"Thank you, sir, we will check into it. Go back to your daughter. I'm glad she is feeling better."

Mark hurried back to his daughter's room, not even saying good-bye to the officer or to Dr. Stein. When he got to the room, he saw that Lisa was still asleep, with Gretchen next to her.

He looked at his daughter and kissed her on the forehead. *She could have died, he thought. Poison? How could she have gotten poisoned?* Mark left his daughter's room and went to see how his dad was doing and tell him what the doctor said.

His dad was sitting up in bed talking to his mom. His color was back, and he looked rested.

"How are you doing, Pop?"

"I'm starting to feel my old self again. It's about time. When do we go home?"

"The doctor says one more day to make sure everything is okay. It is just a precaution."

"Damn, I'm ready for some good home cooking. This hospital food is for the birds. Not sure they would even eat it themselves."

"Has the doctor been in to talk to you about what they found?"

"No, is something wrong? The only person I've seen today has been this good woman." He pointed to his wife.

"A policeman stopped by a few minutes ago. He said they got the test results back and found poison in both you and Lisa."

"Poison!" his mom cried out.

"Yes, that is what he said. Dr. Stein said they tested the samples twice and got the same results."

"How the hell did we get poison?" his dad asked.

"That is what the police want to know. He specifically mentioned pyrethrum poison. I don't think we have any poison anywhere on the farm. And how the hell would both you and Lisa get it at the same time? They want to check out the farm and see if they can find the source. I said it was okay.

"Mom, they wanted to know if we still had the food that we ate on the picnic. I remember we packed up and went back to the house because the bugs were bothering Lisa. What did you do with the food?"

"I put it in the refrigerator, and most of it is still there. I had a little of the potato salad yesterday when I went home to get a change of clothes, but I feel fine. The rest is still there."

"The police want to test the food to make sure it is okay. I told them to go ahead. Will you go with them?"

"Oh my lord. Do they think something is wrong with the food?"

"Don't worry, Mom. There is nothing wrong with your food. They just want to cover all bases. Let me take you to the policeman, Mom, and you go home with him and show him the food. I would do it myself, but I don't want Lisa to wake up and I'm not there."

"You two go. I will be okay. Give my granddaughter a big kiss from Grandpa."

Mark took his mom to the policeman and watched as they left to go home. This is probably the first time his mom has ever been in a police car. Was he right in sending her with the police? He couldn't think about that. He had to go back to his daughter's room.

CHAPTER 18

On Monday morning, Alex arrived at the airport two hours before his departure and ended up waiting for over an hour once he got to the boarding area. He didn't like to be rushed at the airport. He had breakfast at a café and was reviewing his notes about the farm while waiting to board. This is the third year the farm has been in operation, and it was run by Don Brown, a permanent employee of Sterling.

Once on the plane, he fell asleep, only to be awakened when they announced the landing. After retrieving his luggage, he headed to the car rental area, paid the extra fee for the GPS systems, and was on his way to the farm. The farm was only fifty miles from the airport, so it was a short ride.

As he was sitting in traffic, his mind kept going back to the phone call from Cindy Hudson and the note he found in his desk drawer.

Were they in any way connected?

But something was gnawing at him.

Why would Cindy want to talk to him about her husband? He hadn't met him. On the other hand, her husband was a chemical statistician like him. Maybe she had some notes from her husband related to work that she thought Alex should have. But why call him and ask to meet? Why not just mail them or drop them off at the front desk?

His inner voice told him that something else was bothering her that she wanted to talk about. With that, he decided to make a date to meet with her when he got back in town. If he didn't, it would drive him crazy wondering what she wanted.

As he neared the turn into the farm, he saw a large billboard sign with a Norman Rockwell–like picture setting of a farmhouse, people on the front porch, a dog sitting at their feet, and corn and wheat in the background. At the top of the billboard was the Sterling Chemicals logo and slogan: Better Food to Keep People Well. Kind of corny, but people remembered it.

He turned into the gravel driveway, passing rows of cotton, tobacco, corn, soybeans, and various vegetables. He saw a man standing out front of a white building at the end of the road. He pulled up, parked the car, and got out to a blast of hot air hitting his face. He had forgotten how hot it gets in North Carolina in the summer.

"Good morning, Dr. Gregory. Hope you had no trouble finding us."

"No problem. I just followed the GPS. I assume you are Don Brown." He stretched out his hand. "And call me Alex. No need for formalities."

"Good to meet you. We are glad to have you on board. Dr. Hudson liked to be called Doctor. He said he worked hard for it and liked hearing it. Come on in, and we can talk where it is cooler. It gets hot here during the summer. Welcome to North Carolina heat."

"I know how hot it gets here in the summer. I went to school at NC State."

"You don't have a North Carolina accent."

"I was raised in Minnesota . . . no accent."

Don stood at about six feet tall, full head of hair, scruffy shaved face, and was very tan. His clothes were loose fitting on his lean body and soiled with dirt and paint.

As Don opened the front door, a blast of cool air hit him in the face. It felt good. They were standing in a large room that ran the length of the building.

"This is our main office building where everything gets done. It is our meeting place, bug sorting and counting area, and where we plan our workday."

Alex looked around. The front wall of the room had four large windows looking out over the farm. He could see workers in the field taking some kind of measurements. The room had two desks with computers against one wall and a long table in the center with chairs around it. There were filing cabinets and bookshelves along another wall, and benches and chairs scattered through. None of the furniture matched.

On the back wall were three doors that apparently led to other rooms. One door was open. Through it, he could see what appeared to be a lunch room.

"How about some coffee before we start? I haven't had my morning limit yet. Or maybe you would rather have something cold?" Alex put his knapsack on the center table and followed Don into the lunch room. On the way, he passed the two other doors. One looked like an office, and the other had the door closed.

"I like the labels on the doors." He pointed to two doors next to each other along the back wall of the lunch room. One was labeled Farmers and the other Maidens.

"That was Max's idea. He came up with the names and made the signs."

Don walked over to the counter, picked up a cup, and filled it with coffee. Who knows how long the coffee had been sitting there. Things were looking up, however. They were using real cups for coffee, not paper cups. There were many cups of different shapes and sizes hanging from hooks under one cabinet. Each one had a different logo on it.

"This is our break room as you probably guessed. Not the Four Seasons, but it serves the purpose."

"Coffee is what I need. I can't start the day without it."

"I know what you mean. This is probably my fifth cup already. Let's go to my office where it is more comfortable and talk. Then we can tour the farm."

They left the room, coffee in hand, and moved to the next room. On the way, Alex picked up his knapsack.

"Although this is called an office, I just use it for paperwork and phone calls. I spend most of my time outside. Have a seat, Alex." He motioned to a chair. None of the furniture matched, but it served its purpose. There was a copy and fax machine on a table behind the desk. A laptop computer sat on the corner of the desk.

"Thanks for allowing me to stop by on such short notice. I've only been with the company for a week and have a lot to learn. I'm just here to get a better understanding how things are set up. I'm not here to make any changes."

"We are glad to have you part of the team. Dr. Hudson was great, and he is missed. We are not data people and not always sure we are doing things the most efficient way or collecting the data correctly. He was very good in keeping us on track with our mission. We welcome any suggestions."

"I'm sure Dr. Hudson gave you good directions. Do you have the procedure written anyplace so I can review them?"

Don turned around and pulled a binder off the shelf behind him. The title read "Protocol for Field Testing." "When I heard you were coming, I put this together for you," Don said, pushing the binder across the desk. "This binder was developed by the person before Dr. Hudson, and he just updated it as he saw fit. I'm sure there is one back at the corporate office someplace."

Alex didn't remember seeing one, but then again, he wasn't looking for it specifically. He will do that when he gets back. Hopefully it is not only in hard copy but also on a computer someplace.

"Thanks. I'll review the protocol manual at a later time. First I'd like to have a tour of the farm and see firsthand how things are done. Before we do that, however, can you tell me about the setup, starting with the employees?"

"We have two permanent workers, Max and Jose, who take care of the planting, seeding, harvest, machine repair . . . essentially responsible for keeping the farm running. They also help in preparing the chemicals we are testing and applying them to the crops. They don't get involved with the data collection unless we are shorthanded."

"How long have they been with you?"

"Max has been here since the farm started, and this is Jose's second year. Both come from a farming background, and we are lucky to have them. They keep the place running and all the equipment in working order with very little direction."

"It is good to have people who are knowledgeable in how to run a farm and also enjoy what they are doing. Who does the data collecting then?"

"We hire locals to help with that. We have twelve people that rotate through the year."

"Where do you get these workers, and what type of background do you look for?"

"Most of them are students from the local colleges where we have a good working relationship with the agriculture departments. Some are from your alma mater. The students get practical experience and some extra cash. The people we get are usually undergrads with an entomologist major so they help with bug identification or plant specialists who can help with yield and disease samples. They are here twice a week to collect the data. Some of them are here today, so you will see our methods firsthand."

"After the data is collected, what do you do with it?"

"We collect the bugs in the field, and they are brought back here to identify and count. We enter the information on special forms that Dr. Hudson developed for us. We also record the plant sampled, date and time of sample, weather conditions, height of plant, and insecticide used on the plant. We then enter the data into the computer. Basically our role at this farm is to get data on as many different crops as we can and submit it. It was Dr. Hudson's job to analyze the information and make some sense out of it. What he did with the information I don't know. He was also instrumental in telling us which crops we need to add to our test or which we can cut back on."

"I'll review Dr. Hudson's procedures when I get back and update or revise them as I see necessary. Then we can meet again and review them together. Until then, continue on with what you are doing. I'm sure that I will agree totally with Dr. Hudson's methodology. Sounds like you have a good system going here."

"That sounds good to me. Let me give you a tour of the farm. After that, you might have more questions."

"I'd also like to meet the workers so they know who I am. Nothing worse than hearing a person's name and have no idea what he looks like."

"I know they are anxious to meet you too. They keep asking me when the new guy will be here. Today's that day."

Don led the way to the closed door at the end of the large room. They went through a small entrance foyer and then a second door to a back room. There were two long tables with scales on them. In one corner was a sink. Next to that was a door leading to the outside.

"This is our chemical room where we mix the chemical to spray on the plants. We usually test three different concentrations of each product. Right now we are testing three new products. One is in its third year of testing. The other two are new this year."

"How are the products looking so far?"

"57126 is kicking butt. It seems to kill any bug that gets near it. Not only that, but we are seeing significant increases in yield on every crop at the end of the season, and in many cases we can harvest weeks earlier than the control cops. On some crops, the yield is doubled. The other two new products don't have the same effects, but we are seeing some disease control on crops in storage for these two. We will know more as the summer wears on."

"Do you store the chemicals in this room too?"

"No, the chemicals are stored in a shed out back. We only measure them here and prepare the spray. The chemical is brought here through the back door, so no chemicals are ever in any other areas of this building.

"We always wear facial protective gear when working in this room. There is a shower room through that door"—he pointed to a door in the corner—"in case of emergencies. So far we have not had a need to use it."

"Looks like you are taking good precautions to protect the employees from exposure to the chemicals. After all, they are working with unknown products. Has anyone complained about any medical issues that might be related to exposure to them?"

"Max and Jose are required to be checked by a doctor every six months. Max has been complaining of being more tired than usual this season. And he has trouble breathing from time to time. We've had him checked out, but the docs can't find anything wrong. Max just says he is getting old. No one else has complained of anything."

"Great, looks like you have things well in hand. Let's go see the rest of the farm."

They exited out the back door. At the bottom of the steps, they turned left. A mosquito landed on Alex's arm. He was able to smash it before it had time to take some of his blood. A second one buzzed around his head, and he swatted at it.

"You learn to wear long sleeves or use mosquito spray when you spend a lot of time outside."

"They seem to have radar for me."

By now they were at the edge of the crops. "The crops are divided into sections we call pods. Each pod contains four rows each of five different crops. That is twenty rows of crops running the length of the field. We are testing on corn, soybeans, potatoes, tobacco, and peas. We test the three products at three different concentrations. That makes nine pods. Then we have pods that don't get any products, used as a control."

Don walked over to the edge of the field where there was a blue flag stuck in the ground. "Each flag color represents a different product. We write the product number and spray concentration on the flag to identify the beginning of each spray concentration. We only spray the middle two rows of each crop to avoid drift issues from crop to crop," Don pointed out.

Alex bent over and looked at the blue flag. It had "57126 @ 1 lb/acre" written on it.

Alex looked down the row of crops. He estimated that each row ran about a hundred feet. "How are they sprayed?"

"All the crops are sprayed by hand in order to direct the spray right on the plants. And we don't spray on windy days."

Alex walked over to a red flag. He looked at the plants and back at the plants in the blue area. "Wow, there is a significant difference in the size of the plants in the blue area."

"That is what we have been seeing the past three years. Not only in size and growth rate, but we have also been getting a significant increase in yield on plants treated with 57126. And we see little difference between the concentrations we use when it comes to yield. And it appears to kill all the insect pests equally at all concentrations. We have a winner there."

Alex started walking down the rows of the crops in the blue area. A mosquito buzzed around his head. "It doesn't appear to control the mosquitoes." He continued to walk down the field looking at the crops. He noticed that he started to breathe heavier and was aware of taking deeper breaths than earlier. It was more evident when he walked through the taller crops of corn. He chalked it up to being tired from his flight and the hot day. He looked over at Don, and he noticed that his chest was moving in and out as if taking deep breaths. He hadn't noticed that before.

"What kind of samples are you collecting?"

"Twice a week, we take fifty swings of a net across the top of the plants in each of the crops in the pods. The bugs are then transferred to killing jars. You can see the guys out there collecting samples now."

There were three guys in the different areas swinging nets and then stopping to put their catch in jars.

"The samples are taken back in the office to count and record what they caught. We try to sample in the morning when it is not so hot and count the catch in the afternoon."

Don continued on. "The rest of the farm is used for regular farming. Jose and Max take care of that, and we harvest and sell our yields locally. This year we mostly have soybean and corn. We grow some vegetables that I take to the local farmers' market on Saturdays. We grow them far away from the test crops. The plants sprayed with the chemicals are not sold. They are for testing purposes only."

Alex stood and watched the workers swinging the nets and working their way down the rows of crops.

"It is almost time for lunch," Don said. "Let's head back to the office. The guys will be coming in soon, and I'd like to introduce you to them. Then we can head into town and get something to eat."

As Alex left the field and headed back to the office, he noticed that his breathing had gone back to normal. He looked over at Don and noticed his chest wasn't moving in and out as much as before. Alex swatted at another mosquito as they entered the building.

It was good to get back inside where it was cool. The workers started coming in one by one, placing their jars on the worktable before heading to the break room. Don took Alex around and introduced him to the workers. Soon Max and Jose joined them.

"Dr. Gregory will be taking over Dr. Hudson's role and analyzing the data we send to him."

"Call me Alex, no formalities necessary. I'm impressed with the work you are doing, so continue on. I will be reviewing the procedures over the next couple of weeks and let you know if we need to make any alterations. Right now just enjoy your lunch."

"Alex and I are heading into town. We'll be back in about an hour."

With that, they turned and headed to the car and went to a small diner in town. The diner was a throwback to the fifties. The only thing missing were waitresses on roller skates. They got a booth and ordered hamburgers.

"Looks like you have things well in hand. If it is okay with you, I'd like to spend the afternoon going through the procedures manual and looking at the data entry program."

"No problem. You can use my office. I'll be working outside anyway the rest of the day. Got any plans for tonight?"

"A fraternity buddy of mine lives about an hour away. I haven't seen him in a couple of years, so I'm going to head there later this afternoon and catch up with him. I can finish up here tomorrow before catching my flight back Wednesday morning."

"Hey, good to keep in touch with school buddies."

Alex had to ask. "Have you noticed any physical effects on you personally while working with these new products?"

"No, I haven't noticed anything. Why do you ask?"

"No special reason. Just wondering."

Apparently Don was not aware or concerned about the change in his breathing that Alex noticed. Or maybe it was nothing. They ate their lunch and headed back to the farm. The field workers were at the conference table sorting through the day's catch and entering the data.

Alex set up in Don's office and began reviewing the procedures manual, making notes in areas that needed further instructions or changes. The afternoon went by quickly. He looked up, and it was already 4:00 p.m. He decided to wrap it up and head out. He had hoped to look at the computer programs before the end of the day, but that could wait until tomorrow.

Alex went outside and saw Don was in the blue flag area. As he walked over to him, Alex again noticed the difference in the size of the crops compared to the other areas. He also noticed that he was again taking deeper breaths the closer he got to the row of crops.

"I'm heading out now to try to find my buddy's place. I'll be back tomorrow morning. Thanks for your help today. Good to actually see how things work," Alex said.

"No problem. Have a good trip, and I'll see you in the morning," Don said.

Alex headed to his car, swatting at a mosquito as he got in. "Damn bugs." He set the GPS and headed out to his friend's farm.

CHAPTER 19

Mark went to the cafeteria to get some dinner for Diane. She didn't want to leave Lisa's bedside. As he waited for the food, he thought about the police going through his home. His mom must be terrified. What was he thinking sending her there alone?

He picked up the food and headed back to his daughter's room. Diane was sitting in the chair next to the bed holding Lisa's hand. Lisa was awake. He walked over to Lisa and gave her a hug.

"Are you feeling better? Daddy's here now."

"I want to go home."

"The doctor said you can go home tomorrow. Mommy and I will stay here with you. And Gretchen is getting better too. You must be taking good care of her."

"She was sick too, Daddy. Can she go home tomorrow?"

"That's what the doctor said."

He turned to Diane. "How are you doing?"

"I'm fine. Any idea what is going on? I haven't heard anything from the doctor."

"They are still checking the test results. They will let us know when they have something conclusive. I brought you some dinner from the cafeteria. I knew you wouldn't leave Lisa to get something for yourself."

"How is Dad doing?"

"He is much better. He says he is back to his old self," Mark replied.

"That's a good sign. I just wish we knew what caused this so suddenly."

Just then there was a knock on the door behind them. They both looked toward the door.

"Hi, Mark. Remember me?"

Mark hesitated for a moment and then recognized his old fraternity brother standing behind his mom. "Alex Gregory, what are you doing here? You are the last person I expected to show up here."

They greeted each other with a handshake that turned into a big bear hug.

"I am in town on business and stopped by your place to surprise you and catch up. Your mom told me you are all at the hospital and that your dad and daughter were here. She wanted to come back, so I gave her a ride and came by to see if there is anything I can do. She told me what happened. How are your daughter and dad doing?"

"Thanks for bringing Mom back. I didn't want to leave Lisa. Everyone is getting better and will be going home tomorrow."

Alex looked toward Lisa. "She looks just like her mother, the prettiest thing around."

Mark gleamed with pride.

"Yes, she is."

Alex turned to Diane. "You haven't changed since your wedding. You're still as pretty as ever."

Diane gave Alex a hug. "Thanks for coming by. It is good to see you too. I wish it was under better circumstances though."

"Lisa, this is my friend, Alex. He came to the hospital just to see if you are getting better," Mark said, turning to Lisa.

"How are you feeling, Lisa? Is your baby doll sick too?" Alex said, moving closer to the bed.

"Gretchen is sick, but she is going home tomorrow when she is better," Lisa said, holding on to Gretchen.

"That is so good to hear, Lisa. You are taking good care of her."

Alex turned back to Mark and Diane. "This is not the place I wanted to be to see you two. But I'm glad everything is looking good."

Mark turned back to Alex. "I'm just surprised to see you, Alex."

"The company I work for has a research farm about an hour from here. I'm here to check it out, one of my new responsibilities. While I was in the area, I thought I'd pop over and check up on you. The last time we saw each other was at your wedding. I didn't know you had a daughter. Congratulations."

"Thanks, buddy."

"So how are you doing? Do you need anything? What's going on?"

Mark turned to Diane. "I have some more information about what they found with Lisa and Dad. Mom, can you sit with Lisa so we can go someplace and talk?"

"Hey, I'll get out of your way so you two can talk. We can catch up another time," Alex said.

"No, Alex, I want you to be part of this conversation. You might be able to shed some light on what is happening."

"Anything, Mark, but I can't imagine how I can be of any help," Alex replied.

Diane and Alex both looked at each other with puzzled looks.

"Lisa, Mommy and I need to go talk. Grandma will stay with you. We'll be right back."

"Take your time. I'll stay here as long as you want me to," his mom responded.

"Thanks, Mom."

With that, Mark headed to the door with Diane and Alex following close behind. They headed to the nurses' desk on the floor with Mark leading the way. "Is there a place we can go and talk privately?"

"At the end of the hall is a conference room," the nurse said as she pointed to the left. "You can use that."

Mark headed toward the room at a rapid pace with Diane and Alex on his heels. They entered the room, and Mark shut the door behind them.

"What's going on, Mark? You are scaring me," Diane said.

Mark told Diane and Alex everything he knew.

"How could this happen?" Diane said.

"I don't know."

Mark turned to Alex. "I read in the newsletter that you are working for Sterling Chemicals."

"Yes, I started last week. The farm I'm visiting is one of theirs."

"The farm next to us is leased by your company to test new chemicals. Is there any way that any of the products that you are using there could be the cause for Lisa's and my dad's condition? Could they have gotten in the water or in the air? I can't think of any other source. Are you using pyrethrum products as part of your tests?"

"I'm sure that isn't the source, Mark. I haven't seen any reports of any problem. But then again, I have only been there a week. But I promise to personally look into it right away. If they are causing this, we need to know as soon as possible. I will call you and keep you informed of anything I find, I promise."

"I gave the police your name, so they may be contacting you. I didn't know anyone else for them to contact," Mark added.

"It was okay to give them my name. I'm sure that Sterling Chemicals, with the reputation it has, would not do anything that would be potentially harmful to people. The company is very concerned about the environment and the effect its products have on living things."

"Thanks, Alex. I hope that is not just corporate talk and they really mean what they advertise. I hope they aren't hiding anything. Right now I'm at a loss. I'm only glad that nothing serious happened to Lisa or Dad. And I sure don't want anyone else to go through what we just went through."

"You and Diane need to get back to Lisa. I will head back to the research farm so I can get back before it is too dark. You don't need me hanging around. I promise to look into this, and next time I'm in town, we'll all get together on a happier note," Alex said.

"Thanks, Alex. Sorry we didn't have more time this time, but we will."

"Say good-bye to your mom and dad for me, and give that sweet child a big kiss for me."

Alex turned and gave Diane a hug. "Take care of your family," he said into her ear.

"Thanks, Alex, I always do."

Alex watched as Mark and Diane hurried down the hall. He turned and headed toward the entrance of the hospital. As he got into the car and headed back to the research farm, more questions were running through his head.

Is there any connection to the testing of the new products?

Are the Sterling chemicals dangerous?

Are there other instances like this at any of the other locations?

Could the products be changing, mutating? No, that can't be it, chemicals don't mutate.

Is this in any way connected to the note I found in my desk . . . or the call from Cindy?

Am I being paranoid?

It couldn't be the chemicals. Not when only two people are ill. It has to be something else. A virus they both got. Or maybe there was something they both ate.

Although he couldn't see any logical connection, there was that gnawing feeling in his stomach. He knew that tonight he would not sleep well and that he had to call Cindy when he got back.

The next day Alex called his boss to tell him what happened to his friend and his concern about the leased land next to his farm. His boss was out of the office for the day, so he left a voice message for him and also a message for Jeanette to have him call when he had a chance.

Alex spent the second day at the farm going over the procedures manual, helping the guys in the field take samples and looking at the computer programs used to enter the data.

On Wednesday morning while he was wrapping up things at the farm to get ready to head to the airport, his boss called.

"I understand that you wanted to talk me yesterday and felt it was important. I'm sorry I didn't get back to you, but I was out of the office all day and didn't check my voice mail. Jeanette told me this morning that you were anxious to talk to me. So what is going on?"

Alex gave him a quick synopsis of his visit to the hospital since he had to leave for the airport. He wanted to make sure that his boss understood his concerns and reassure him that the Sterling products were not responsible for what happened to his friend's family. His boss told him to meet with him as soon as he got back to the office—first thing—and that there was nothing wrong with the Sterling products. He then hung up. Alex sensed that there was concern in his voice.

CHAPTER 20

Leslie was busy working on proofing a document. She was in her second week now and starting to feel part of the organization. Her boss had kept her busy. She started thinking about all that had happened since she started a week ago. Every time Alex came into her thoughts, she got a warm feeling inside. She hadn't talk to him since last week. All of a sudden her thoughts were interrupted by some commotion behind her. She turned and saw Brianna running to the glass door. On the other side of the door was a man with an anxious look on his face. Barb had opened the door to let the man in.

"Can I help you, Mr. Matthews?"

"I need to see Mr. Gianti right away."

"This way, Mr. Matthews," Brianna said, leading him to Mr. Gianti's office. Brianna returned to her work area, leaving the door to her boss's office open.

Leslie heard Mr. Matthews and her boss exchange greetings. Then they were talking softly, so she couldn't make out what they were saying.

"Brianna, get Alan and Curtis and have them come to my office immediately!" Mr. Gianti yelled from his office.

Brianna rushed to the get the other vice presidents. They immediately went into Mr. Gianti's office. Brianna entered behind them.

"Start from the beginning and repeat everything that Alex told you. Leave nothing out."

When Leslie heard Alex's name, she turned to the office, trying to hear if they were talking about her Alex.

"Alex Gregory is the new guy in our department. He was at our research farm in North Carolina. He is responsible for analyzing the data collected on new products. He was at the farm reviewing procedures. Last night he went to visit a college buddy who lives close by. This friend was in the hospital with his daughter who was . . ."

Just then Brianna shut the door. As she shut the door, she saw Leslie staring back at her.

Leslie went back to proofing the document. She couldn't hear anything that was being said, but it involved Alex. Hearing loud footsteps behind her, she turned and saw the security guy whom she had noticed in the cafeteria coming through the closed door at a fast pace.

He looked at Leslie but quickly glanced away. She knew though that in that quick glance, he had recognized her. He went into the office without knocking, shutting the door behind him.

But before the door closed, she heard someone say, "That the child and the father had been poisoned."

What is going on? Is Alex involved? Is he in trouble for taking personal time while on a business trip? That can't be it. That would be between him and his boss. Poison? Someone was poisoned? Is Alex okay?

Leslie felt a shiver go through her body.

Who is Mr. Matthews?

Leslie opened her company directory and found three Matthews: one in IT, one in Distribution, and one in Marketing. Alex was in Marketing.

Questions went through Leslie's head, none of them good.

Is this the Mr. Matthews that works with Alex?

Is Alex poisoned?

Is Alex exposed to poison?

How is Alex involved?

Is Alex okay?

Leslie wasn't able to concentrate on proofing the document. She kept reading the same paragraph over and over again, looking up at the door and straining to hear what was going on. She couldn't stand not knowing. She picked up the phone and dialed Alex's cell phone number.

"Good morning, Alex Gregory."

"Oh, Alex, you're okay."

"Hi, Leslie. Why wouldn't I be?"

"There is a big meeting behind closed doors going on up here, and I heard them mention your name and the research farm and something about poison. All the senior vice presidents were called into the meeting behind closed doors. I didn't know what to think."

"I'm fine, not to worry. Thank you for worrying about me, but I am okay."

"That's good. Now I can go back to work."

"I'll be back in the office tomorrow. How about meeting for lunch?"

"I'd love to meet you for lunch."

"How about I meet you at twelve fifteen, outside the cafeteria? And thanks for worrying about me. You don't need to. I'm okay."

"I'll see you tomorrow."

Leslie hung up the phone and heard a noise behind her. She turned and saw Brianna moving back to her desk. She didn't look happy. On the way to her desk, she gave Leslie the strangest look. But who cares, Alex was okay.

Alex hung up the phone, sat back, and rethought the events of the past two days. He also felt good that Leslie was worried about him. A smile came over his face.

Alex said good-bye to the farm personnel and headed to the airport. First thing in the morning, he will see his boss and get verification that nothing is wrong with the product so he can report back to Mark. And then there will be lunch with Leslie. That will be the best part of the day.

As soon he got to work the next day, Alex went immediately to Gene Matthew's office. He discussed what he did while at the farm and the results he witnessed on the growth stimulant of the new product.

Gene didn't seem all that interested in his analysis of the farm but listened to what Alex told him.

As soon as Alex started talking about the events in the hospital and what led up to them, Gene seemed to pay more attention. His boss reassured him that the chemicals were safe and there were procedures in place for storage and distribution of the chemicals at each location. Those facts made Alex feel better. He returned to his office, shutting the door behind him.

Then what was the emergency meeting about yesterday morning with his boss and the people on the sixty-first floor? Leslie seemed agitated when she called. Something just wasn't right. Four things came to mind: Cindy Hudson's phone call, the note he found in his desk drawer, the poisoning of Mark's daughter and father, and Dr. Hudson's sudden death.

Were they all related in some way? Or were they just coincidences? Was he reading too much into the events? Were these related to 57126 in any way?

Now more than ever, he had to talk to Cindy Hudson. Alex found her number, headed to the elevator, and headed outside the building to make the call.

"Hello?"

"Is this Cindy Hudson?"

"Yes, it is. Who is this?"

"This is Alex Gregory from Sterling Chemicals. You called me last week and said you wanted to talk about your husband. Again, I'm sorry about his sudden death. I don't mean to bother you, but you were insistent that we talk soon. If this is not a good time, I can call at another that is convenient to you."

"No, that is okay. Thanks for returning my call. But I prefer we meet and talk face-to-face someplace away from the company."

"I'm free this evening or any evening this week if that works for you"

"Tonight would be fine. Do you live in the city?"

"I live on the Upper West Side."

"Good, you are in the city. I live on East Eighty-second. There is a coffee shop on the corner of Eighty-second and Second Avenue. How about meeting there tonight? About 8:00 p.m.?"

"That works for me. How will I recognize you?"

"I have long brown hair and will be wearing a red blouse and jeans. I'll be one of the few people there not working on a computer."

"All right, I'll see you there at eight."

"Can I ask a favor of you? It may sound strange, but I insist."

"Sure, if I can do it."

"Make sure that you are not followed. I'll see you tonight."

Alex heard the phone hang up. Why was she worried about him being followed? Another question to add to his growing list . . . *Am I being watched? How does that affect her?*

CHAPTER 21

Alex's first seven days had been eventful. The events of the past three days kept running through this head. He had to put them aside so he could get some work done.

He was eventually able to clear his mind and go back to work. He started analyzing some of the data collected at the farm. Two of the new products had no significant advantage over current products already being sold in the data that he had looked. Maybe the yield taken at the end of the season will prove some advantage to continue testing them.

But 57126 was a superior pesticide against almost all destructive insects that attack all types of crops. It constantly showed a better-than-95-percent kill rate. These crops also showed a significant growth advantage. Alex had observed that himself. The product acted both as an insecticide and a growth hormone. If the yield data showed the same results, Sterling Chemicals had a huge winner with 57126.

Alex now wanted to know more about this product. What were the financials associated with this product? Would it be profitable to the company to manufacture and sell it? He was sure that someone had already done a cost-benefit analysis. But he wanted to see the numbers for himself. How about production? Could they make it with current facilities? What about the environmental tests? What studies and tests had been done? Since this product had been around for at least three years, all of these reports must be available. He got up and went to the file room and pull out all the folders he could find on 57126 and took them back to his desk.

The first folder was entitled "Development of 57126." Alex opened the folder and started reading the documents.

57126 was developed in 2010 by Dr. Michael Mohanna in the chemistry lab of Sterling Chemicals in Charleston, West Virginia. It contains 7 hydrocarbon components. The patent number is 8975122 (patent pending) and the formula is:

The product has been tested in the labs at Charleston, West Virginia and shows potential not only working as an insecticide, but also as a growth hormone for the plant. In greenhouse tests, the product had a 99.8% mortality rate on all insects tested with the exception of flies and mosquitoes for which it only had 5% mortality rate. This is the natural mortality rate for these insects, hence we concluded that there was no effect on these pests. The next phase of development is to field test the product at our research facilities and University affiliates. Environment impact tests are pending and will be completed in the next phase.

Signed: Michael Mohanna
Signed: Tony Sossat

The field tests so far seemed to support the greenhouse findings. Alex shuffled through the folder to look for the results of the environmental tests, but he could not find anything. There was no environmental impact statement anyplace in the files. He made a mental note to ask his boss.

Something about the formula looked familiar. Then he remembered the piece of paper he found taped to the back of his desk drawer. He pulled the paper out of his desk drawer. Sure enough, one of the formulas on the paper was 57126. Now what was the other formula, and what did it have to do with 57126?

The next document he pulled out was the cost-benefit analysis done by the finance department.

A preliminary cost/benefit analysis was completed by Andrew Steffel in 2013, one year into the field testing of the product. These analyses are based on one year of field research so they are only preliminary. Based on the information from the field, this product kills insects that feed on food crops at the 99% confidence level when applied at a low rate, twice in the growing season. It also shows the same properties against pests that attack crops in storage. In addition, those crops that have been treated with this pesticide also show an increase in yield from 100% to 150% over the untreated crops (these are preliminary numbers, further test results are needed). The rate applied to the crops for this type of control is ¼ - ½ pound of product per acre. For this analysis I will use the upper rate of ½ pound per acre.

Preliminary results show that we can produce 100 pounds of the product for $12.50 using current facilities. This includes all costs associated with the manufacturing, and packaging and distribution of the product.

The major agriculture crops grown in the US cover an estimated 231 million acres. The table below shows the number of acres by crop, the average harvest rate per acre (Unit/Acre) and the average yield on treated crops (Increase column) realized at the test farms for treated crops.

Crop	Acres	Unit/Acre	Increase	Unit
corn	83,100,000	171	362	bushel
soybeans	83,100,000	48	105	bushel
Cotton	9,710,000	795	1,596	pounds
Sorghum	6,400,000	68	138	bushel
Rice	2,940,000	7,572	18,682	pounds
Wheat	40,500,000	49	122	bushes
Citrus	782,300	12	29	tons
Misc.	4,682,500	Vegetables, melons, potatoes	
Total	231,214,800			

The following chart shows the net profit at different market share values. The calculation used the value of 231 million acres of crop, sprayed at the rate of ½ pound per acre and list price of $50 per 100 pounds bag of products. Production and Distribution costs set at $12.50 per 100 pounds.

Market Share	10%	20%	40%	50%
Acres	23,121,480	46,242,960	92,485,920	115,607,400
1 lb./acre	11,560,740	23,121,480	46,242,960	57,803,700
100 lb. bag	115,607	231,215	462,430	578,037
Gross ($50.00)	$5,780,370	$11,560,740	$23,121,480	$28,901,850
Cost ($12.5)	$1,445,093	$2,890,185	$5,780,370	$7,225,463
Net	$4,335,278	$8,670,555	$17,341,110	$21,676,388

The numbers are for the United States only. It is estimated that based on current competition we should be able to get 40%-50% market share, especially with the potential of increased yield.

Signed: Andrew Steffel

Alex looked at the numbers and thought to himself,

That is some profit. That comes to seventeen to twenty-one million dollars' profit per year. And this is for the US only.

Looking at his watch, he noticed that it was almost time to meet Leslie for lunch. On his way to the cafeteria, he stopped by his boss's office to ask about the environmental report for 57126.

"Why do you need the environmental report?" his boss asked.

"I want to make sure that the results specified in the report are supported by the data. We don't want this to come back later and cause a delay in the selling and distribution of this product. Looking at the financial data, this product will be millions of dollars of profit for the company. And if it goes worldwide, you can easily double that or maybe even triple the profit."

"I'll see if I can find it for you" was all Gene said. With that, he picked up his phone to make a call. Alex took that as a sign that the conversation was over. Alex felt that Gene was not interested in the conversation but wanted Alex out of his office.

Alex left to meet Leslie for lunch. After a few steps, he realized that he had forgotten to ask if there was any update on the poisoning. He returned to his boss's office. As he approached the office, he heard his boss on the phone. "Rachael, Alex has been looking at the 57126 files." Alex stopped short of going into the office when he heard his name. "He wants to see the environmental impact research results. What do I tell him?"

Alex turned and left. He didn't see any need in asking his boss for the document again. He would have to find it himself. His inner voice told him that something is going on here, but he couldn't put his finger on it.

Leslie was waiting for him by the entrance of the cafeteria.

"You are a little late, Alex. I'm hungry."

"Sorry, I got sidetracked looking at some data on one of the products. Hey, look, there's a table by the window. Let's grab it."

They quickly headed to the table and sat down. "You go first," Leslie said. "I'm sure you are hungrier than I am." As she watched Alex walk away, she scanned the room to see if there was anyone she recognized.

There he was again, sitting at a table against the wall in direct sight of where she was sitting. But he was watching Alex as he stood in line to order his food. As Alex returned to the table, the man's eyes followed him.

"I've got my food. Go get yours, and I'll wait," Alex said.

"Start without me. You don't want it to get cold."

Leslie got up and headed to the salad area. From there, she had a clean view of the guy watching Alex. The man was just sitting there glancing around the room, but his eyes always came back to Alex. It was Alex that he was interested in, not her.

"Are you going to get something or just stand there?" the person behind her said.

"Oh, I'm sorry." Leslie started to fill her plate. As she moved to the cashier, she glanced over and noticed that the man was still looking in Alex's direction. She returned to the table and sat across from Alex.

"Don't look now, but there is a guy sitting behind you against the wall wearing a blue shirt. He isn't eating. He is just sitting there. But he seems to be watching you. Don't turn or he will know I'm talking about him."

"Why would he be watching me?" Alex was tempted to look and see who it was.

"This is the third time I've seen Mr. Blue Shirt watching us."

"Third time?"

"The first time was our first day when we went for a drink after work. I didn't think anything of it until today. He was in the bar leaning against the back wall. I remember seeing him as we left. I also noticed him another time when we were having lunch here. He wasn't eating, just sitting there watching us. And yesterday he met with my boss."

"Is Ms. Paranoia settling in?"

"Seriously, Alex, I think he is spying on you. Remember when I called you yesterday to see if you were okay?"

"Yes, and I thank you for your concern."

"Your boss was called to a meeting yesterday by Brianna's boss, and before they closed the door, I hear them say, 'Tell me everything that Alex told you.' And then they mentioned someone getting poisoned. Then Mr. Blue Shirt joined the meeting. I know he recognized me as he passed my desk but tried not to show it. He also had the entrance code for our area. I was told that only eight people had that code: three VPs; three assistants; Barb, our receptionist, and of course, Mr. Sterling. Apparently nine people have the code. I asked Barb who he was. She didn't know his name but said he was from security."

Alex had stopped eating and was listening intently to what Leslie was saying. What had he done that could have caused such an uproar upstairs? More questions to add to his growing list.

"I have an idea. Let's see if he really is following me. I'm going to look at my watch and react as if I have something to do right now. I'm going to get up and leave quickly. If the guy gets up and leaves right after me, then you text me. Just say, 'DRINKS TONIGHT.' If he doesn't leave when I leave, then text me, 'I CAN'T MAKE IT TONIGHT.' Got that?"

"Yes."

Alex finished his food, looked at this watch, said a few words to Leslie about leaving, picked up his tray, and headed to the disposal area, turning to wave at Leslie. He then headed out of the cafeteria and took the elevator to the first floor and out of the building. Just then he heard his cell phone buzz with a text message. He took it out of his pocket.

DRINKS TONIGHT?

He put the phone back in his pocket, walked to the drugstore across the street, and bought a candy bar. He glanced toward the door, and in walked Mr. Blue Shirt.

CHAPTER 22

Alex spent the afternoon reading the files on 57126. There were production schedules, distribution plans, pricing modules, and return on investment analyses. But there was nothing on the environmental effects. He read some of the results documents by Peter Hudson to review his conclusions. Peter had documented the same performance he had seen.

By why were there no documents about effects of the product on the environment? Degradation, pollution, air quality, groundwater impact... nothing. Maybe they were filed someplace else? Alex went back to the file room and looked to see if he could find some more documents. Nothing was there. He then pulled out the files for 62541 and 67689 that were also being tested at the farm. Both of them had extensive documentation of the effect of the product on the environment and had a copy of the environmental impact document. These documents had been signed by the person doing the analysis and countersigned by Rachael Phillips. There were also documentations stating that the documents had been sent to Environmental Protection Agency (EPA) and the Department of Agriculture in Washington DC.

But there was no document for 57126. And this product had been around for three years and getting ready for manufacturing and the marketplace. Alex checked all the file cabinets to see if maybe it had been misfiled. He turned up nothing.

There has to be a reason why nothing is here. Maybe someone borrowed the folder, and it is sitting on a desk. That has to be it. But who might have it? He couldn't think of anyone who would need the information. And what about the dismissal from his boss when he brought up the subject?

Was he being paranoid? There had to be a logical reason why it was not in the file room. But his instincts told him something was not right. And over the years he had learned to trust his instincts.

Alex returned to his office.

Did Peter also look for the missing document?
Had he seen it?
Did he have it?

Alex took out the piece of paper he had found in the desk drawer, unfolded it, placed it on his desk, and looked at it again. He still didn't recognize the other compound on the paper. He would have to try to figure it out. And what did the question mark mean? He sat there staring at the paper.

"I called our farm manager in North Carolina to have him contact your friend to see how his daughter is doing. I told him to call you with any information."

Alex looked up and saw his boss standing in his doorway staring at the piece of paper Alex had in front of him. Alex quickly put his hand over it, but he knew that his boss had already seen it. But did he see enough to make it out?

"Any update?"

"According to the report I got, your friend brought his daughter and father home from the hospital this morning, and everyone is doing fine."

"That's good to hear. I'm sure Mark is relieved. I hope they find out what caused it so it won't happen again. He wants to find out too. He said he doesn't want any other parent to go through what he went through. I'll give him a call tonight and report on his condition."

"Yes, of course, and let me know what he says." It was nice that Mr. Mathews was concerned about his friend. Or did he have a different reason for wanting to know about his friend? He didn't come across as a caring man when it comes to other people.

Alex decided to make one last attempt to find out about the missing document.

"Any update on the whereabouts of the environmental impact document for 57126? I want to review it and include pertinent information in my report to Charleston at the end of the month. I saw the performance of that product while at the farm, and it really looks like a winner."

"No, I have no idea where the documents are. If I hear anything, I'll let you know."

Gene turned and exited the office briskly.

Alex spent the rest of the afternoon documenting some of the data and filling out his expense report from his trip. He was glad to see the day end.

He caught the crowded subway and headed home. Picking up a pizza at a neighborhood pizzeria, he walked the two blocks to his apartment, rehashing everything that had happened over and over in his mind. He hardly remembered eating. He showered, changed into a pair of jeans, and headed out to meet Cindy Hudson.

He decided to take the bus across town to the coffee shop. He walked the six blocks to the bus stop, stopping occasionally to look in the store window. It was not for the purpose of window-shopping but to see if anyone was following him in the reflection of the glass. He wouldn't have given this a second thought if it hadn't been for Cindy's warning and the incident in the cafeteria. Nothing looked out of place in the reflection.

There was a subway entrance across the street from the bus stop. He walked down the stairs as if going to take the subway and then ran quickly through the tunnel and out the opposite exit across the street. He went around the corner of the building and stood in the shadows of a doorway watching the subway entrance. If anyone had been following him, he would have thought he got on the subway and would have followed him through the turnstile. No one came up the stairs.

He saw his bus arrive at the corner where he was hiding. He quickly stepped out of the shadows and boarded the bus and headed to the back. He didn't notice anyone checking him out. He looked out the window and didn't see anyone watching the bus. He was sure that he wasn't being followed.

It took the bus about twenty minutes to get across town. Only four people got out at the Second Avenue stop with him. He got out and stood there to see if anyone else came along. He could see the coffee shop across the street on the corner. He waited five minutes before heading across the street.

As he passed the window of the coffee shop, he looked in, scanning the customers. Only two people were at tables without computers. One was a man, reading a paper, and the other was a woman staring at the front door wearing a red shirt. That had to be Cindy.

She was much younger than Alex had pictured. She was about Alex's age. She sat there with her hands wrapped around her paper cup. Her brown hair hung to her shoulders. Her skin was flawless, and from time to time, she bit on her lower lip. He couldn't see her figure, but he suspected from what he saw that it was perfect.

Alex pulled the door open. He saw her look at him and a hint of a smile. He walked over to her table.

"Hi, Cindy, I'm Alex."

"Hi, Alex, thank you for coming."

"Let me get some coffee first. Do you want a refill?"

"No, I'm fine. Any more and I won't be able to sleep." There was the lip biting again. It was kind of sexy.

Alex walked over to the counter. For some strange reason, he felt she was watching every step he took. When he looked her way, she was staring at him. He got his coffee and returned to the table.

"Again, thank you for coming. Were you followed?"

"I don't think so, but why would anyone follow me?"

"I'm just being careful."

"I have to admit I was surprised to get your call. After all, I didn't know your husband. Again, I'm sorry for your loss. How are you doing?"

"I'm doing fine, taking one day at a time. I have a good support system in my friends, so that helps. The nights are just long."

Cindy continued to hold on to her coffee cup. Her hand hadn't left the cup since he had entered.

"You probably want to know why I called you."

"Yes, I am very curious about that."

"Let me tell you about my husband first. We had only been married for three years. We are both from Omaha and dated through most of college. We got married right after college. Peter got this offer to come to New York and work at Sterling. We were both excited. When we got here and started looking for a place to live, we didn't realize how expensive apartments were. We did find a small one bedroom around the corner from here. I have a degree in accounting and found a job right away as a loan officer in a bank to help with the rent. So we thought we were set."

"You are right, apartments are expensive here. I have a small place, and it takes a big chunk of my paycheck each month to pay the rent. The only saving grace is that you don't need a car here."

"We enjoyed the city and took advantage of what was here. We couldn't afford Broadway plays, but we loved the museums. On weekends, we helped clean up parks and common areas around the city as part of the Beautify the City organization."

"That is very admirable of you," Alex remarked.

"Peter was very big into the environment and worked on committees outside of work that are involved with saving the planet. He was also a health nut. He ran almost every day and was working up to running in the New York marathon again. But he never got that chance."

Alex noticed that she talked about Peter in the past tense. That was a sign that she had moved on.

"I was told he was an avid runner, and that is why it was so strange when he had a heart attack. But you never know what's going on inside your body."

Cindy finally took a sip of her coffee.

"Are you sure you don't want something else? That coffee has to be cold."

"I could use some water, if you don't mind."

Alex got up and went to the cooler and returned to the table with a cup of ice and a bottle of water.

"Thank you."

She opened the bottle and filled the cup. Again, he noticed her biting her lower lip right before she took a drink. He felt she didn't know how to begin or afraid to begin.

"So tell me about Peter at work."

"About eight months ago, I noticed a change in his attitude towards work. He mentioned that Sterling was working on a new product that would increase food production and would be a huge moneymaker for the company."

Alex just sat and listened. He knew she was talking about 57126.

"Peter said that he had a feeling that something was wrong with the product, but he couldn't put his finger on what it was. Just a gut feeling, he said. I told him he was being silly. After all, the company would never manufacture something that would be harmful or dangerous. One of the reasons he joined the company was because of their concern for the environment."

"That philosophy is one of the reasons I joined the company too," Alex added.

Cindy continued to look at Alex. "Peter mentioned that he couldn't find any documents on the effects of the product on the environment. He asked everyone, but no one had any answers. I think that is what caused him to have concerns about the product.

"He said his boss kept avoiding the question, no matter how many times he asked. He said he even contacted the people in West Virginia and got no answer as to the whereabouts of the document."

"Why do you think he thought something was wrong with the product? Did he say anything specific?"

"Not in so many words. He said he just had a feeling. Small things that he said combined together led him to believe something was wrong.

I remember him telling me that when he went to the research farm and walked through crops that had been sprayed with that product, he seemed to breathe heavier. He brushed it off as exhaustion. But then later he said he experienced that every time he went to the farm. And only when he walked through rows of crops sprayed with the new product."

Alex had a similar feeling when he was at the farm and was sure Don Brown did also. But he didn't remember where he was at the time.

"So every time he went to the farm, he would walk through the fields. And sure enough, the same shortness of breath happened every time or he had the same shortness of breath every time."

"Did he tell anyone about his experience and concerns?"

"He documented all this and told his boss, but nothing seemed to come of it. His boss, Gene Matthews, said it was probably due to jet lag or exhaustion. But Peter didn't accept that reason. When he got on to something, he would not let go, especially if he felt it was important. He needed to find the answer."

"So no one got back to him?"

"No one. He was almost obsessed trying to find out what was going on. He also mentioned that sometimes after being at the research farms, he would feel a little nauseous at night. He wondered if the chemicals had anything to do with it."

"Just being around chemicals can cause that."

"Peter was sure something was wrong. He kept pushing his boss and the people in Charleston to provide any information on how the product might affect people and the environment. I told him to just let it go."

Alex didn't know how to respond. He sat there listening, not aware of what was happening around him. People had entered and left the coffee shop, but he didn't notice.

"Do you know if he ever saw the environmental document?"

"As far as I know, he never saw the document. I'm sure that if he had, he would have mentioned it to me. I think he just kept getting the brush-off."

Alex knew the feeling. Alex was sure now that Peter never saw the document.

"Does this all sound strange to you, or was Peter just concerned with something that was all built up in his head?" Cindy said, looking straight at Alex with a concerned look on her face.

"I'm still rather new to the company, so I can't provide you with any insight. First, I didn't know Peter so can't speak for him. Only you could answer that. But I can tell you that I have not been able to find any documents on the effects on the environment. I've asked for that information, and everyone seems to avoid the question."

"That is what Peter kept asking for."

"Can I ask you why you thought this was important for me to know? After all, you don't know me."

"I heard from a friend who still works at the company that they had hired a new person to fill Peter's position. She is the only person I keep in contact with there. I felt that you should know the circumstances around Peter's life and his death."

"His death? Is there more you want to tell me?"

"There's more."

Cindy took a breath and continued. "I'm not sure if what I'm about to tell you really happened, but since you asked."

Alex had long finished his coffee but was holding the empty cup in his hand, waiting for her to continue.

"First of all when I called you last week, it wasn't a mistake. I called that number on purpose so we could meet. But I had to leave it up to you to decide if you wanted to meet me."

"Well, it worked."

Cindy took a deep breath. "I have no evidence for what I'm going to tell you, just a feeling I have and the sequence of events that took place. Chalk it up to paranoia or intuition or whatever you want to call it."

"I've found that sometimes gut feelings are based on facts that you're not always aware of," Alex interjected.

"Peter told me that he felt he was being watched and sometimes followed during the last couple of months. He said he never saw anyone, but he just felt it."

"Why did he think someone was following him? And for what reason would they be spying on him?"

"He thought that maybe he was getting close to something that the company didn't want him to know about."

"If that was the case, why didn't they just fire him and he would be gone?"

"We talked about that. If he still worked there, it's easier for them to watch him and have better control over his actions."

Alex decided best not to tell her that Leslie thought he was being followed too.

"But there is more. Peter was an avid runner and an athlete. He had a physical a couple of weeks before we went on vacation. His doctor said he was in perfect health. In fact, his doctor said he had the body of an eighteen-year-old, and his heart was strong. Peter was thirty-two."

"What are you trying to tell me?"

"Peter would not have a heart attack on his own. I think he was getting too close to something, and they had to stop him."

She stopped talking to let that sink in.

Alex just sat there staring at her. "Stop him? Do you think he was murdered because he was getting close to something?"

"That is the only conclusion that I can come to for what happened to us, to him. He must have found something that would have hurt the company in a big way. And they couldn't let that happen. That is why I called you and asked to meet. To warn you so the same thing won't happen to you and also to see if you have uncovered anything. I don't trust anyone there."

"If you feel that way, why not go to the police or someone else other than me?"

"You know they won't listen to someone with a gut feel. I have no evidence."

"Didn't an autopsy show anything? If he died of a heart attack when there was no evidence, it had to be poison or something like that they could trace."

"I took the word of the doctor and thought it was a heart attack so didn't authorize an autopsy. And I had him cremated. That is what Peter had wanted. I wish now that I had not rushed it so. There was so much going on, getting him back to New York, making all the arrangements . . . I just never thought something like that could have been the cause."

"What happened to prompt you to change your mind and think that he didn't die of a heart attack?" Peter asked.

"It wasn't until I went to the bank to put his death certificate away that I found a sealed envelope with my name on it. I opened it and found pages documenting Peter's findings and concerns. Also, there was a letter to me. He had also created a file on his computer that was password protected. The letter included the password. I went into his computer and found the same documents I found in the safety-deposit box. It was at that time that I thought something other than a heart attack could have been the cause. By then it was too late to look for evidence."

"I can't believe a major corporation like Sterling would be involved in something like this," Alex responded.

"Peter really thought he was on to something, and I really think it might have led to his death. Almost sounds like a mystery novel."

"Aren't most mystery novels based on real-life experiences?" Alex said.

"Also, a few weeks after the funeral, my apartment was broken into, and the only thing missing was Peter's computer. And there was no evidence of a random break-in according to the police. I suspect that Sterling has Peter's computer."

"Why do you think Sterling would be interested in the computer? Maybe it was a real thief?"

"Because in the desk drawer was an envelope with almost $500, and it was still there. The drawer was right below the computer. If it was a real break-in, wouldn't the money have been taken too? If Sterling took the computer, they probably feel safe now because there is no paper trail. They don't know that Peter had a hard copy of everything."

Alex thought about that last statement and all that he had just heard. "I just can't see anyone at Sterling murdering someone over concerns about a product. And as you said, there is no evidence."

"Peter said that the new products were going to make millions of dollars for the company, and the company had overextended itself and needed an influx of cash. He said they were on the verge of a financial collapse. In his research, he found evidence to that fact. He said a new product like this would save the company. Maybe it wasn't the company itself, but someone in the company who thought Peter might discover something that would hurt the company, or the person himself."

Alex had researched the company before he joined, and he saw no evidence that Sterling was in financial trouble. *Is there a cover-up? Are they in financial trouble?* Alex had seen the finance projections and knew that 57126 would bring in millions of dollars after introduction.

"Why do you feel it necessary to tell me this? What do you want from me?" Alex asked.

"I just want you to be careful, and maybe you will find something that will help me to finally put these thoughts I'm having to bed so I can move on."

"Thank you for your concern for me. But I'm not sure what I can do. I'm just new to the company and just getting my feet wet."

"I made a copy of everything for you that Peter left in the envelope. You read the documents and make your own conclusions. You can tell me that you have no interest and that I'm just fantasizing or wishful thinking. Or you might come to the same conclusion." Cindy reached into a bag she had set on the floor by her chair and pulled out a large envelope and pushed it across the table to Alex.

Alex stared at the envelope for a few seconds and then looked into her eyes. "If you didn't think the police would be of any interest, why tell me?"

"There was nothing concrete in the documents Peter had filed away. I suppose he was hoping to be around longer to gather more proof. But I know my husband, and I think he was on to something. But I have no idea what. That is when I thought I should call you and warn you or at least tell you. I would like to have you look at what he left behind and see if you feel I should go to the police. Then maybe they will start some type of investigation."

Alex again looked at the envelope lying on the table in front of him then looked up and saw the concern on Cindy's face. Alex thought about the man who followed him out of the cafeteria today. If it hadn't been for the recent observations that Leslie made, he would have thought that Cindy was just imagining things.

"I'll look at what you have and see if it makes any sense to me. I can't promise you anything though. As you know, I'm new to the company and am still learning my way around."

"That is all I can ask."

"I'll contact you and give you my thoughts. That's the least I can do since you've shared your concerns with me."

"That is all I'm asking. But call me on your personal phone, not on the company phone, in case you are being bugged. I've taken enough of your time, Alex. I have to go now." She got up from her chair to leave. She turned and looked at Alex, again with that concerned expression. "Thanks, Alex."

Alex picked up the envelope, and they headed to the door, Alex to go to the bus stop and Cindy to go home.

As they left the coffee shop, neither one of them noticed the man in the blue shirt across the street, leaning on the building staring into the coffee shop. He had taken out his cell phone and was making a call.

CHAPTER 23

Cindy walked to the corner with Alex.

"Thanks for coming, Alex. I hope I have not frightened you. It was not my intent."

"I'm glad we did meet. And again I'm sorry about your husband. I'm sorry I couldn't have been more helpful."

"Just someone to talk to helps."

"How are you doing otherwise?"

"I'm fine. Every day is easier. I miss Peter, but I know he would want me to get on with my life, and that is what I am trying to do. My job keeps me busy, and I do volunteer work in the parks on weekends. My days are full. The nights are just long, but it is getting easier."

"That is all you can do. If you need anything, let know. I'm new to the city so don't have a lot on my social calendar." He reached into his pocket and took out a piece of paper, wrote a number, and handed the paper to her.

"Here is my personal cell number. Call me anytime."

"Thank you." She opened her purse and dropped the piece of paper in. "You better get going. You need to get across the city, and it is getting late. Workday tomorrow." She leaned forward and gave Alex a hug while whispering in his ear, "Thank you." As she pulled away, she looked over Alex's shoulder and saw a man across the street leaning on the wall looking at them. He looked vaguely familiar, but she couldn't place him.

She watched Alex cross the street and head to the bus stop, envelope under his arm. He turned and waved, and she returned the wave and then turned around and headed to her apartment. At the corner, she crossed the street and turned left and headed down the block.

Was the guy watching them, or was she being paranoid?

She stopped to look into a store window. In the reflection, she saw the guy across the street about a half block back. She picked up her pace and headed toward her apartment.

As she entered her building, she turned and looked through the glass. There he was, a half a block away walking in her direction on the other side of the street. He must also have picked up his pace, keeping the distance between them the same. She rushed past the doorman without saying anything, taking the stairs to her apartment on the second floor. After entering the apartment, she double locked the door and moved to the front window without turning on the lights, keeping in the shadows to avoid being seen. There he was, across the street. As he passed her building, he slowed down, turned and looked up at her window, and then continued down the street. Although he could not see her, she instinctively jumped back further into the shadows. Slowly she moved back to the window and saw him disappear around the corner. She continued watching, but he didn't come back. Wrapping her arms around herself, she stood there shaking. Maybe Peter was right. Maybe he was being followed, and now someone is following her, and he knows where she lives.

As soon as Alex got home, he opened the envelope at his desk and pulled out the documents.

Just then his cell phone rang. "Hello."

"Alex, it's Cindy. I think we were being watched." She paused, letting that sink in.

"What?"

"There was a man standing across the street as we left the coffee shop. He appeared to be watching us. He looked familiar, but I couldn't place him."

"Why do you think he was watching us?"

"As I turned the corner from the coffee shop and headed down the street, I glanced back, and he was behind me about a half block back on the other side of the street. His eyes appeared to be fixed on me. When I got to my apartment, I looked out the window and saw him walk past my building. He slowed down and looked up at my window. I was standing there in the dark, so he couldn't see me. I watched him go to the end of the block and turn the corner. He glanced back in my direction and then disappeared. I waited awhile, but he never came back."

"Did you get a good look at him?"

"He was about six feet tall, short brown hair, and was wearing a blue shirt and black pants. I couldn't see his face, but I would put his age at late thirties or early forties based on the way he walked. Maybe Peter was right. Maybe he was being followed. I just wanted to let you know so you can be careful. But I'm sure he saw me give you the envelope."

"Are you okay? Do you want me to come over?"

"No, I'm fine. I'm locked in here, and we have a doorman downstairs. No one can come up without being announced first. Just be careful. Good night, Alex." The phone went dead.

Her description sounded like Mr. Blue Shirt. Maybe something really is going on.

Alex put the phone down and took the pile of papers from his desk and moved to the sofa. There were about thirty to forty pieces of paper in the envelope. He started going through the stacks of paper, one page at a time.

Peter had documented all his thoughts and suspicions. He suspected that he was being watched, his phone monitored, and his office bugged. He even thought his home was bugged. He wrote that he searched everything in his home but wasn't sure what to look for. He even tried several times to set traps or ways to get evidence that he was being watched. But he had never found anything.

Was something going on, or did Peter just have a vivid imagination? Alex thought to himself. *Maybe he was being watched. And now it is my turn.*

Alex continued reading the documents. Peter suspected that all of this revolved around the new product, 57126, that Sterling was getting ready to market and distribute worldwide.

Peter had talked to people from the research farms, the universities that were also testing the product, and even the research center that had worked with the product since it had been developed three years ago. He kept detailed notes of each conversation.

From his conversations, he found out that the employee absentee rate was 70 percent higher for those who had worked with 57126 than the rest of the company. But this increase in absentee rate only applied to those workers who worked with the product in the field—the farmhands from the research farms and the hired students from the universities that collected the field data. They all experienced similar symptoms: nausea and headache.

There were a few reported shortness of breath from time to time. After a few days, they felt better and went back to work. Those who worked with the product in an enclosed area, like in the chemistry labs and greenhouses, did not experience these symptoms. Nothing was found for those employees who had been checked by a doctor.

Peter had suggested that the interaction with the outside elements might have caused a change in 57126 and that the new product might have affected the workers when they came in contact with plants that have been treated with it. Air, water, sun? So far no deaths . . . but Peter was concerned about possible long-term effects. He compared it to smoking and the long-term effects on smokers.

Peter had talked to this boss about his findings and concerns. His boss dismissed it as coincidence and told him not to worry about it. His boss told him that there were people in the company who handled those tests and had found nothing. Yet Peter would not give up. He had requested more environmental studies on the product before it was released, but everyone ignored him.

Alex saw a list of dates that Peter had asked for the environmental impact research along with the names of the people he had requested them from. He had never received the reports. He had requested them from Gene Mathews, Rachael Phillips, Alan Milton, and Curtis Clark.

Curtis Clark was Leslie's boss. Alex had asked his boss for the studies and had also gotten the brush-off. Alex had not contacted anyone else but was going to e-mail Rachael to see if she had the documents. But now he had second thoughts.

Alex continued going through the documents. Peter had been very thorough. There was information on the financial status of the company. Peter was convinced that without a new product, the company was in financial trouble. He surmised that the company would survive but that upper management might not. Was Peter suggesting that it was upper management that was behind this scheme? That included Leslie's boss.

The next page was a copy of the letter that Peter had written to Cindy. Peter wasn't sure he should read it since it appeared to be a personal note. But if Cindy didn't want him to see it, she would have left if out of the envelope. Alex sat back on the sofa.

My darling wife,

If you are reading this letter, then something has happened to me. First of all I want to tell you how much I love you and was hoping to spend my life with you. Believe me when I tell you that I will always love you, and one day we will be together again. I don't want you to grieve me. I know that we will meet again someday and pick up right where we left off. Until that time, I want you to enjoy your life on earth while I get everything prepared for you here in heaven. Forgive me for getting you involved in this.

As you are aware, I have been suspicious of one of the new products being developed at work. If you feel my death is suspicious in any way, contact the police and give them the information that you find in the envelope. I also have the data in a file on my computer. The file is locked. The password to the file is "mystic95." I have no concrete evidence of any of my conclusions but feel something is wrong. This is all I have.

Remember, I will always love you and will always be with you.

Peter

Alex picked up the last piece of paper and saw the same diagram he found taped to his desk drawer.

57126

Pyrethrum

At the bottom of the page was written: "The composition of 57126 is very close to the structure of pyrethrums. Is there a connection?" Alex now knew the name of the other compound on the page.

Alex went to his computer and searched for "pyrethrums."

Pyrethrums are used in insecticides but also used topically for the treatment of head lice. If ingested it can be harmful to people. It causes sore throat, nausea, vomiting and abdominal pain almost immediately upon ingestion.

Alex started thinking about Lisa. *Sterling has a research testing site next to Mark's farm. Since 57126 is close in structure to pyrethrums, it might also cause the same symptoms if ingested. Did Lisa somehow accidentally get into some 57126?*

That couldn't be it. She got sick while on a picnic, and pyrethrum poison happens almost immediately. And what about Mark's dad? He got sick too. That couldn't have been an accident, two people at the same time. One being an adult who should know better. It doesn't make any sense that it could have been an accidental ingestion. And Mark and Diane had no symptoms and were with them when the symptoms occurred. And they all ate the same food, so the poison couldn't have been in the food. Maybe there is no connection between 57126 and Lisa after all. Maybe Mark is just looking for a connection that doesn't exist.

But what if there is something there? If 57126 has the same symptoms as a pyrethrum, there would be no reason for Sterling to hide that fact and refuse the publication of the environmental impact statements. The company would just need a disclaimer on the labels along with treatment, and everything would meet the legal requirements for an insecticide. All pesticides have these declarations as a precaution to protect the consumer and the company.

Alex needed to get more information from Mark. He checked his watch. Too late to call tonight. He would call tomorrow and find out more about Lisa's and his dad's symptoms. He also wanted to make sure that they were getting better.

He'd also call Don Brown at the research farm and see if any of the workers had complained or had been sick right after interacting with the product.

It was late, and he needed to try to get some sleep. But he had trouble falling asleep. Everything was going through his head: 57126, Peter's death, Lisa's illness, his being followed. Are all these events connected with 57126? Should he be taking some precautions?

CHAPTER 24

Mark was sitting at the kitchen table finishing his morning coffee, watching his family around him. It was a good day. His dad was sitting in his favorite chair reading the paper, and his mom was fussing over him as usual. Lisa was playing on the floor with Gretchen. Diane was at the kitchen sink humming away. The family was all back home. Just then the phone rang.

"Hello?"

"Good morning, Mark. This is Alex. I wanted to call to see how everyone is doing."

"Hi, Alex. We are doing much better. Everyone is home. It has been a stressful week, but I am thankful that everyone is okay and back home."

"That's good to hear. I'm sorry I had to leave in such a hurry, but I was working, and with a new job, I didn't feel I could take any more time off. How are you and Diane doing?"

"We are fine, thank you. Diane spent as much time as she could at the hospital. In fact, she slept in the room with Lisa both nights. She is the perfect mom . . . and wife. I stayed home with Mom at night but spent the days in the hospital. We were worried about Dad for a while. He seemed to be sicker than Lisa and didn't respond to the drugs like Lisa did. I guess his age had something to do with that."

"Do you mind telling me what happened after I left?"

"As you know, the lab took blood and urine samples, and they found traces of pyrethrum poisoning. We still don't know where they got the poison. I have all my chemicals locked up in a separate room in the barn. I checked them all, and none of them were pyrethrum products. And Diane and I didn't get sick. I keep coming back to the research farm next door run by your company thinking that maybe something was going on there. Did you find out anything?"

"So far I haven't found out anything, but I promise to keep looking, and I'll let you know anything I find. Did anything else happen after I left?" Alex asked.

"Well, the police came by. I think they thought that I might have had something to do with what happened. How could anyone think that?"

"They were only doing their job, Mark. They have to rule out everything so they can find the real cause."

"The food that we had at the picnic was in the refrigerator. They took it and sent it to a lab for testing. They didn't find anything wrong with the food. They spent a day at the farm looking around, taking samples, but didn't find anything. I guess I should be happy about that. But I still want to know what caused them to get sick."

"I know you've told the story a dozen times, but can you tell me what happened before you went to the hospital? When you first noticed something was wrong and what you were doing before that," Alex asked.

"We went on a picnic in the grove not far from the house. Diane and Mom made a picnic lunch. We started eating, and Lisa was running around. It was a beautiful day, and we were having a good time. Everything was perfect except for the mosquitoes. We have had so much rain this year that it is a natural breeding ground for them. But the crops sure look good. Anyway, Lisa started complaining about all the mosquitoes and that they were biting her. She was covered in mosquito bites. We could see red welts on her arms and legs from the bites. So we decided to pack up and go back home and finish the picnic. On the way home, Lisa said her stomach hurt. By the time we got home, she was vomiting and had a fever. We thought it was just the start of the flu or maybe she was just tired from running around. We put her to bed just to be sure. But then Dad started getting the same symptoms. I called the doctor, and he said to bring them to the hospital. He met us there."

"Do you know if they checked the research farm next door?"

"Yes. The police told me they checked them out too and found that all their chemicals were locked. The police were going to contact the university and see if there was any possibility that the chemicals would cause that reaction."

"Have you heard back from them?" Alex asked.

"They reported back that the poisoning could not have happened by coming in contact with the skin. It had to be ingested to cause that reaction that we saw. Also, it was probably not airborne since Diane and I didn't get sick."

"Let me ask you one more thing. At any time, did Lisa or your dad complain about having trouble breathing?"

"No, they never mentioned that. Why do you ask?"

"I'm just curious. Did the doctor take blood and urine samples after they had been in the hospital awhile?"

"Yes, they took more samples during the day and night, and they found less poison in the blood than the prior sample. The antibiotics helped them once they found out the cause."

"So no one has any ideas how they got the poison?" Alex asked.

"It is a mystery to all of us."

"That is a strange story, Mark. I'm glad though that everyone is better and home now.

"One more question, Mark. Did the doctor take blood and urine samples from you, your mom, and Diane as a precaution?"

"Yes, he did."

"Did they find anything?"

"They found small amounts of pyrethrums in our blood as well, but nowhere near the level that Lisa and Dad had. Now isn't that a kicker. So they treated us as well. They took samples yesterday, and there are no traces in any of us. I am glad this is over."

"I am too, Mark."

"Alex, keep me informed if you find anything. After all, fraternity brothers watch out for each other."

"I promise I will. Give my best to Diane and give that little Lisa a big hug for me."

"I think she is all hugged out, but I'll give her one for you. Bye, Alex. Thanks for everything."

"And I promise to spend more time with you next time I am in town, when we can rehash old times and not be so stressed out."

"We look forward to it. Thanks for calling, Alex. Keep in touch."

Alex hung up the phone. There was too much information going around in his head: Lisa getting poisoned, Peter may be murdered, and someone following him and the same guy spying on Cindy. Are they all connected?

Alex had gone outside to make the phone call. He didn't want to take the chance that someone could overhear his conversations. He looked at his watch and saw it was ten thirty.

He spent the rest of the morning going over the data he had received from the research farms and writing up some reports for R&D. But he had a hard time concentrating. He kept going back to the events of the past week. Had all of this happened in just a week? At eleven thirty, he called Leslie.

"Good morning, Alex," Leslie said as she picked up the phone.

"I'm just calling to see if you have lunch plans today."

"If I did, I'd cancel them if you are calling for a lunch date."

"You bet I am. Same place at noon?"

"I'll be there." The phone went dead.

Alex hung on to the phone a little longer. That woman was starting to get to him. There was something about her that kept bringing him back to her. She was so down to earth and easy to talk to. Not only did his heart feel that, but there was a stirring someplace else. He sat there awhile waiting for the erection to go down. He didn't want a tent as he headed to the elevator.

A little before noon, he felt safe to head to the cafeteria. He reached into his pocket and pulled out a penny. He checked to see if anyone could see him from the hallway. Lindsey had already left for lunch, and no one was around. Bending over, he quickly leaned the penny on its edge to rest against the wheel of his chair. He closed the door behind him and took a final look to make sure that the penny was still leaning against his chair wheel.

He headed to the elevator. It was full by the time it got to his floor. He squeezed in, not wanting to keep Leslie waiting. She was waiting for him as he got off the elevator looking as beautiful as ever. He looked around to see if Mr. Blue Shirt was anywhere in sight. It looked like they were alone.

"You hungry?" he said as he approached Leslie.

"Always."

"Let's do it. Hey, look, the same table is free." They headed toward it.

"This is our table," Leslie said. "Go get your lunch, and I'll hold the table."

Alex headed off to the food line. Leslie looked around to see if they were being watched. Not seeing anyone interested in them, she let out a sigh of relief and looked for Alex. He was in the hamburger line waiting for his order. He looked over at her and smiled. She gave a little wave back.

As she sat there watching him, she felt a little shiver come over her. She can't remember when she had ever felt so comfortable with a man. She had dated many men, but for some reason, Alex seemed special. She didn't understand the feelings she had right now. No other man had ever affected her this way. How could she feel this way having only known him for a short time? But she liked the feeling and hoped it would continue and he felt the same way. She wanted the relationship to continue to see where it might go.

"Your turn," Alex said as he sat his tray on the table. "You seem to be deep in thoughts. Hope I didn't frighten you."

"No, just thinking about all the work I have to do this afternoon," she lied.

"Then you better get a hardy lunch so you have the energy."

As Leslie headed toward the salad bar, Alex looked around to see if Mr. Blue Shirt was anywhere watching them. Not seeing him, he sat back in his seat, waiting for Leslie to return. She was in line for the salad bar. He watched as she moved down the line, looking at her perfect figure and firm ass.

"Down, boy," he said to himself, hoping not to give away his body's reaction when she returns. But he had no control over that part—it had a mind of its own. Just like when he was in high school.

"Damn," he said out loud to no one in particular.

Leslie had her tray and headed back to the table. She noticed that Alex hadn't started yet.

"Alex, you didn't have to wait for me. Your food is getting cold."

"Who said I don't like a cold burger," he said with a smile. "So have you settled in your job yet?"

"I'm still finding my way around. But I'm getting into the routine."

"Same here," he responded. "Every time I turn around, there is something new thrown at me to do or learn. But it is better to be busy than sit around with nothing to do."

"I agree with you there," she said, taking a bite of her salad.

"I just had a thought," Alex said.

"Thinking during lunch? I hope it isn't contagious."

"We've had lunch several times the past two weeks and one dinner after work. How about we go out on a real date?" Alex stopped, waiting for some type of reaction.

He didn't have to wait long for a response.

"Now those thoughts I like, and you can have them anytime. That sounds like a good idea. What do you have in mind?"

"How about having dinner or going to a movie Saturday night? That will be a perfect thing to do on a weekend. I can head out to Brooklyn so you won't have to come back into the city. That gives me a reason to get off this island and see something else."

"I'd like that very much. And I think a dinner would be nice. A place where we can be alone and just talk so we get to know each other outside of work."

"Great. How about 8:00 p.m.?"

"I'll be ready. Let me text you the address and landmarks so you have it. We don't want a city boy to get lost in the country."

"I will need your personal cell phone number. I want to send the address to that phone," she said. She pulled out her cell phone and sent him the information. "You have the address now, and I have your private phone number," she said with a wink

"I'm surprised I hadn't given it to you before now."

They finished their lunch, and after saying good-bye at the elevator, they headed back to work.

"You seem to be happier than when you went to lunch," Barb said as Leslie walked past her.

"I should be," she responded, looking back as she walked through the glass door. "I just got asked out by a handsome man."

"Anyone I know?"

"I hope not," she responded with a snicker. "I don't like competition. But his name is Alex, and he works in Marketing."

"Don't worry, I'm married. All I can do is look, not touch."

Leslie sat down and turned on her computer. As it was booting up, she heard the glass door open. She turned in her chair see to Mr. Blue Shirt come through the door and go into Mr. Gianti's office. As he turned to close the door, he glanced over at Leslie. Their eyes met for a second. His eyes seemed cold. He slowly closed the door, knowing that Leslie was watching him.

At about the same moment, Alex had returned to his office. As he walked in, everything looked like when he'd left. He looked at the wheel on his chair. The penny was not leaning against the wheel. It was lying flat on floor, about a foot from the chair wheel. Someone had been in his office while he was at lunch.

CHAPTER 25

Alex sat on the subway, traveling toward Brooklyn. He looked forward to seeing Leslie away from the office. It took him a long time to decide what to wear, longer than for any of his dates in college. He ended up with a blue-striped open-collar shirt and gray slacks. He was excited about this evening and didn't want to screw it up.

He never felt this way about a person so early on in a relationship. He wanted to see where this relationship would go. Was he in a relationship, and did Leslie feel the same toward him?

He knew it would be about forty minutes to get to Brooklyn, so he gave himself an hour. If he was early, he would walk around the neighborhood. He didn't want to be late, nor did he want to be early. Everything had to be perfect.

As the train pulled into the Fourteenth Street subway station, a group of tourists got on carrying maps, discussing where to go next and wondered if they were on the right subway. He heard them mention they wanted to go to Ground Zero while trying to read the subway map. From their accent, he figured they were from the Midwest. They sounded just like people from home. Alex turned to the female tourist sitting next to him.

"Excuse me. I hear you want to go to Ground Zero. You are on the right train. You will get off at Park Place. It is the second stop from here. When you get off the train, you will be at the Woolworth Building. Ground Zero is only a couple of blocks from there. You will see signs guiding you to the location, and people will point the way for you if you need help."

"Thank you. And people told me that New Yorkers are not friendly."

"There are a lot of us here. Don't let the news or what you hear scare you. And while you are in the area, check out Trinity Church. It is one of the oldest churches in the country and has great architecture. Walk through the cemetery and see the names of a lot of famous Americans. Alexander Hamilton is buried there."

"Thank you very much. We definitely will check that out."

The woman opened the tour book, looked up the church, and read the history about the church to her family. They then switched their conversation to dinner plans, trying to determine what type of food they wanted.

Alex sat back and listened to the sound of the subway as it sped through the tunnel to the next stop. As it approached Park Place, the tourists got up and headed to the door. The lady turned around and thanked Alex again.

"Have a good evening, and enjoy the city," he replied. He felt like a true New Yorker now.

The train left Manhattan and went under the East River to Brooklyn. It slowed as it pulled into the first stop in Brooklyn, Clark Street. He got up, climbed the stairs to the surface, and pulled out the map he had drawn from the text that Leslie had sent him. Now he was a tourist.

He walked two blocks down Henry Street and found the tree-lined street she described, Orange Street. He stopped and looked up and down the street. Both sides of the street were lined with red-bricked row houses, three stories high, and with shade trees for those hot days. The street was narrow, and there was no traffic, unlike the streets in his neighborhood. It was so quiet and peaceful. Many of the row houses had window boxes full of blooming flowers, and there were large decorative pots with flowers of all colors on the front steps. People were sitting on the steps talking to each other or enjoying the evening, catching the evening breeze. Although it was beginning to get dark, there were still children playing hopscotch, young boys playing catch in the street, and two girls roller-skating over the sidewalk. Everyone was taking advantage of the last rays of sunlight.

As he looked further down the street, three blocks away, he could see the East River and across from it Manhattan. The lights of the tall buildings were beginning to show up against the evening sky.

He heard a mother yell from an open window, "Maria, time to come in now." He watched as a pretty little girl stopped playing with her friends, waved good-bye, and headed up the front steps of her building. It was a totally different environment than you would find in the high-rise apartment buildings in Manhattan. Alex just stood there and watched for a while. This was a real neighborhood.

He continued one block farther and turned on Cranberry Street. On the corner was an Italian restaurant that Leslie had given as a landmark.

He stopped and looked in the window. People were eating and seemed to be having a good time. This was probably a neighborhood favorite, and being Saturday night, it was already full. Alex continued down the street looking for number 33.

Leslie buzzed him in, and he walked up the stairs to the second floor. She was standing in the doorway waiting for him, looking as beautiful as she did the first day he saw her in the conference room.

"This way, young man," she said with that perfect smile.

"What a beautiful street. Seems like a family neighborhood. I don't get that feeling in my neighborhood."

"That is why I like it here. People know each other and seem to care about their neighbors."

She was wearing a salmon-colored skirt with a matching sleeveless blouse that draped across the front and flowed when she walked.

"Come in and let me show you my home."

Alex followed her as she led the way into her home, his eyes on her perfect figure.

"Just a small two-bedroom place as you can see. I like this front bay window. I often stand here and watch what is happening on my street."

Alex joined her at the window. He looked to the left and saw the tavern that he passed, people going in and out. Across the street on the corner was a small deli. A man and a woman were standing out front talking while a young boy had his face plastered against the window of the store looking inside.

Her apartment was put together with class. It was just what Alex had expected from her. There was a large high-backed sofa with large stuffed pillows. It looked like the type that you want to sit in and never leave. It faced a fireplace that gave the room a homey feeling with built-in bookcases on either side and matching wing chairs sitting in front of each bookcase. A lithograph of four guys on a sailboat in a black frame hung over the fireplace. The wood floor was covered with a black-and-gold rug, and a glass coffee table held a vase of fresh flowers. A small dining area was set up outside the kitchen area with more flowers in a crystal vase in the center of a glass table. Through a door, he could see a kitchen, and down a hall he suspected were the bedrooms.

"How about a glass of wine before we leave?" she asked. "I don't have much other than that in the way of alcohol."

"Wine will be fine. I have reservations at River Café. Have you been there? I wasn't sure what your taste is in regard to food so thought something American would be best. All I've ever seen you eat at work was a salad."

"I've never been there but have heard good things about it. And as far as taste in food, I eat almost anything, except sardines."

"I'll make sure not to order a sardine salad then. It was my first choice, but I will find something else on the menu," he responded jokingly.

"Sit down, let me get the wine."

Alex sat on sofa and watched her go to the kitchen to get the glasses. As she reached up to the top shelf, her skirt rose up, and he saw more of her thighs. They were smooth and firm. She pulled down the glasses and filled them half full with wine. Sitting next to him, she handed him a glass. Alex raised his glass. "To a wonderful evening."

"I'm sure it will be." There was that smile again.

He closed his eyes as he tasted the smoothness of the wine. "Very nice," he replied.

"Did you have any trouble finding the place?"

"Your directions were perfect. I stopped on Orange Street and watched some kids playing outside their home. And people sitting on their steps just enjoying themselves. It just felt so good to watch. It gives you a warm feeling inside. Kind of reminds me of back home in Minnesota."

"It is a nice neighborhood. I really like it here. Well, let's finish up and get on our way. It's about a fifteen-minute walk from here. That will help us build up an appetite."

They finished the wine, and Leslie took the glasses to the kitchen, rinsed them, and put them in the sink drainer. She turned and headed to the door, handing Alex the key to lock up behind them.

They left the building and headed toward the river. Leslie took his arm as they strolled down the sidewalk.

"Such a nice evening," she said, tossing her hair as she looked at him.

"I can see why you like living here. It is so peaceful, and the sidewalks aren't crowded."

"People tend to slow down when they get out of the city and seem to enjoy the things around them more," she added.

"I do feel more relaxed," Alex added, smiling back at her.

"Most of the people in the neighborhood have lived here a long time. Some were even raised in the homes they are now raising their children. I know almost everyone by sight and many by name. There are block parties during the spring and summer to allow new people to get to know their neighbors."

Leslie pointed out many interesting tidbits about the neighborhood as they walked down the street.

"We are not in Manhattan, but we are right next door. We have the advantage of both locations: the high energy of the city when we want it, yet the quiet neighborhood feeling when we need our solitude. I can't imagine living anyplace else right now."

They came to the entrance of the restaurant. They entered, and Alex gave him his name. He said "Dr. Gregory" hoping he would get a little extra service since this was a special night. They were seated at a table by a window where they could see the river and the lights of the city in the distance. The sun was just setting, so the sight was something to enjoy. Off to the right, they could see the Brooklyn Bridge.

"May I get you something from the bar?" asked a waiter dressed in a white shirt, black pants, bow tie, and white apron.

"May we see the wine list?"

Alex checked the list and ordered a bottle similar to what he had at Leslie's place.

"It is hard to believe that a million and half people actually live on that island that is only twenty square miles," Alex said, looking out the window across the East River to Manhattan. "And almost double that during the week when all the commuters come in for work. It really is the city that never sleeps." They both sat and looked out the window as it got darker and more and more of the building lights glowed against the dark sky.

The wine came, and they looked at the menu while the waiter opened and poured. After placing their order, they turned back to look at the view.

"So are you getting used to the commute to work each day?" Alex asked, trying to break the silence.

"It has only been a couple of weeks, but I'm getting used to it. The hardest part is scheduling around the subway schedule."

"How are the other people on your floor?" Alex asked. "Are they accepting you as one of them yet?"

"I'm the new kid on the block, so it will take a while before everyone accepts me as one of them. Brianna seems to run the floor and will have nothing to do with me other than a casual hello and good night . . . but only if I initiate it first. Barb is great and so helpful. And Rob has been helpful too. He is very quiet and keeps to himself though, so know nothing about him."

"Hang in there. Before you know it, you will be one of the gang, and maybe the leader of the gang."

"That's something I don't want," she replied.

Their salads arrived, and they started eating. Over the next forty minutes, they talked about their jobs, their upbringing, their likes and dislikes.

"I find it so easy to talk to you, Alex. It is as if we have known each other for a long time."

"I feel the same way."

Again, there was that stirring in his pants. Dinner was finished, and Alex asked for the check.

"Let's walk for a while," Alex said. "This is such a nice evening and nice neighborhood. I want to enjoy it as long as I can. I can see why you like it."

"You are welcome to come over anything you want," she said.

"Is that an invitation?" he asked, looking at her.

"Of course it is," she responded.

Alex reached over and took her hand, hoping she wouldn't pull away. She took a firm grip of his hand, turned, and smiled at him. They walked along the boardwalk looking at Manhattan in the distance and then headed back to Leslie's apartment. Never once did she let go of his hand. They passed other people out walking along the boardwalk and on the street, but he hardly noticed them.

"Want to come in for a glass of wine?"

"I would like that very much."

She gave him the key, he unlocked the door, and they entered, Alex moving to the sofa while she walked into the kitchen to get the wine. On the way back, she stopped by a radio and turned on a station with soft music.

"I didn't think anyone else ever listened to radio music in their homes. I thought I was the only crazy one."

"It is just so relaxing when I come home from work and making dinner. Most people just turn on the TV. The radio relaxes me."

Alex sat in the center of the sofa so no matter where she sat, she would be close to him. She handed him the glass and sat next to him.

"Cheers," he said, lifting his glass. "Thanks for a wonderful evening."

Alex took a drink and then put his glass on the coffee table and leaned into her. She leaned toward him, and their lips met. Her mouth opened slightly, and her tongue moved into his mouth. He had his arms around her, and the kiss seemed to go on forever. She pulled back and put her glass down, and they remained close, looking into each other's eyes.

"I've thought about this moment all evening," she said, pulling back a little.

"You didn't have a monopoly on that feeling," he said, moving into her again, her moist lips pressing into his. This time her body was closer, and he could feel her hard nipples pressing against his chest. That was not the only thing in the room that was hard at this moment. The kiss lasted longer and was done with more passion.

Alex felt like a schoolboy. He had kissed many women through his college days, but he never felt like he felt now. He wanted her, yet he did not want her in the same moment. He didn't want to ruin something that could turn into something better by rushing it. Yet his body was telling him a different story, and so were her hands.

Her hand ran along the inside of his thigh in a circular motion, caressing it softly as they continued exploring each other's mouths with their tongues. She then moved her hand from his leg, pushed it under his shirt up to his chest, and softly caressed his chest. His body was responding to her touch, and his penis was harder than he had ever remembered. He didn't want the feeling to ever end.

"Are you sure you want to do this?" he asked, hoping to get the answer he wanted.

"Yes, I've wanted this for a long time," she responded with a wicked smile. "Will you stay the night?"

"Well, it is late and a long way home. I don't want to get lost since I've had lots of wine."

"You're right, it is a long way home, and it is dark. After all, being your host, it is my responsibility to make sure that you get home safely."

She grabbed his hand and led him into the bedroom. She turned toward him, and he pulled her to him, his arms around her back and her arms around his neck. He slowly moved his hand down her back and then down to the ass he had admired so often. It was better than he had imagined. She continued to explore his mouth with her tongue.

He was enjoying every minute. They slowly pulled apart, and her hands went up under his shirt and pulled it off over his head. He stood there bare chested as she ran her tongue over his chest and gently bit into each nipple, first one and then the other. Alex's hands were on the back of her head, not to guide her, but simply to feel her. He ran his fingers through her hair as she ran her tongue over his chest and then back up his neck, into his ears, and then ending on his lips.

Alex reached under her blouse and gently undid her bra. Her breasts stood there firm without any support. He moved his hand to her breasts and found her nipples with his thumbs and forefingers. She moaned softly as he pinched them, her mouth still on his. They pulled apart.

"The bed would be much more comfortable," she said as she reached down and unbuckled his belt. His pants dropped swiftly around his ankles. He sat on the bed and removed his shoes as he watched her remove everything down to her panties. She stood as a goddess in front of him, as he sat on the edge of the bed, a total erection pushing up against his underwear.

"That must be uncomfortable," she remarked as she kneeled in front him, reaching up and removing his underwear.

"That's much better," she said. One hand wrapped around his shaft while the other gently stroked his balls. Alex closed his eyes and spread his legs further apart so he could enjoy the sensation to its fullest. She continued to stroke. Then he felt something wet and warm around his cock. He opened his eyes to see her mouth moving up and down, and he could hear a deep moan come from deep inside her. He didn't want this to stop.

She removed her mouth from him and looked up. Alex stared into her face. He then pulled her up to the bed and coaxed her onto her back on the bed. He turned toward her and pressed his lips against hers. At the same time, his hand moved to her breasts and then down across her flat stomach to the top of her panties.

She raised her hips; and he pulled her panties down, over her legs, and threw them on the floor. His hand moved back up her legs, slowly stroking one thigh and then the other. She opened her legs, and his hand moved up and started caressing her before putting a finger inside her, moving slowly in and out. She arched her hips, begging him to continue and go deeper. He had no intention of stopping.

He now moved his mouth down her neck to her breasts, taking in each nipple and sucking and chewing on them gently. They were already hard and begging for more. His fingers found her G-spot, and she started to moan more. He looked up and saw her eyes closed and her lips slightly parted.

A peaceful yet erotic look was on her face. His tongue went back to her nipples, and then he started working down her stomach, stopping at her navel. He continued south, ending at her womanhood. He found the treasure and didn't want to leave it. He needed to make her happy and take her to a place she had never been before. From the sounds he heard coming from her, she was there.

"Oh, Alex, I've fantasized about this moment, and it is better than my fantasies. But I want you inside me now."

Alex reached for his pants and took out a condom that he brought with him. Quickly he pulled it out of the package, ready to put it on.

"No, let me put it on for you. I want to feel your hard shaft again."

She took the condom from him, and he lay back on the bed, his erection standing straight up. She crouched over him and gently rolled the condom down his shaft. Then she moved up over him lying on top, their lips meeting again, tongues once more exploring.

Alex rolled her over onto her back, pressing her legs apart at the same time. Slowly he entered her, and their hips moved in perfect unison that seemed to go on forever.

"I can't hold back any longer," she moaned, and Alex felt her tighten up, at the same time grabbing his ass and pulling him further into her.

Alex was on the edge, and he exploded deep inside her at the same time. It felt as if it was the first time, all the sensations he had ever felt wrapped up in this single moment. He hoped the sensation would never stop. He looked at her and knew that she reached the height of pleasure at the same time he did. He gently kissed her on her lips as she made one last thrust of her hips. Slowly she relaxed.

Alex pulled out slowly, rolling onto his back and pulled her to him. They both lay back onto the bed, his arms around her, her head nuzzled in his neck. They lay there in silence, enjoying the moment. He heard her breathing go shallow as she moved closer to him.

He reached down and pulled the covers up over them. She felt so natural in his arms, and he enjoyed it. Her breathing became even, and he knew she was falling asleep. He smiled as he closed his eyes to sleep, happy that he was here.

CHAPTER 26

Alex turned over in bed to put his arms around Leslie, but the bed was empty. He opened his eyes to see that he was alone. The sun was streaming in through the windows, and he could hear the sounds of the city outside. He pulled back the covers, found his pants, and put them on. He followed the aroma of the coffee to the kitchen where Leslie was standing next to the kitchen counter.

"Good morning. How long have you been up?"

"Good morning. I've been up for about an hour. I thought I would let you sleep."

She walked over to him. He took her in his arms and kissed her on the lips. She responded by pushing her body into his.

"Thank you for last night, and I'm not talking about the dinner," she said as she pulled away.

"No, thank you. I had a great time. And the dinner was good too."

"You want to shower before breakfast? I put out a towel for you in the bathroom. I've already showered."

"I'd like that."

He gave her a kiss on the lips and headed to the bathroom. She had laid out a towel, a soap, and a toothbrush for him. He removed his pants and stepped into the shower. He stood there and let the water run down his body. He found himself humming, something that was not typical of him. He had enjoyed last night, not just the sex but just being here and having Leslie around him. He stepped out of the shower, dried himself off, and brushed his teeth. He would have to wait until he got home to shave. But he felt refreshed. Hanging the towel over the shower door, he headed back to the kitchen.

Leslie was at the stove stirring what appeared to be scrambled eggs. He walked over, put his arms around her waist, and kissed her on her neck.

"Sit down at the table before I burn these eggs."

Alex moved to the bay window. Looking up and down the street, he saw a couple sitting on their front steps with coffee in their hands talking to a passing neighbor.

Leslie came from the kitchen with two plates in her hand. Alex moved to the table and sat down. She placed a plate in front of him that was filled with scrambled eggs, hash browns, and buttered toast. A glass of orange juice sat next to the plate.

"I slept with you and I'm not even sure how you take your coffee. What does that say about me?"

"It says you are a good hostess. And I take it black. I need all the caffeine I can get in the morning to get going."

"I'll fill the first cup for you, but if you want more, you'll need to get yourself."

"That works for me."

She sat, and they enjoyed their first and what he hoped to be many breakfasts together.

"This breakfast looks great. Thanks for making it."

"Some mornings I expect to wake up and you have breakfast waiting for me."

"Deal. But you are taking your life in your hands. Cooking is not one of my strengths," Alex replied.

"Let me be the judge of that."

Alex ate as if it was the first breakfast he had ever had. He usually only had a bagel in the morning as he ran out the door to work. And on weekends, he would sleep in and then head to the gym. His first meal on weekends was usually lunch.

After they finished eating, they took their coffee and moved to the sofa in the living room. She sat next to him, sitting with her legs wrapped under her. She looked so beautiful. They both sat and looked out the window at the buildings across the street. The window was opened, and they could hear the street waking up.

"I really had a good time yesterday. And thanks for letting me stay the night." Alex paused, wanting to continue with what he was feeling, but didn't want to frighten her.

"I had a good time too."

He decided to take a chance. "I'm not sure where this relationship is going, but I'd like to find out. I'm not talking about only at work but outside of the office."

"I would like that too."

"With that said, I want to tell you some things that have been happening at work to get your opinion of a situation. In some ways, you have been a part of it."

"I'm all ears," she said, taking another sip of coffee.

"Okay, here goes. On my first day of work, I received a call from a woman, Cindy Hudson, who was the wife of the person who had my job. Her husband had died of a heart attack. She said she called me by mistake, and she wished me well in my new job. She then said she would like to meet with me to tell me about her husband. I let it pass until something happened later."

Leslie sat, listening intently. "You mentioned that when we were at dinner the first day. Did you call?"

"I'll get to that. Last week I found a note in my desk that was taped to the top of the inside of my desk drawer. I suspect it was written and placed there by her husband. Again, I thought nothing of it at that time."

"How do you know it was from him?" she asked.

"I just assumed it was since he occupied my office before me and it was his desk. Anyway, when I was at the research farm this past week, I found out that one of the employees had trouble breathing while on the job. He claimed it was just due to getting old. I later realized that I had a similar experience while there and also noticed that the farm manager was also breathing heavily. I didn't think anything of it at the time. I assumed it was due to the heat and being tired."

"Did you find out the cause?"

"I still don't know, but I don't think it was due to the heat."

"What else happened?" Leslie asked.

"I went to college in North Carolina. That is one reason I wanted to visit that farm rather than the one in Texas or Florida. A frat brother of mine lives close by, so I decided to make a surprise visit while there. I hadn't seen him in several years so thought it would be fun to catch up."

"I'm sure that he was surprised to see you."

"Well, it didn't turn out the way I had hoped it would."

"Why, what happened?" Leslie asked.

"When I got to his farm, his mother was there alone. She told me that Mark's daughter and father were in the hospital. She asked if I would take her back to the hospital so she could be there with the family. I went to the hospital to see if there was anything I could do."

"That was nice of you. Is everyone okay?"

"Mark was surprised to see me, but he had other concerns on his mind at that time. Blood tests taken at the hospital indicated that his daughter and dad had been poisoned."

"Poisoned? So that is what the conversation was with Mr. Gianti last week at work. Are your friends okay?"

"Yes, they are home and doing well. But it is still a mystery how they got the poison. It was a poison called pyrethrum that is found in insecticides. Mark said they had no poison like that on this farm for his daughter and dad to get. Then he told me that their farm was next to the land that is being leased by Sterling to test new products. He wanted to know if we were testing pyrethrum products. The police checked the farm, and all the chemicals there are locked up at all times."

"All of that could have been a coincidence, couldn't it? I don't see any connection."

"That is what I thought at first. But this got me thinking of the other events that have taken place."

"What other events?" she asked.

"I'll get to that. I need to give you some background so you can see where I'm coming from."

"Go on," she replied, with a serious look in her eyes.

"Part of my job is to review the results of the tests at the farms and make recommendations to the company on the new products. One product being tested is showing dramatic results that will make the company millions of dollars once it reaches the market. The product doesn't have a name yet, but it's referred to as 57126. The company wants to have it in the market for spring next year. So I started looking through the files for all the documents on the product. There was no environmental impact statement associated with this product."

"What is that document?"

"It is a document required by the federal government for new products. It describes the positive and negative environmental effects. It is one of the first documents needed for a new product to be registered. I have been looking and asking for the document but keep getting the runaround from everyone I ask."

"Maybe they haven't done it yet."

"It is completed early on in the field tests. This is the third year of testing this product in the field, so something should be in the files, especially if it is going into the market next year. It can take the EPA a year to approve a product. So if they want it for the market for next year, it has to be completed and sent to the government. But I can't find it anyplace in the files."

"Is there any way you can check with the government to see if it has been filed?"

"You can send a request, but it has to be on company stationery and signed by an executive since the product is not yet being sold. And that could take months before you can get an answer."

"Do you have any ideas why you can't find it?"

"I've come up with three reasons. First, like you said, it hasn't been done yet. Second, someone else has it and forgot about returning it to the files. Third, the impact on the environment is bad, so they don't want to have it published for others to see."

"But can they get permission to sell the product without it?"

"No, they can't. But they can make a phony one and submit that, and no one will be the wiser. The government doesn't do their own studies. They depend on the companies to be honest."

"But eventually someone will find out."

"True... but what if the dangers cause long-term effects but nothing now? Like cigarettes. No one thought there would be a problem. At the time of filing, everything looked good. But people in the tobacco companies knew there was a long-term effect."

"That sounds scary, but you have no evidence."

"That's true, but there's more."

"More?" she asked. "What else?"

"You pointed out that twice I was being followed or thought I was being followed."

"Now you are starting to scare me, Alex."

"I don't mean to scare you. I just want to let you know what is going on. I decided to call Cindy and see what she wanted. We arranged to meet at a coffee shop near her home. She told me to make sure that I was not being followed when I came to meet her. I thought that was a strange request but did what she asked."

"Where you followed?"

"I didn't think so then, but I do now."

A look of concern appeared on Leslie's face. She grabbed Alex's hand.

"She lives on the east side. She suggested we meet at a coffee shop on East Eighty-second Street. I took a bus across town making sure that no one was following me, especially keeping an eye out for Mr. Blue Shirt. I didn't see him, so I was sure I did a good job at evading anyone following me."

"Was Cindy there when you got there?"

"Yes, I could see her thorough the windows of the coffee shop, and she looked nervous."

"How could anyone be nervous around you?" Leslie added to lighten the conversation a bit.

"I think you are a little biased," Alex added.

"So what did Cindy want?"

"Her husband, Peter, had the job that I now have. She told me that he felt that he was being watched, that his home was being bugged and his cell phone monitored. He had been collecting documents about 57126 and was concerned about its impact on the environment. Kind of what I am now going through."

"Does she know if he ever saw the document?"

"From what she said, he never saw it and that he had the same concerns that I have about the safety of the product. She believes there is a possibility that her husband was murdered because he was getting close to finding out something about this new product, something that the company didn't want known. But she only has a suspicion. She has no evidence to that fact."

"Murdered!" Leslie responded with fear in her eyes. "Did you say murdered?"

"That's what she said. Peter had collected a lot of documents about the product and had them filed away. She gave me a copy of all the documents he had."

Alex waited for the last few statements to sink in. Leslie sat there clutching her coffee cup, her eyes on Alex.

Alex continued. "Peter found out that the company had overextended itself financially and needed an influx of cash. This new product was their answer to their financial problems."

"Alex, are you in danger?" He could see concern on her face.

"I'm okay. Don't worry."

"You may not be worried, but I am," she responded.

"Don't worry about me."

Alex waited a few seconds and then said, "There's more."

"I hope it gets better. You are scaring me."

"You have been clutching that coffee mug for a long time. Would you like me to fill it?" he said, trying to calm her down a little.

"No, I'm fine," she said as she put the cup on the table next to her. "You said there was more?"

"When I got home from meeting with Cindy, she called me and said that we were being watched while in the coffee shop. From her description, I believe it was Mr. Blue Shirt. She also said he followed her home."

"Oh my, is she okay?" Leslie asked.

"She is fine. She is a strong woman. The next day, you and I met for lunch. Before I left to join you, I set up a trap to see if anyone went into my office when I was not there. I leaned a penny against the wheel of my desk chair, and when I came back from lunch, the penny was lying flat on the floor away from the wheel of the chair. I suspect that someone had been in my office looking for something and moved my chair and, in the process, disturbed the penny. I think they might have been looking for the notes Cindy gave me. I left the notes at home in a safe place. So maybe someone is watching me and trying to find out what I know or what Cindy told me."

Alex sat back to catch her reaction. She just continued to look at him. No reaction. It was like she was deep in thought.

"Are you okay, Leslie?" Alex asked after a few minutes. He had noticed that her expression had gone from fearful to thoughtful.

"Maybe I have something to add," she finally said.

"What?" Alex asked.

"I'm not sure if it has anything to do with this, but since we are sharing strange happenings, the other day while I was working at my desk, Mr. Blue Shirt came to Mr. Gianti's office in a hurry. I know he saw me but let on that he didn't recognize me. Mr. Gianti is Brianna's boss. The strange thing is that Rob, the other assistant on the floor, was in the meeting, and Brianna wasn't invited to join them. I could see that Brianna was furious."

"Do you have any idea what they were talking about?"

"I tried to hear, but I was too far away, and the door was closed. But Mr. Blue Shirt knew the code to get through the glass partition. Brianna said he works for security. I thought he then knew the code because of that. I mentioned it to Barb, and she was surprised that he had the code. She said the head of security doesn't even have the code for the doors. So if the head doesn't have the code, why would someone who works for him have it?"

"I wonder how we can find out who Mr. Blue Shirt is. That way we can see if he works in security and who he works for," Alex asked. "Anything else happen?"

"About thirty minutes later, Mr. Blue Shirt came out of Mr. Gianti's office, and while the door was open, I heard someone from the inside say,

'In the same way.' I have no idea what they were talking about. About fifteen minutes later, Rob came out. Brianna looked angry and demanded to know what he was talking about with her boss. Rob shrugged it off and said it was none of her business and that it was personal. I know this really upset Brianna. What kind of personal relationship would Rob have with an executive vice president? He doesn't work for him, and I've never heard him talk about any connection with him."

"Maybe he is buttering him up to take over Brianna's job."

"I doubt that. Brianna would never let that happen, and I'm sure that Mr. Gianti thinks very highly of her."

"With everything we know so far, or suspect, something is going on at Sterling. I don't know if my imagination is getting the best of me, but I'm starting to think that maybe Peter was on to something. I think I need to go back to Cindy with all this information and see if she can add anything. I'll go alone. I don't want you to get mixed up with this."

"I'm already mixed up with it. I'm with you, and I care about you. Let's call Cindy and see if she is available now. Do you have her number?"

"Yes, I have it in my wallet. But let's play safe and call from a public phone in case our phones are bugged."

"There is a public phone on the corner, or we can go into the deli there and use the one there. I know the manager, and he will let me use his phone."

They got dressed and headed to the deli, both of them looking around to see if they could see if anyone was paying any attention to them. It was still early on Sunday and not many people on the street. At the corner deli, Leslie found the manager, and he was happy to let them use his office phone. There were only two other people in the store at this hour. Leslie recognized them from the neighborhood . . . no strangers, and definitely no Mr. Blue Shirt.

Alex took out the phone number and dialed. After three rings, he heard someone pick up the phone.

"Hello?" Cindy answered.

"Hi, Cindy, this is Alex. I was wondering if we could meet again now. Some things have happened, and we want to bring you up to date and see if any of it makes sense to you."

"Where are you?"

"We are in Brooklyn Heights."

"We?"

"I'm sorry, I'm here with Leslie, my girlfriend. She also works at Sterling and has added some more information to the pot."

It just slipped off his tongue, "my girlfriend."

Leslie looked at him after that statement and smiled at the "my girlfriend" remark.

"Can you come to my place? We can talk here. Just make sure you aren't being followed. You know how paranoid I am."

"We will be careful. I thought it strange when you asked me last time. But you were right."

Cindy gave them the address.

"We are on our way," Alex said and hung up the phone.

CHAPTER 27

Alex and Leslie took a cab from Brooklyn Heights to Penn Station, constantly looking to make sure no car or cab was following them. At Penn Station, they walked through the underground tunnel to the subway stop for the number one train. The tunnel was long and straight, was full of people, and had many exits. They kept looking behind to see if anyone was following them. They quickly went through the turnstile for the subway train. When they got to the track, the train was just pulling into the station, and they hopped on, and the door closed behind them. If anyone was following them, they would not have made the train.

"Whew. I feel like I'm on an espionage mission," Leslie said.

"In a way you are."

They took the subway to Eighty-sixth Street and then the crosstown bus through Central Park. Exiting on the other side of the park, they walked to Cindy's apartment, again watching to make sure that no suspicious person was following them. The doorman called up to make sure she was expecting them and then directed them to the elevator.

Cindy met them at the door, holding a cup of coffee in her hand.

"I hope you have more of that coffee available or I'll have to send out for some," Alex said. "Thanks for having us over on such short notice."

"The tone of your voice left me with no choice. My curiosity got the best of me. How do you take your coffee?"

"Black, thank you."

"Same for you?" she said, looking at Leslie. "By the way, I'm Cindy. It's nice to meet you, Leslie. I'll get the coffee."

"Nice meeting you, Cindy. Alex has told me all about you. I'm sorry about your husband. No coffee for me. I'm shaking enough. A glass of water would be nice."

Cindy left the room and returned with a pot of coffee, two mugs, a pitcher of iced water, and a glass on a tray. Alex and Leslie were still standing by the door.

"Come in, sit down. No need to stand there."

Alex sat on the sofa, and Leslie sat next to him. Cindy put the tray on the coffee table in front of the sofa and sat down opposite Alex.

The room was large with a bay window across the front. The furniture consisted of a high-backed sofa with rounded arms in a floral pattern. A round Chinese-carved coffee table with a glass top was in front of the sofa. Two high-backed chairs faced the sofa, with the same floral pattern. On the wall behind the two chairs was a large cabinet that probably housed a television. On either side were shelves full of books. A dining area and open kitchen comprised the rest of the area. Artwork hung on the walls. The room was eloquently done yet felt homey and comfortable.

Cindy poured Alex some coffee, handed the mug to him, and then handed Leslie a glass of water. Grabbing the other mug and filling it, she sat back.

"Okay, so what's going on?" Cindy asked, sitting on the edge of the chair.

Alex repeated what he had told Leslie earlier. The note with the two formulas that he found in his desk was similar to what Cindy gave him. Also that he felt he had been followed and someone had also been in his office looking for something. He told her about the poisoning of his friend's daughter and father. And everything seemed to point to the new product, 57126. And then Leslie's account of what happened at work. Cindy sat there listening intently, not saying a word, and barely moving a muscle. When he was finished, he sat back. Cindy sat very quiet as if synthesizing all that had been said. Alex waited for a response.

"Peter kept saying that there was a potential problem with one of the new products. I don't remember him saying the name. Just that it was a new product that Sterling has been testing for several years and getting ready to market."

"They only have one new product, and that is 57126. Everything points to that product."

"The puzzle is starting to come together. There must be something really bad about this product to make Peter risk his job and career to uncover. He loved his job at first, and in the beginning, he was sure that this was a 'for life' job."

"I think Peter was on to something."

"Are you're convinced that someone has been following you, Alex?" Cindy asked.

"Yes. I wasn't at first but am now. I must be getting close to something or asking too many questions. Maybe we are putting too much into what is happening or have read too many mystery books. But my gut tells me something is going on, and I won't rest until I know one way or the other. It may be nothing at all."

"That is the same feeling that Peter had. He told me he felt something was wrong but couldn't put his finger on it. He was too much of a scientist to brush it off, even if it was nothing. He had to be sure. And now I have to find out for sure for Peter's sake," Cindy said.

"I think I would have passed being followed as coincidence until you told me that we were being watched when we met at the coffee shop. And then someone searched my office last week, probably looking for the documents you gave me. Probably the same guy who has been following us. We know he works for Sterling."

"Mr. Blue Shirt?" Leslie asked.

"Yes, I think the same guy is following Cindy and me, based on your description the other night," Alex said, looking at Cindy. "At first I think they were just watching me, to see how I worked and if I had the same curiosity as Peter. I think their curiosity increased after the incident at the farm and my continued inquiry about the environmental impact document. And then that fact that Mr. Blue Shirt saw you pass me some documents at the coffee shop."

"Do you think our phones are being monitored? In this day of electronics, everyone knows everyone's business."

"I have a company phone, so I'm sure they are monitoring my calls. That is why we called you from an outside phone."

"Do you think that my home phone here is bugged? Peter thought we might."

"Probably not. They probably just monitored Peter through his company phone and saw no reason to do anything to your phone. But who knows."

Leslie just sat there listening, taking in everything.

"They have no idea what is in the envelope you gave me, but they have to believe that Peter found something and you passed it on to me last week. However, didn't find anything we can prove in the papers you gave me. But since they are concerned, there must be something they are afraid we know."

"So where do we go from here?" Cindy asked. "This isn't going to go away."

Alex thought awhile, and Leslie and Cindy just sat there waiting, knowing that he needed some time to think.

Alex broke the silence. "So what do we know or think we know? One, Peter might have been murdered because of what they think he found; two, it all points to the new product, 57126, that is to go into distribution in the spring; three, there must be something wrong with the product from an environmental point of view since those documents are missing; four, they think we have information about the product; and five, there might be some connection between 57126 and pyrethrum poisons. Is there anything else?"

"Six, they know that you have the documents that Peter had," Leslie added. "And seven, if Peter was murdered because of what he knows, you might be in danger."

"Pyrethrum poisons? What's that?" Cindy asked.

"Pyrethrums are a class of organic chemicals that are used in insecticides. They are similar to a natural product found in chrysanthemums. They are used to kill all types of insects, both good and bad. It is also poisonous to fish and other water creatures, so it isn't used around water. Usually they aren't harmful to humans unless ingested and in large amounts. And they are more dangerous to younger children and older people."

"Didn't you say that with your college friend only his daughter and father were affected?" Leslie asked.

"You're right. This is another indication that pesticide poisoning might be involved. The doctor did say the test showed that they had been poisoned with a pyrethrum poison. Also, Diane and Mark showed low levels of pyrethrum poison in their blood, so they also came in contact with the poison."

"What are you talking about?" Cindy asked.

Alex told Cindy about what happened to his fraternity brother's family recently.

"I just had a thought." Alex took out his personal cell phone and made a call.

"Hey, Mark. This is Alex. I hope everyone is back to normal. I just want to follow up and see how everyone is doing."

Pause.

"That's good to hear. As promised, I'm following up with our conversation, and I want to have all the facts. Can you tell me what symptoms your daughter and father had before they went to the hospital and also when they were in the hospital?"

Alex listened for a while. "Thanks, Mark. I'll let you know if I find anything. Give another big hug to that daughter of yours for me."

Alex turned to Leslie and Cindy. "He said they had fever, nausea, stuffiness, and stiffness. All of these are symptoms of pyrethrum poisoning. But lots of things have these symptoms. This is just another piece of the puzzle."

"So what do we do now?" Cindy asked.

"Let's list the people who we think are part of this scheme or whatever it is or might have knowledge of 57126 and its effect on people or the environment."

"I can only think of two: Mr. Blue Shirt and Mr. Gianti," Leslie said. "I don't know about your boss, Alex. From the expression on Brianna's face, I don't think she knows anything. If there are any documents, then my boss, Mr. Clark, has to know. He is in charge of Marketing."

"I would add my boss, Gene Matthews, and Rachael Phillips from R&D to that list."

"What if Rob is also involved someway in the cover-up and that is what the closed meeting was all about the other day? I can't believe he is, but should we add him to the list?" Leslie asked.

"That is a stretch. Why would they involve an assistant in this? What does he have to gain?"

"I don't know, but I don't think we should count him out," Leslie said.

"Okay, that's a total of six people," Alex counted. "That's a lot of people. There has to be documents of some sort that have been passing back and forth. I'm sure there are no e-mails or text messages. They are too easy for someone else to get access. And since most of those people are on the sixty-first floor, any documents have to be there someplace."

"I'm sure they have all types of security on those documents, if they even have them," Cindy added. "We have no way to get them."

"That's not exactly true. I have access to the locked file room on that floor," Leslie interjected.

Alex and Cindy looked at her.

"Let me go see what I can find," Leslie said.

"Absolutely not, Leslie," Alex blurted out.

"It is the only way we can find if anything exists. I'll just go into the office this afternoon as if I'm going to do some work. I'll sit at my desk for a while working on a project in case security is watching. After a while,

I'll go into the file room and file some documents, and while I'm there, I'll see what I can find. It will just be a day of work. And if it is nothing, no one will care. What other options do we have?"

Neither one could come up with anything else.

"It is too dangerous, Leslie. I can't ask you to do that. There has to be another way."

"Alex, I'll be fine. The longer we wait, the more time they have to destroy any evidence, especially if they think we are on to them. As far as we know, everything might already be destroyed."

"I doubt if they have been destroyed. They have to still be around or they wouldn't be following us."

"Alex, I don't see any other way. Let her try it," Cindy added.

"Are there security cameras there?"

"There are cameras where I work, but none in the offices or the file room. I'll get in and out fast yet spend enough time so it looks as if I did come in to catch up on some work. I'll be okay. No one will be there Sunday afternoon. I can also go up on the private elevator so no one will see me."

"I still don't like it, Leslie," Alex said with concern on his face.

"I'll be okay, Alex. And anyway, what can they do? I'm just at work."

"Okay . . . but be careful and get out of there if you feel uncomfortable."

"Don't worry, I can take care of myself. So tell me what I should be looking for."

"We are only interested in 57126. There might be some documents from R&D. Look for anything on the effects of the product in relationship to the environment or anything harmful. We don't need production, marketing, or manufacturing information."

"I got it. Let me get on my way. Want me to call you when I'm done?'

"Let's not take any chance that our phones are monitored. Just go home when you are done. Cindy and I will be at your place waiting for you to return."

Leslie reached into her purse, took out a set of keys, and handed them to Alex. "Here are my house keys. Just let yourself in."

Alex rode down the elevator with Leslie. He wanted to stop her from going, but he knew she was determined to do this. "We'll see you in a couple of hours." He leaned over and gave her a quick kiss. "Be careful."

"I will. Wish me luck."

He watched as she left the building and walk to the corner. When she reached the corner, she turned and gave him a wave and was then gone.

Alex could only stand there and watch as she disappeared. He should not have let her go alone.

Alex headed back to Cindy's apartment by taking the stairs. Cindy was standing in the doorway.

"She will be okay, Alex. She is a determined lady," Cindy said.

"I know, but I'm concerned for her."

"Love does that to a person," Cindy responded with a smile.

"Yes, it does," Alex said, standing in the window, looking at the empty street below. *She will be okay*, he kept saying to himself over and over. *It is going to be a long day of waiting.*

CHAPTER 28

The subway train arrived at the station just as Leslie got down the stairs to the platform. It was about half full. She looked around to see if she recognized anyone following her or someone taking special interest. No one looked suspicious. Thirty-five minutes later, she arrived at the front door of Sterling Chemicals, the tall glass building looming above her on Park Avenue.

She took a deep breath as she entered the lobby, showed her employee pass to the guard on duty, and went directly to the executive elevator. The door opened; she entered and pressed the floor number followed by the code. The door closed and started up. The first part of her journey was over.

Leslie knew that there were cameras watching the floor. She needed to make sure it appeared that she was here to catch up on work. She went to her desk, turned on her computer, and pulled out some papers that she had placed in her desk drawer and then pulled out some more documents from her inbox. Turning to her computer, she pulled up a program and started working. To anyone watching, it would appear that she was doing normal work.

The office was cold because of the air-conditioning. Leslie had a sweater on the back of her chair. She put it on and buttoned it in the front. She had another purpose for this sweater other than keeping warm.

She got up and went to the restroom, looking around to see if anyone else was working today. She looked into the breakout room and the empty offices and conference rooms. She was alone. She waited a few minutes in the restroom and then headed back to her desk and did some work that she had left on Friday.

After about thirty minutes, she sent a few documents to the printer and walked over to get them.

She then entered her boss's office as if she was going to leave the documents on his desk. She knew there were no cameras in his office. His desk was totally void of any documents.

Leslie picked up his phone and wrote down the codes for the file room and for his personal file cabinet in the file room. There was another code there that she didn't recognize.

Returning to her desk, she started going through a pile of documents, putting them in order for filing. She put several documents on top and behind that a number of blank pages to make it look like she had a lot of documents to file.

Walking to the file room with the stack of documents, she entered the security code. She casually looked around to again make sure there were no cameras in the file room. She figured she would have ten to fifteen minutes to find any documents. She quickly filed the few documents she had on top of the pile and put the blank pages in the paper tray of the copy machine. She entered the code she found on the bottom of the phone in the computer and heard her boss's file drawer click open. As she pulled the drawer open, she noticed an empty coffee mug sitting on top of the file cabinet. There was a chip on the rim of the cup. It had a college team logo on the side. No time to wash cups today.

Leslie looked at her watch. She had about nine minutes left. The top file drawer contained correspondences by department. She pulled out the one marked R&D. There were several folders inside this folder, each labeled with a product number. She quickly scanned the files, grabbing the one labeled 57126. She then saw a folder marked SECURITY in bold letters. Inside that folder were other folders, each with a label. She scanned the folder and pulled out three folders and added them to her pile, mentally noting where she found them in the folder. Nothing else in this drawer was of any interest. Six minutes left.

She opened the second drawer. This drawer contained product information by product name. It was easy to find the file marked 57126. It was too thick to take the entire folder. She pulled it out and started going through the documents, pulling out a few. Only three minutes left.

She opened the third drawer. This contained documents on current products. She closed that drawer and opened the bottom file cabinet drawer. This drawer contained personal letters about her boss and letters about other people in the office. She saw one labeled Leslie Sherwood. Quickly looking in that file, she only saw her resume and salary information. No need for that file. She looked at her watch. One minute left. There was nothing else in this drawer. It was time to go.

She shut the file drawer and made sure the cabinet was locked. Unbuttoning the top button of her blouse, she put the files inside, buttoning the sweater in front to hide the documents. She left the room, checked to make sure the door was locked, and walked back to her desk, covering her chest as much as she could with her arms.

As she sat down at her desk, she realized that the other code she found under the phone was probably for her boss's private file cabinet in his office. Did she dare go in a second and see if there was anything in that file? She had to risk it. She entered the office and opened his private file cabinet. She found one folder marked 57126. There were only a few documents in the folder. She quickly removed them, took them to the printer, made a copy, and returned them back to the file cabinet. Stepping back, she looked around the room to make sure that everything was exactly as it was when she entered.

She returned to her desk and worked about fifteen more minutes. It was difficult with all the documents she had hidden under her blouse pushing against her chest. She turned off her computer, got up, pushed her chair under her desk, and headed to the elevator with the documents still against her chest. She had been there almost an hour.

Just as she approached the executive elevator, she heard it start descending to the first floor. Someone else was coming, and she didn't want to be caught here. She quickly ran to the front elevator and pushed the bottom. She watched the numbers on the elevator above the door, hoping it would come directly up so she could get on before the executive elevator door opened. She felt panic mounting and her breathing getting shallower.

Finally the elevator arrived. She jumped in and pressed the button for the first floor, stepping to the side to hide as much as she could. Just as the door started to close, the executive elevator door started to open. She pushed herself against the side wall, hoping not to be seen by anyone getting off the executive elevator. But as a result, she was not able to see if anyone was on the other elevator. The door opened in the lobby, and she walked quickly toward the front door, the documents still in her blouse. The guard at the front desk was on the phone. She gave him a wave as she continued toward the revolving door. She didn't look back.

She walked quickly to the subway, down the steps to wait for the train to arrive. She kept looking at the steps to see if anyone she recognized followed her. In the distance, she saw the lights of the train approaching. The train stopped, and she got on again, checking the stairs. She gave a sigh of relief as the doors closed and the train started. As the train left the station, she saw him descend down the stairs to the platform . . . Mr. Blue Shirt.

Had he been following her, or was it a coincidence that he was there? Or was it someone who looked like him? She started to shake. She had been so careful and hadn't seen anyone in the office or anyone following her.

Leslie got off the train at her stop and quickly walked home. As she turned the corner of her street, she looked back and didn't see anyone behind her. She rang the bell to her apartment. She waited, but there was no answer. A little over two hours had passed since she left to go to the office. She had given Alex her keys, so she had no way to get in. She rang again, hoping Alex would buzz her in. Still no answer. She buzzed again. There was still no answer. Maybe Alex wasn't there yet. Where could he be?

She started to panic. Where was Alex? She was just about to ring the neighbor to let her in the building when the front door opened, and Alex was standing there. She was so happy to see him that she fell into his arms. He could feel her trembling, so he held her tightly.

"I should not have let you go," he said. "Are you okay?"

"I am now that I am home."

He walked her up the stairs to her apartment, and he sat her down on the sofa, sitting next to her, holding her hand. She continued to tremble.

"I should never have let you do this," he repeated. "I've been here the entire time worrying about you."

"No, I had to do this. There was no one else who could have gotten into the files without being noticed."

Alex held her hand. They were still shaking.

"I'm glad I'm back. Thanks for waiting, Alex."

"You should have seen him, Leslie. He paced the floor like an expectant father," Cindy added.

Leslie didn't even notice that Cindy was in the room. She was sitting at the dining table, a magazine on the table in front of her.

"Did you find anything?" Cindy asked.

Reaching into her blouse, she pulled out the documents and put them on the coffee table in front of her. Her hand was shaking. "I grabbed a bunch of documents. I have no idea what's in them or if they are what you want. I just wanted to get out of there. But I might have been seen. I'm not sure."

"What do you mean you might have been seen?" Alex asked, looking into her eyes. He saw fear for the first time on her face. He moved closer to her and held her hand even tighter. She continued to shake. "Take a deep breath and sit back. Tell us what happened."

Leslie went through everything she had done to get the documents, being careful not to be seen by any camera. She told them about the executive elevator and seeing who she thought was Mr. Blue Shirt on the subway platform.

"From what you said, I don't think he saw you in your office area. And if he did, you were there working. You did well, Leslie. But I'm also glad you're home," Alex added to assure her.

"I'm fine. Okay, let's see if anything I brought back is what we are looking for. I didn't have a chance to look at any of the documents. I just pulled folders."

Alex picked up the folders, and they all moved to the dining table and laid them out.

"Let's do one folder at a time together in order to get three opinions of what we find."

Alex pulled the folder marked R&D. He opened the first document and started reading. "There is nothing here that we don't already know." He moved to the next and the next. Cindy and Leslie sat back and watched as he went to the documents, one at a time. All of a sudden he sat up, and there was a look of concern on his face.

"Now here's something that doesn't look good." He continued reading. Leslie and Cindy leaned forward, waiting for him to continue.

"What is it, Alex?" Leslie asked.

Silence.

Alex put several documents down and sat back in the chair, looking at the table in deep thought. More silence.

"What did you find, Alex?" Leslie said.

No response.

"Alex?" Cindy interjected, trying to get him to tell them what he found.

"Sorry. I was just processing. I found the environmental impact statement. It was in one of these folders. There were some other documents that were more important in this folder as well. I was just processing."

"What did you find?" Cindy asked.

"Most of the documents in the folders describe the test results done in the greenhouse and the farms showing how effective 57126 is on plants.

Things we already know. The other documents talk about the financials, production, distribution, and marketing surrounding 57126."

"So you found nothing that can help us," Cindy said.

"That's not exactly true," Alex said, picking up a red folder. "I found some very interesting documents in this folder."

He was holding the documents that Leslie had found in her boss's office.

"I found a copy of the environmental impact statement that was filed with the government two years ago. But it is not true. It says that all types of tests have been done on 57126 and the product is safe to the environment and to people. But I found no evidence of any research when I looked through the marketing files, and my boss gave no indication that any test had been done. I'm convinced now that nothing has been done and reports sent to the government are false."

"That is why you and Peter had never seen the document," Cindy said. "It is a fake, and they knew that you two would have recognized that it was false or at least ask to look at the test results."

"There were some other documents in the same folder as the environmental impact statement that report some things that are not documented in any files that I have access to," Alex said.

"What did you find?" Cindy asked, looking at Alex and then at Leslie.

"We know that the product does a damn good job. In fact, all the research that I have seen shows that it kills every insect that is exposed to it, except one . . . the mosquito," Alex replied.

"That's good, isn't it?" Leslie asked.

"That wouldn't be an issue, if that was the only problem," Alex replied, looking first at Leslie and then at Cindy.

Alex continued. "One document in this folder describes a test that was done in a research lab in Charleston. The results speculate that the mosquito actually takes in the product and synthesizes it into a weak form of pyrethrums. Although the pyrethrums are used in insecticides and used to kill insects, this weak form does not kill the mosquitoes. This research was conducted by Dr. Rachael Phillips herself. So she is aware of this phenomenon."

"How is that a danger to the environment? Many products currently being sold contain pyrethrums," Leslie asked.

"That's true, Leslie. But it is not sprayed over large areas of crops. And the skin protects the body if the product gets on the skin. That is why it can be used in bug sprays with no problem."

"I feel you have some other concern, Alex?" Cindy said.

"Not only does the product kill all the bugs on food crops but also doubles the crop yield," Alex started. "Imagine doubling the food supply and killing all harmful bugs with just one product. Think of the value of this product to the company that develops it. We are talking millions of dollars of profit for that company in the United States alone. Imagine if it went worldwide. That could mean tens of millions of dollars of profit, especially for a company that is having financial problems. Increased food supply will also cause decreased prices for the consumer. Everybody wins."

"That sounds good, isn't it?" Leslie asked.

"Yes, that would be great, if that was the only issue."

"What do you mean?" Leslie replied.

"There is no proof here, but what about this scenario. The plants are sprayed in the field. Mosquitoes somehow get exposed to the chemical, walking on the plants, being sprayed, in the water or some other way. The mosquito then converts 57126 to a weak form of pyrethrums, but not strong enough to affect them."

"If it is a weak form that does not kill mosquitoes, how could it hurt a human?" Leslie asked.

"They bite a person and transfer the pyrethrums in their saliva. The dose is so low it doesn't affect the person. Eventually the body will destroy it. So it is not a problem.

"But what if a person gets lots of bites from lots of mosquitoes over a short period of time? It then accumulates in the body faster than the body can destroy it. Eventually it reaches a level where the person gets sick. The person has essentially been poisoned by the mosquitoes."

"Could that have been the source of the poison from your friends?" Leslie asked.

"There is a strong possibility that could have been the cause for them getting poisoned," Alex answered.

"But why would only those two got sick and not everyone?"

"It would affect children, the elderly, and people with compromised immune systems faster."

"Any of that documented there?" Cindy asked.

"No. I'm just speculating. But my fraternity brother's daughter and father were taken to a hospital because of pyrethrum poisoning. And Mark, his wife, and his mother had low levels in their system. There was no poison found on their farm. But their farm was right next to the land leased by Sterling that is testing 57126 on a variety of crops. Mark said his daughter and father both started getting sick while on a picnic. A picnic they had to move indoors because they were being bitten by lots of mosquitoes."

"But wouldn't this eventually come out?" Leslie said.

"It might, but what if Sterling or someone at Sterling is betting on the fact that it won't? It looks just like the flu, and eventually the person gets better. The body would destroy the poison, and everyone would be fine. Remember, you have to be bitten by lots of mosquitoes over a short period of time. I suspect that eventually the poison would be compromised in the mosquito, so they would no longer be a threat. And if that doesn't happen, the adult mosquito only lives about two weeks, so the cycle would end then. So that further diminishes the risk."

Alex looked at Cindy. "Peter was on to this. That was the meaning of the message I found in my desk drawer and also in the notes that you gave me."

Cindy looked at Alex with a look of final comprehension on her face. "Peter told me he was going to talk to his boss about his concerns. Then shortly after, he had a heart attack."

She paused.

"He didn't die of a heart attack. They killed him," she quietly said to herself.

"That's a possibility, but we have no proof. That is a scenario, no evidence."

Leslie reached over and grabbed Cindy's hand. She could see she was shaking.

Cindy looked up at Leslie and then over to Alex. "That means that we may all be in danger if they suspect that we know something."

"That's right, Cindy. This product is too important to the company. They have spent lots of money on it, and it will bring the company out of financial ruin. It is like a miracle drug, with side effects."

"I can see why they want to take it to market," Leslie added.

"But there is something else that I found in these documents that is far worse than the mosquito bites," Alex added.

CHAPTER 29

Leslie and Cindy sat there listening to every word that Alex was saying. It finally registered that what they knew or suspected had put them in danger.

"What are you talking about, Alex? What could be more dangerous than people being poisoned by mosquitoes?"

"That is the immediate danger. But I'm looking at the long-term effect of this product. This product could cause something that will happen after we are dead but could affect everyone on earth in the future."

Leslie and Cindy looked at each other and then returned their total attention back to Alex.

"Remember this new chemical is a miracle product for increasing yield. On every crop that it has been applied, the yield is two to three times the normal. Think of the profit for farmers and the savings for consumers. We could feed the world. And profit for Sterling in the manufacturing and distribution of this new insecticide or growth stimulant is astronomical."

"But if it is dangerous?" Leslie said.

"When it comes to profit over safety, profit usually wins. And remember there is no evidence of this. It is just speculation on our part."

"Leslie, do you have a computer? I want to check some facts that might support something that I remember from my college days."

Leslie went into the bedroom and came back with a laptop. She put it on the dining table and logged in to the network.

She got up, and Alex sat down at the table and started searching.

Cindy and Leslie just watched Alex work, not saying a word.

"Here are some facts. The three most important crops for feeding people are corn, rice, and wheat. An acre of corn produces about sixty bushels per acre, wheat is about sixty pounds per acre, and rice is seven thousand four hundred pounds per acre. Now double or triple that for each of those products and imagine the impact it would have on the world. And at the same time, it controls the insects that damage the crops in the field and in storage. Twenty to thirty percent of a crop is destroyed by insects before or after harvest."

"But you said there was a larger danger," Leslie said.

"Let me continue so you understand my reasoning and how I came to my conclusions.

"So here we have an insecticide that kills all the bugs and increases the yield of the product. Sterling wants to put this into distribution for next spring. Think of the money the company will make over the next five years and the money and bonuses the top executives will earn. And on top of that, countries around the world will be able to feed their people."

"Yes, it will help the world except for the mosquito part," Cindy repeated.

"But remember that is only our speculation and Peter's as well. So I started thinking. There must have been something more they were worried about that we might uncover to have us followed. The mosquito problem isn't that important."

"So what else could it be?" Leslie asked.

"Looking through the documents, I found one letter from R&D that bothers me."

"What did it say?" Cindy said, leaning toward Alex.

"Again, let me preference this by saying there is no proof, just what I interpreted. The letter intimated that plants that have been sprayed with 57126 take in less carbon dioxide than plants that haven't been sprayed. The plants that have been sprayed also take in oxygen and convert it to water internally. Thus, they have a constant supply of water, and this might be one factor that leads to the increase in yield."

"How is that a problem?"

"There is a balance between plants and animals for the use of oxygen and carbon dioxide. Animals breathe in oxygen and exhale carbon dioxide. Plants do the reverse. They take in carbon dioxide, convert it to chlorophyll, and give off oxygen as a by-product. So it is a nice cycle. Plants and animals support each other."

Alex continued. "We know we are in a battle with nature with global warming caused by all the cars and factories that are pouring carbon dioxide into the air. We have some control over these, and we will eventually solve the problems with new technology. But we have no control over how plants use carbon dioxide and oxygen."

Alex could see that what he said started to register with Leslie.

"So what you are saying is that the balance between plants and animals can be affected," Leslie said.

"That is exactly what I am saying. So we fix the factories and cars, but the plants keep competing with us for the oxygen. About 30 percent of the earth is covered with plants. What if they start competing with us and take the oxygen from the air that we need? The atmosphere contains about 20 percent oxygen that we use. If that drops to somewhere between 15 and 19 percent, we start feeling the effects. It will cause less concentration, reduced coordination, increased pulse and breathing rate. Imagine a surgeon under these conditions or someone driving a car?"

"That would be scary."

"These changes would take place over a long period of time, and maybe they would be solved. But what if this product also changes the makeup of the plants? We don't know what will happen then. What if all the plants start using the oxygen too and the concentration eventually goes below 15 percent? At 10 percent, people would start being unconscious, and some would die. And also remember, the population is growing, thus using more oxygen. Do we want a life where we have to run around wearing oxygen masks all the time? Again, I am speculating, but if I have concerns, I'm sure others would have concerns too, and we need to be absolutely sure before the product is introduced into our environment."

"But what if you are wrong and this could be a wonder product?" Leslie asked.

"I read the environmental impact statement that was submitted, and there is nothing in there that says there is a problem in regard to oxygen consumption or mosquitoes converting the product to pyrethrums. Since the effect is long term, they probably decided not to include it in the documents. And there is a low risk in regard to the mosquitoes hurting anyone. Probably no worse than people who get sick and die because of allergies to aspirin. They are betting on the fact that nothing will happen."

"If that is the case, why did they keep the documents that show the effect on the oxygen? Wouldn't it have been better for them to destroy them?" Cindy asked.

"They probably thought that no one would find them and only a limited number of people knew about it. And the documents were locked up," Alex said.

"Well, they underestimated you and Peter," Leslie added.

"I guess the people behind this cover-up were hoping that over time the problems would go away or someone would find something better before it became an issue. The planet wins, the company is saved, and they all get their bonus. It keeps coming back to money as the driving force of this cover-up," Alex said.

"You are probably right. They all want their big bonus at the risk of the rest of us," Leslie stated.

"Also," Alex continued, "no one knows the long-term effects it might have on the plants. Maybe it is irreversible."

"If you are right and it can't be reversed or a solution is not found, they are putting all of us at risk," Cindy added.

"I'm not willing to take that chance," Leslie stated.

"And if it is a long-term effect, they will all be dead before anyone discovered it. All they want is their bonus money and save the company. Let the next generation or the one after that clean up their problem. That is a stupid reason for not doing anything," Cindy said with anger in her voice.

"As you said, when it comes to money or doing something good, money usually wins," Alex said.

"I wonder if Peter came up with the same conclusion," Cindy said.

"I'm not sure he had enough time to come to this conclusion, but I feel he was on the same track and would have eventually gotten here. Remember, he didn't have someone upstairs to get the documents. We had an ace in the hole with Leslie. He was a smart guy."

"Thank you, Alex."

Alex could see a tear forming in Cindy's eyes, not from sadness but from pride. Leslie put her arm around Cindy's shoulder.

"Something else comes to mind. When I was at the research farm, I remember walking through a field of corn that had been sprayed with 57126. I found myself breathing extra hard to get oxygen at that moment. Once I left the field, my breathing went back to normal. I didn't think about it at the time, but now it makes sense. Also, a couple other farm workers had experienced that and reported it. But no one followed up on it. The mentality is 'Let's just bury it and hope it goes away.'"

"But what if we are wrong?" Leslie asked.

"I hope we are wrong. But my gut tells me differently. Do we want to take that chance, putting profit before safety?"

"That's the way the world works," Cindy stated.

"I know that, but I can't live with that if I feel something is wrong and there is no evidence to the contrary. Maybe I'm just too cautious or naive.

I joined Sterling because I thought they were doing something to help the world, not destroy it."

"That's a cynical statement," Leslie said.

"I know. But Sterling has the results, and they have to know that eventually someone would suspect them. Why don't they take the time now to find out for sure rather than rush into production? Did they think it would go away?"

"Maybe they thought that if it was in production and the world food supply increased, everyone would accept it and let it go. It is the same way they treated the automobile and factory emissions. We know it was a problem, but we lived with it. As you said, this won't happen right away but over time. Let the next generation worry about it. Just give me my bonus check," Leslie remarked.

"But we are the next generation. We didn't know the automobile was causing problems when it was developed. If we had, I'm hoping something might have been done back then. Here we are thinking that this product could cause serious damage. And we need to be responsible. Do we want to take the risk of possibly killing the earth and let someone else worry about it? Not me . . . I am that someone else."

"I agree with Alex," Leslie responded. "But what can we do? There are just three of us, and we have no evidence. As you said, all we have are speculations."

"Let's look at what we do know. There are several reasons why I feel the mosquito and environment factors are real problems for Sterling management, and they know about it but are willing to hide it. One, if there wasn't something wrong, why were we being followed? Two, why were they after Peter when he probably came to the same conclusions, conclusions that may have been responsible for his death? Three, why did they hide the environmental impact statement from both of us? Four, why are none of these facts enclosed in the Environmental Statement? Five, two of my friends got sick from what we think might be pyrethrum poisoning from mosquitoes transmitting the poison. Six, my breathing was labored when I entered a field of corn that had been sprayed with 57126. Anything else to add?"

Cindy and Leslie looked at each other and then back to Alex.

"I believe that they know about the potential of this product being dangerous, but they don't care. In fact, they are hiding evidence to justify their position," Alex added.

"But as you said, Alex, there is no evidence, just supposition. Could this all be just a coincidence? Maybe we aren't seeing everything. Maybe there are other tests that have been done to disqualify what we think. Don't we have to trust those in charge to make good, sound decisions?" Leslie questioned.

"I really hope you are right, Leslie," Alex responded with hesitation. "But right now, I can only go on the evidence we have."

There was a moment of silence.

Cindy broke the silence. "So what do we do now?"

"First of all, I need to get these documents back into the file cabinets before anyone realizes they are gone. I can go into work early tomorrow morning and put them back in the file room, and no one will be the wiser. I remember exactly where each one went," Leslie said.

"Yes, we need to get those documents back on place. Just be careful and don't take any chances."

"If I go early enough, no one will be there. I'll be okay."

"I'll try to see if I can find anything else that will shed some light on this situation, one way or the other. Maybe we are overlooking something that will solve this entire problem," Alex added.

"Alex, please be careful."

"Please don't either of you take unnecessary risks," Cindy added.

"Don't worry about me. Let me give you the same advice," Leslie said.

"We don't know what we are working with or who is involved. My advice is not to say anything to anyone. We don't know the extent of this cover-up if that is what it is. And, Leslie, don't take any chances. Get those files put away and then forget about it. Promise?" Alex stated.

"I promise."

"Let's all exchange cell phone numbers and keep in touch if we find anything else."

"That is a good idea," Cindy added.

They gave each other phone numbers, Alex making sure that he gave them his personal cell phone number, not his work one.

"Well, I better get going. After all, I am a working girl," Cindy said. "And I think you two would like some time alone."

"Thanks for your help, Cindy. I hope that I'm wrong about what happened to Peter. Are you going to be okay?"

"I'm fine, Alex. You've given me a reason to go on."

Cindy turned to Leslie and gave her a hug.

"Cindy, if you ever need to talk or need company, please give me a call. I can be on the next train," Leslie said, looking into Cindy's eyes.

"The same goes for me too," Alex added.

"Thank you, and let me offer the same to you," Cindy replied.

Alex opened the door for Cindy to leave, and as she passed him, she turned and gave him a hug.

"Thanks for caring so much, Alex." She pulled away and looked up at him and then turned to Leslie. "Thanks, Leslie. I'll see you soon." With that, she left, and Alex shut the door behind her and walked over to Leslie. He pulled her to the couch and sat down next to her. He felt her shaking, so he reached over and put his arms around her.

"All of a sudden this has become so real. Alex, you may be in danger. What do we do?"

"Right now we do nothing. We just go back to work tomorrow as if it is any other day. This may go away."

Alex held her tightly and could feel her shaking slowly stop. They sat quietly for a moment on the sofa, just taking in each other's presence. But then a new sensation started. Alex leaned over, pulling Leslie to his chest, and kissed her hard on the lips. She gave no resistance but returned the kiss and held on to him tightly. He felt her nipples get hard against his chest. Alex pulled back and looked into her face. "Are you sure you want to do this now?"

"Yes, Alex, I do, very much. I need to be close to you."

"How can I say no to such a beautiful woman?"

"You've been through so much, and right now you are my hero."

"No, Leslie, what you did today makes you a hero in my book."

She pushed herself from him, stood up, and took his hand and led him into the bedroom.

An hour later, they were lying in each other's arms, Leslie's head nestled in Alex's neck, his arms around her.

"We can't spend the rest of the day in bed, although it does sound like a good idea. But tomorrow is a workday, and I need to get back to my place. Can I take a shower before I leave?" Alex asked.

"Only if I can join you," Leslie responded.

"I'll race you to the bathroom."

They both jumped out of bed and headed to the shower. Leslie got in first and got the water nice and warm. Alex pulled back the curtain and joined her. They spent the next thirty minutes washing every part of each other's body.

They stepped out of the shower, dried each other off, and then got dressed. Leslie hung on to him so as not to let him get dressed.

"You are such a temptress, but I do need to get home. I have laundry to do or won't have anything to wear to work tomorrow. But I'll take a rain check." He hoped his excuse didn't sound lame, but he needed to go home and think through what is happening and what his next steps should be.

"How many women have you used that excuse to leave?"

"You're the first," he said as he kissed her on the nose.

They finished dressing and then walked into the living area. Alex walked to the table where the documents were spread out, covering most of the table.

Alex turned toward the table. "I wish I could take these documents with me, but you need to get them back before someone realizes they are gone."

He turned to Leslie. "Be careful tomorrow. Make sure no one is watching."

"I'll be okay. I'll go in to work forty-five minutes early, before anyone else gets there. Meet for lunch?"

"I'll be at our table at noon," he said with a smile. "Thanks for everything, and I mean everything," Alex said with a wink. "I'll see you tomorrow." He walked over to her, took her in his arms, and then gave her a kiss.

"This is for luck." He kissed her again. "This is for me." He then turned and walked out the door, looking back one last time.

Leslie stood alone in the center of the room, looking at the closed door. So much had happened over the past two days. *Was Sterling responsible for Peter's death? Should we be worried? There is no evidence that 57126 is responsible for any of this. Could it be just a coincidence, or is there something really here?*

She sat on the sofa and started to shake. It all became real now; this was not a game.

"No, I can do this," she said out loud to no one in particular.

CHAPTER 30

As the elevator came to a stop on the sixty-first floor, Leslie stepped out and looked around. She wanted to get the files back before anyone noticed that they were missing. She didn't see anyone. As she walked past her boss's office, she heard him in there talking on the phone, his door closed. He always came in early, so it was no surprise that he was there. Right now her mind was on getting the files back into the file room. It was good that he was busy. It would give her a chance to return the documents and get back to her desk without being seen.

She also noticed that Mr. Gianti's office door was shut, and he was in there talking to someone. She couldn't see who was there, but the tone of his voice didn't seem happy.

She punched in the code for the file room and entered. Again, she was alone. She quickly put away all the documents in the same place she had retrieved them and slipped out of the room and back to her desk. She gave a sigh of relief.

She got up to get a cup of coffee to start her day when she heard the elevator open. Brianna stepped out and headed toward her desk. As she passed Leslie, she uttered a monotonic good morning.

"How was your weekend, Brianna? Did anything special?"

"Stayed home" was all she replied as she sat at her desk and started work.

Just then the door opened from Mr. Gianti's office, and Mr. Blue Shirt came out. Leslie watched him as he walked to the glass wall and left without looking back. Leslie turned back to her desk and started work. She felt someone behind her; and when she turned, she saw her boss standing there, holding a cup of coffee. Leslie noticed the cup and realized it was the cup that she saw in the file room yesterday, the one with the chip.

"Can I talk to you a minute, Leslie? Come into my office."

Leslie followed her boss into his office and sat in the leather chair opposite his desk. He sat in his chair, placing the coffee mug on the desk to make sure that Leslie could see it.

"I understand you came in this weekend and did some work."

"Yes, I did. I knew you were leaving town in two days, and I wanted to get caught up so I would be available if you need me to get things ready for your trip."

"That is very commendable, Leslie. I have been watching you and noticed that you are very accurate in your work and seem to enjoy your job and the people here."

"Thank you, sir, I do like it here very much."

"I think it is about time you see more of the company and how it works, especially in the areas that I am responsible. Mr. Gianti suggested you accompany us when we go to Charleston this week. That way you will have an appreciation of the R&D and manufacturing arms of the company. We are heading there on Wednesday. When you make reservations for my trip, make some for yourself. I'd like to have you meet and talk to the people there. Work with Barb for plane and hotel reservations."

"Thank you. I would appreciate that. It will be nice to see the people I actually talk to on the phone or send e-mail."

"Keep up the good work." With that, he picked up the phone as an indication that the meeting was over. She got up and left his office. Leslie walked over to Brianna's desk. Brianna looked up at her as if to ask, "What do you want?"

"Your boss suggested that I go to Charleston to see the R&D facilities this week when he and Mr. Clark travel here. I'm so excited. Can you recommend a hotel so I can tell Barb?"

Brianna looked surprised and just said no and went back to work. Leslie returned to her desk, surprised at the negative response Brianna gave her.

"What was that all about?" Rob asked.

"Mr. Clark wants me to go to Charleston and see the facilities and meet the people there. I've never been to West Virginia, so this will be a fun trip. He said Mr. Gianti suggested it."

"He likes to make sure that his people meet everyone they work with. He likes to think of all of them as family."

"Have you ever been there?"

"In all my years here, I've never been asked to go anywhere. I guess you got the luck of the draw." Rob turned back to his desk and picked up the phone to make a phone call.

Alex was ten minutes early to work. He was glad to get off the subway. Being packed like sardines in a car that has little air-conditioning isn't a good way to start the day. Everyone around him was complaining about how hot it was. Well, it was July, what can you expect.

The subway was crowded, but so was the elevator as it made its way to the forty-second floor. When the door opened, he pushed his way through the crowd and made his way to his office. There he sat down and stretched his legs and relaxed, glad to be alone with no one around him.

As he sat back in his chair, he started to think again about all that happened this past weekend. Did he miss anything? Was he overreacting? Did he read something into something that wasn't there? But he always came back to 57126, and something must be wrong with it. But there was no evidence to support his theory, and without any type of evidence, there was nothing he could do. Was Peter's death really the results of him asking too many questions, or did he really have a heart attack? If so, is he in danger? What a way to start a new job. Is there anything he can do to get the company to delay the introduction of 57126 so they can study the effect on the environment more?

He could hear people coming to work and moving to the coffee room to get their caffeine fix. He got up, closed this office door, and picked up the phone. He dialed a ten-digit number and sat back waiting for someone to answer.

"Sterling Research Farm, Don Brown here."

"Hi, Don. This is Alex from corporate."

"Good morning, Alex. How is everything in the Big Apple?"

"Just another hot Monday morning."

"What can I do for you?"

"I've been going over the results of the data that you and the other farms have been sending me. I have a few questions about the methodology you are using. I saw some of the procedures when I was there but wanted to follow up to make sure I didn't miss anything. Just want to make my reports complete."

"Fire away."

"When you apply the chemicals, do you spray all the crops with all chemicals on the same day?"

"Yes, we prepare the chemicals in the morning and spray in the afternoon. Each chemical has its own spray canister so we don't have a chance of contamination, and we have them color coded. In each test, we spray three concentrations of each chemical. That way you can see the results of different application rates."

"So everything is sprayed by hand? The guys walk up and down the rows spraying the tops of the plants?"

"Yup, that is the only way we feel we can get an even concentration on all parts of the plants."

"I assume also you don't spray on windy days."

"If the wind is more than ten miles per hour, we don't apply the chemical."

"What do you do when the plants get so tall, above the waist when it is hard to spray?"

"At that point we use the tractor and go up and down the rows. But the critical time for the plants is when they are young. When they get older, they tend to take care of themselves, and the chemical is still there. Corn is really the only crop that we spray by tractor."

"And the data is collected on a scheduled basis?"

"Yes, we sample all crops for both pests and growth. At harvest time, we keep track of yield by crop."

"How protected are the workers when they apply the chemicals?"

"I tell them all to wear long-sleeved shirts, but on hot days, they don't always adhere to that. But they always wear gloves."

"Any face masks?"

"No, R&D assures us that there is no danger in the chemicals that we are testing, so no masks are required."

"Are the employees tested in any way to make sure that the chemicals aren't in their bodies? That is just as important as the efficacy of the chemicals. We have to make sure they are safe to humans."

"Yes, we try to run urine tests a couple of times during the season to monitor if there are any residual chemicals in them. But between you and me, we don't follow the rules here. We only test if the employees complain about not feeling well."

"Have you found anything?"

"We've never found anything."

Alex was writing this down. Now it was time to ask the questions that led to this phone call in the first place.

"Has anyone complained of anything or discussed changes that they have noticed while working with the chemicals?"

"What kind of changes are we talking about?"

"Has anyone complained of experiencing headaches more than usual or being nauseous? Or feeling tired after applying the chemicals or while they are working the field? Any breathing issues that they were aware of? I'm really interested to see if they experience changes in the field compared to when they are not in the field. We just want to make sure that we are aware of any effect these chemicals may have on a person."

Don answered but didn't answer the questions asked. "We assume that anything that has been sent to us to test is safe under field conditions. But we do take some precautions to protect ourselves. Things like no spraying on windy days and always wearing long-sleeved shirts and gloves. And they are not allowed to wear shorts even on hot days."

"But has anyone mentioned anything out of the ordinary to you?"

"That is a strange question to ask. What is behind that question?"

"I'm just trying to cover all bases. Since these products will be eventually going to market, I just want to make sure that everything is okay and the company isn't open to any lawsuits."

"I remember a couple of times that some of the farm workers complained of shortness of breath after taking samples from the crops. But that was probably due to the workload and hot weather."

"Did anyone follow up on it?"

"It seemed to go away after about an hour, so we thought nothing of it."

"Do you remember how many times it happened and where they were when it happened?"

"I would only be guessing, but probably five to six times. If I recall, it happened shortly after they were working in the tall crops. Should I be worried about anything?"

"No, I'm just following up. Do you remember what product was used on the tall crops?"

"Hang on."

Alex heard some talking in the background. Don was talking to the farm workers.

"I asked Jose and Max, and they think it happened mostly when they were taking samples from corn that was sprayed with 57126. As I said before, it was probably due to being tired and the hot weather, and it went away over time. We always take samples from corn last, so we are winding down. Also, it is tough walking through the rows of cornstalks."

"Did any other strange things happen to any of the workers?"

"That is all they recall. Is something wrong, something I should be worried about?"

"As I said, I'm just following up. I had a great time while I was there, and again, I want to thank you for showing me around. Give my regards to everyone." With that, Alex hung up the phone.

Sounds like the same feeling that he had when he walked through the corn rows that had been sprayed with 57126. His heavy breathing might have been because of less oxygen in the air around him. That just further confirmed what Alex speculated was happening.

But how could he stop it? He felt that no one would listen to him or wanted to listen to him. Too much was at stake for the company. He can't go to his boss with this since it is only a hunch. And if there is a conspiracy, his boss might be in on it. After all, he did meet with Mr. Gianti and Mr. Blue Shirt right after he called him.

He got up, opened his door, and tried to get some work done. But he could not concentrate on the numbers in front of him. There was a knock on his door. He looked up to see his boss standing in the doorway

"Hi, Gene. Come on in."

His boss entered the room and sat in a chair across from him.

"I've read some of your analyses and am quite impressed. The information is clear and concise. It is well written, and the data supports your conclusion in a way that no one can question the results of our test and field trials. Good job."

"Thanks, Gene" was all he could say.

"I know you have been asking for the environmental impact document."

Now he was going to find out about the document. "I just want to make sure that we have all the necessary documentation before we go into production. And also that we meet all the guidelines set by the Department of Agriculture, EPA, and NEPA. We don't want this to come back and bite us in the ass later."

"You're right. We don't want that to happen after the fact. Not only would it delay our planned introduction, but it would be costly to the corporation."

"That is what I want to avoid too."

"Since we can't seem to find it here at corporate, I think you should go to Charleston this week and talk to the people there. They should have what you want, and it will also give you a firsthand look at our operations. You've already met Rachael Phillips. I'll give her a call and let her know that you are heading there and to set up some meetings and tours."

"That's a good idea. It will be good to meet and talk to those people involved with our products, especially those responsible for the first round of testing in the greenhouses. I'd also like to spend an extra day and get a tour of the production facilities."

"Take whatever time you need to see everything. It is always good to understand the entire process from the chemists who develop the products to those in the greenhouse who screen them out and decide which ones to continue testing. And then see the manufacturing process. After all, you are a key person in the product development cycle helping us decide whether or not the product is really worthwhile to move to production and market. And keep in mind that hundreds of millions of dollars ride on your recommendations. We need to make sure we take the right product to market. We owe that to our shareholders."

With that statement, Gene got up and left the room.

What did Gene mean by that last statement? Should Alex put aside his suspicions and help bring 57126 to market, thus bringing profit to the company and shareholders? Or should he keep it from going to market until further research has been done, thus saving the company millions of dollars of potential lawsuits? And did Gene know that there were potential problems with the product? Who actually knew what is going on?

Every question led to more questions. Alex just sat back in his chair with question after question going through his head. Maybe his trip to the research center in Charleston would clear some of this up.

He looked at his watch and realized it was time to meet Leslie for lunch. Finally there was a bright side to his stressful morning. On the way to the elevator, he stopped by Lindsey's desk and asked her to make his plane and hotel reservations for his trip to Charleston, West Virginia.

CHAPTER 31

When Alex stepped off the elevator, he saw Leslie standing there looking as beautiful as ever. He was anxious to find out if she got all the documents back okay.

"Have you been waiting long?"

"I just got here."

"Good, I'd hate to have you wait for me."

"Don't worry, I wouldn't," she said, nudging Alex in the stomach at the same time.

They both got their lunch and headed to a table close to the windows.

"So how did it go this morning?"

"Everything went fine. I got to work early before anyone was here. I put all the documents back without anyone knowing."

"So no one saw you?"

"No one was around. Everything is back where it started."

"That's good."

"When I got here this morning, my boss was already here. That is not unusual. He normally gets here before anyone else arrives. Mr. Gianti, Brianna's boss, was also in early. I heard him talking to someone in a loud voice, so I knew I had some time to get the documents back before he noticed I was there. When I got back to my desk, he was still talking. But soon after that, his guest left. You will never guess who he was talking to."

"Who?"

"Mr. Blue Shirt."

"I don't trust that guy."

Alex followed Leslie through the lunch line, both getting a sandwich and moving to an empty table.

"Guess what? I'm going on a trip," Leslie said, changing the subject. "Mr. Clark wants me to accompany him this week when he goes to the production plant in Charleston. That will be exciting. Meeting all the people I talk to or send things to. It will also be a chance to see how the products are made."

"That's great. My boss asked me to go to Charleston this week too and talk to the people in R&D. We should try to get on the same plane. Maybe we can share a room and save the company some money."

"I doubt that, Alex. I think they would frown on that. But that doesn't stop us from maybe staying in the same hotel and having dinner together," she said with wink.

"Lindsey is making my reservations for me. Have you made yours yet?"

"No, I haven't. I was going to talk to Barb this afternoon and get her to help me."

"Don't do anything until I talk to you. I'll find out from Lindsey after lunch where I'm staying and call you. You can then check to see if we can stay at the same hotel. And maybe even get an adjoining room with a door connected them."

"You horny devil."

"Nah. I just like being with you. But if something unexpected happens, who am I to go against nature?"

Leslie looked up, and there he was—Mr. Blue Shirt leaning against the wall, looking their way. Just then he took out his cell phone and answered it. He hung up and immediately headed to the exit door at a fast pace.

"Don't look now, but our friend was standing by the entrance checking us out, or so it seems. He took a call on his phone and then immediately left. Sends shivers up my spine. He is starting to scare me."

"You are spending far too much time on Mr. Blue Shirt. He isn't worth the time," he responded, trying to get Leslie to feel at ease. Alex wanted to look, but he didn't want to frighten Leslie. He was concerned about all the attention Mr. Blue Shirt was giving them. He continued on with his sandwich.

"I talked to the farm manager this morning in North Carolina. I wanted to find out if any of the employees or hourly people were experiencing any unexpected health issues, like headaches or feeling nauseous."

"And are they?"

"He told me that some of his workers expressed trouble breathing after they walked through a field of crops that had been repeatedly sprayed with 57126. Sounded like the same reaction I got when I was there. But once I got out of the field, my breathing returned to normal. He told me they had the same results. I didn't want to alarm him but told him I was just following up to make sure that all the products they are using are safe and meet US standards. Part of the report I'm required to complete for new products."

"Did he show any concern or worry about his workers as a result of what he told you or that you had some concerns with the product?"

"No, I think he was okay with my purpose of the call," Alex said.

"What if the product is causing breathing issues? Won't that just get worse as it is used more?"

"There is no evidence of that, but it is a good point. I feel that the chemical itself isn't causing any direct problems. It is just that we are competing with the plants for the oxygen when we are around those that have been sprayed. As I said yesterday, it is the long-term effects that I'm concerned about. But we have no proof of it or evidence that it is happening."

Leslie sat there listening to every word Alex said. She barely touched her lunch.

Alex continued after taking a bite of his sandwich. "I wish there was a way that I could go back to the farm to take another look at the product. But I think upper management has decided to go on with it and hope for the best. After all, it means a lot of money for the company and to them personally in bonuses. I think they believe they are home free."

"Can't you go to your boss?"

"Go with what? I have no proof. It is just a feeling and bits and pieces here and there. If we only had some concrete information or something that links to the death of Peter, then we would have something. And what if my boss is hiding the truth too?"

"Alex, you scare me when you talk like that. Are you in any danger?"

"Don't worry. I can take care of myself. Since I know something is wrong, I am very careful. They don't know that we have seen the information. Don't worry about me."

"But I do worry. It is my nature."

He could see the concern on her face. He smiled back at her, hoping it would assure her that she doesn't have to worry. "I only wish we had a copy of the documents we saw." He turned back to his lunch, looking at his sandwich but not eating it.

"Alex, I have a surprise for you."

He looked up. "What is that?"

"I have a copy of the documents. There is a copy place close to where I live, and they are open early in the morning. Before I came in this morning, I made copies of everything. They are at my place."

She could see a look of excitement come over his face, followed by a look of concern.

"Don't worry Alex, they are in a safe place."

"I'm not worried about the documents. I'm worried about you," Alex said.

"Like you said . . . I can take care of myself too."

He reached across the table and grabbed her hand and mouthed, "Just be careful."

"I just had a thought," Leslie said.

"What is that?"

"I wonder what role Mr. Blue Shirt might have had in Peter's death. I wonder if he was in Canada at the same time Peter was. Is there any way we could find out?"

"That's a good thought. Let me think about that," Alex added.

They finished their lunch and headed out of the cafeteria. Mr. Blue Shirt was no longer standing at the entrance. As they headed toward the elevator, Alex noticed him standing down the hall on his cell phone. The elevator doors opened, and they both got in. As Alex turned around to face the elevator doors, he noticed Mr. Blue Shirt looking at him. The door closed, putting a wall between them.

As Alex entered his office, he saw his itinerary and plane tickets on his desk. Picking them up, he called Leslie and gave her his flight and hotel information.

"Make sure to get adjoining rooms with a connecting door," he repeated.

"You are bad!" she responded.

"How about we have dinner tonight?"

"I'd love that. Can you come to Brooklyn and we'll go from there? I have some things to do after work. Seven o'clock work for you?"

"I'll be there at seven with bells on."

"No bells please. See you later. Bye, Alex."

Alex hung up and went back to work. His mind kept going back and forth between work and what he learned this morning and discovered this weekend. Five o'clock finally arrived. He packed up and left the building to get home, looking around to make sure he was not being tailed.

He showered, got dressed, and headed to the subway. He arrived at Leslie's door a little before seven. He rang the bell and waited. No answer. He rang the bell again. No answer and waited. He started to worry when he heard the buzzer to the door. When he got to her apartment, he found the door open. He walked in, shutting the door behind him. Leslie was sitting on the couch staring up at him with a look of fear on her face.

"What's wrong?" He walked over to her, sat next to her, and put his arm around her shoulders. She fell into his chest and started to shake.

"Someone broke into my place while I was at work."

Alex looked around. Everything looked in place. "Are you okay?" He put his arms around her and held her close to him. "Can you tell me what happened?"

"When I got home, I found that the papers on my desk and in my desk drawers were all messed up. I'm very organized, so I know that someone had been here looking for something specific. Nothing else had been touched."

Alex thought, The documents!

"I had nothing of any importance. I had a few dollars in the drawer, and they were still there. Nothing else in the apartment seemed to be touched that I know of. I looked all over, and only the desk was touched."

"Leslie, did you have the copies of the documents in your desk?"

"No, I told you I had them in a safe place."

"Do you still have them? Did you check?"

"No, I haven't checked, but I know they are safe."

Just then there was a knock on the door. They both looked at the door. "Who could that be? I wasn't expecting anyone."

Leslie got up and opened the door.

Leslie gasped and took a step back.

CHAPTER 32

"May I come in?" Brianna asked.

"Of course, I'm just surprised to see you." Leslie stepped back to let Brianna enter.

"Thank you."

"Brianna, do you know Alex? He also works at Sterling."

Alex had gotten up when Leslie opened the door. When he heard the name Brianna, he stepped back, away from the sofa, looking in the direction of the door.

"I know him by name only." Brianna walked over to Alex and put out her hand. "It is nice to meet you, Alex."

"It's nice to meet you too, Brianna. I've heard a lot about you." Alex wished he had not said that, but it was too late.

"I'm sure nothing good. I know my reputation around the office."

"Have a seat. Can I get you something to drink? I don't have much but can offer you a soda or some juice."

Brianna sat on the sofa, moving all the way to the end, sitting erect, her hands in her lap. Although appearing calm, Leslie could sense that something was bothering her.

"Water would be fine, if it isn't too much trouble."

Leslie brought a glass of iced water to Brianna. As she handed it to her, she noticed that her hand was shaking.

"Would you like something, Alex?"

"I'm fine, Leslie, thanks."

Alex sat in a chair opposite Brianna, and Leslie sat at the other end of the sofa. Brianna was still looking straight ahead. She held the glass in her hand but didn't take a drink.

"I'm surprised to see you here. We never really talked at work. In fact, you seem to be standoffish. Is there something wrong at work that would bring you here?"

Brianna looked over at Leslie and then turned toward Alex. She took a drink of the water, put it on the glass coffee table, and turned back to Alex. Alex and Leslie waited for some type of response.

"Rumor has it that you are concerned about a new product that Sterling is about to manufacture."

That's Brianna, right to business.

"Why do you think that?" Leslie asked.

"I've been in some meetings when the new product is discussed, and in most cases, Alex's name is brought up. That seemed strange that they even knew who you are. You are so new to the company."

Alex noticed that Brianna was being very careful in her choice of words, not giving very much information.

"What kind of meetings?" Alex asked, wanting to find out what was said and who was there.

"Staff meetings, executive meetings, talk in the hallway. Just bits and pieces of information I've picked up."

"What kind of concerns do they think that I have about the product?"

Brianna took a drink of water and put the glass back on the table then looked back at Alex. "That you feel the product could be dangerous and you want more testing done."

"Anything in particular led you to this conclusion?"

"I heard Mr. Matthews say that you are obsessed with finding the environmental impact statement. It seems that you have asked everyone for it. And I also heard something about people getting sick and in the hospital. I don't know if that has anything to do with the product. It was just part of the conversation."

"It is only natural that I would want to see that document," Alex interrupted. "After all, it is part of the package needed to submit for approval by NEPA. I have been asking for it, but no one seems to be able to put their hands on the document. My job is to analyze the data about the product and make recommendations to management on its potential. Part of my recommendation has to include the effects of the product on the environment."

There was silence. Alex continued to stare at Brianna.

"That is not enough for you to come all the way out here," Leslie added. "There has to be more."

More silence.

"What else? Something that was said or something that you sensed that brought you here? From what Leslie has told me, you two aren't exactly friends," Alex said.

Brianna looked at Leslie. "You're right. But in my defense, I'm not really friends with anyone at work. I like to keep my business life and personal life separate."

"So why are you here?" Alex asked.

"I didn't know how to contact you without raising suspicions. I know that you have been seeing Leslie, so I thought if I talked to her and told her what I suspect, she would contact you. It is good that you are here so you can hear firsthand what I have to say. Believe it or not, I don't want anyone to get hurt."

"What other things did you hear?" Alex asked.

"I think management is worried that you will cause a delay in the introduction of the new product into the market. There is a lot of money involved with this product, not only for the company but huge bonuses for the executives. They don't want that put in danger. I think that is what the conversation around you is all about."

"Aren't they concerned about how the product will affect people and the environment? Isn't that the company's motto? Are you here to try to convince me that everything is okay and persuade me to stop asking questions?" Alex asked.

"Don't underestimate these executives. When it comes to money, especially when it affects them personally, money comes first. I've seen some strange things over the years I've been there."

Alex was silent. He was wondering if he should tell Brianna what they found and their suspicions. But now is not the time.

"How do we know we can trust you? Maybe you were sent here to find out what we know since, as you say, they are concerned about what I know," Alex said.

Brianna took another drink of water and then looked at Alex. "Security has a suspicion that some documents were taken from the private file cabinet and Leslie has them. I believe that someone might be sent here to see if you have them."

Alex looked at Leslie. She had a look of surprise on her face as she looked at him.

"Why do they think that Leslie would have taken some documents?"

"Someone from security saw her in the office yesterday. He checked the file room and noticed that one of the drawers was slightly open. He put two and two together."

"Couldn't it have been left open on Friday?" Leslie said. "Did security tell you that he suspected me of taking some documents? Is anything missing from the file room?"

"No, he didn't tell me, but Mr. Clark mentioned it to me. He said he heard that you were in this weekend working. He thought that was admirable of you since you are still very new to the company."

"That still doesn't explain why they think I took some documents," Leslie added.

"There's more. I stayed around at lunch today to get some work done. Tony Neuman showed up to talk to Mr. Gianti. He didn't look happy. The door was shut, so I couldn't hear what they were saying. I can assure you though that it wasn't a polite conversation."

"Who is this Tony Neuman?" Alex interjected.

"Oh, I thought you knew who he was. Until today I thought he was part of the company's security staff. Security rarely comes up to the floor. And if they do, it is usually only the director. But the past weeks this security person has been coming to see Mr. Gianti on a regular basis. I'm sure you've seen him on the floor, Leslie."

Leslie now has a name for Mr. Blue Shirt—Tony Neuman.

"Yes, I've seen him several times but didn't know his name." She looked at Alex, and he gave a look that he also realized that Tony Neuman and Mr. Blue Shirt were the same person.

"Meetings were always behind closed doors," Brianna said. "I didn't think anything of it at first. But when I see the same person here several times, I started to get curious. He seemed to know his way around the floor too. He had the security codes to get through the glass doors. That information was only supposed to be known by those who work on the floor. Sam Hanson, director of security, is the only other person who knows the codes. I have a good relationship with Donna Holland, so today I asked her about Mr. Neuman. She told me in confidence that he was hired by Mr. Gianti as a consultant."

"You find that unusual?"

"Tony's office is in the security area of the building, so I assumed he was part of the security team at Sterling, yet he is a consultant."

"So did anything cause you to question why he was hired?"

"Not at first. I thought maybe he was hired as a security guy to protect Mr. Gianti. After all, he is a VP of a large corporation. I also assumed that Mr. Gianti gave him the codes to the door and elevator."

"That makes sense," Leslie said.

Brianna looked at Leslie and continued. "But I didn't understand why he would be given the codes to the file room. He has no need for anything in there. Any files Tony needed he could have gotten through me. And why would Mr. Gianti need a security guy and no one else in the company has one, including Mr. Sterling?"

"That's interesting, but let's go back to the original question . . . why do they think Leslie took some documents?" Alex asked.

"Today while I was working during lunch, Rob's phone rang, and he immediately got up and went into Mr. Gianti's office without even knocking. He just walked in. While the door was open, I heard Tony say, 'I think she took some documents for him.' Then the door closed, and I didn't hear anything else. A little bit later, both Tony and Rob came out and took the executive elevator down."

"So why do you think they were talking about Leslie?"

"She is the only other female on the floor. And I know that you two are good friends, so I just put two and two together. Also, the fact that she was in the office this past weekend led me to think they were talking about her. And I don't know why Rob would be involved anyway. He doesn't work for Mr. Gianti."

"Well, I don't have any company documents here, Brianna," Leslie blurted out. "And I think Tony was in my apartment this afternoon. When I got home from work, I noticed things in my desk had been ransacked through."

"I'm sorry, Leslie, are you okay?" Brianna asked.

"I'm fine, thank you. Alex came by to be with me."

Alex thought he could now trust Brianna with some information.

"It is true, I do have a suspicion that something is wrong with 57126, and it could be harmful to people and the environment if we release this product now. Unlike them, I'd like to solve the problem before anyone gets hurt. We have to be responsible to our environment. But I have no evidence. It is just my gut feel. But I'd rather be safe than sorry."

"Believe it or not, I'm very concerned with what is happening to our planet. On weekends, I volunteer at the parks picking up trash and replacing dead plants."

"That's so commendable, Brianna. I would never have thought that of you. You don't come across that way at work."

"As I said, I keep work separate from my private life."

"What else? I sense there is something else you want to tell us," Alex interrupted.

"As I said, Tony Neuman has been up to the floor many times this past week. Prior to this week, I hadn't seen him up there for months."

"Are you saying he was there prior to the past two weeks on a regular basis?"

"Yes, I remember seeing him there six or seven months ago. I started to think when I had seen Mr. Neuman before. His visits started a few weeks before Dr. Hudson went on vacation. And again he had the security codes and just walked in. We change the codes often on that floor to prevent people from coming up who shouldn't be there and because of the company confidential documents stored there."

"So did anything cause you to question Tony's presence?"

"I know that Dr. Hudson was asking questions about the new product. He kept pestering management about more research on the product and recommending that the company postpone any introduction. He was sending all types of e-mails about his concern with the product."

"How do you know that? Did you see the e-mails?" Alex asked.

"Yes. When you work with these people for as long as I have, you tend to notice changes in their movements and personalities when things aren't going their way. There seems to be the same type of activities going on now that I saw happening when Dr. Hudson was questioning the product."

"What does all of this mean to you?" Alex asked.

"I don't think they trusted Dr. Hudson and underestimated his tenacity to find the truth. With what I found in my boss's office, I'm sure he was being watched. Also, Mr. Neuman was hired only three weeks before Dr. Hudson's death."

Alex and Leslie looked at each other.

"Do you think that Tony had something to do with Dr. Hudson's death?"

"I'm not sure, but there are so many strange things happening right now. And they seem to be the same things I saw right before Dr. Hudson went on vacation. I also checked with Donna Holland and found out that Tony was out of the office the days that Dr. Hudson was on vacation."

Brianna turned to Alex and then back to Leslie. She opened her purse and pulled out an envelope.

"On Friday I worked late, and after everyone was gone, I went into my boss's office and looked through his private files. I had to see if my suspicions were right or if I am reading too much into what is happening. He has a locked safe in his inner office where he keeps important papers. No one knows the combination of the safe. However, a year ago he gave me the combination because he needed some information overnighted to him and it was in the safe. I think he forgot that I had the combination."

"What did you find in the safe, Brianna?" Alex asked.

"I found copies of e-mails and notes from Dr. Hudson stating that he was concerned with the release of 57126. He stated that he thought there were not enough studies done on the impact to the environment and to human health. He recommended that more studies be done. Then he had some chemical formulas written on a piece of paper that I didn't understand."

Alex looked at Leslie and back at Brianna. "Anything else?

"There was an e-mail from a bank in Miami showing three deposits of $50,000 to a company called Schafter Inc. I started to think to myself, why would he keep that locked up in his safe? It should have been in the regular files with all the other company financial documents. I looked up Schafter, and we don't have any dealings with any company by that name and address. The date on one e-mail was five days before Dr. Hudson and his family went on vacation. Another deposit was dated last week on Thursday for $50,000."

"And what did this lead you to believe?"

"With everything going on about this product, and all the security meetings, and this letter, I think it was money to have Dr. Hudson stopped. And also the fact that Tony was not in the office then."

"Oh my god. Do you think that is possible, Brianna?" Leslie blurted out. "That Tony killed Dr. Hudson?"

"I don't know. Maybe I have seen too many movies or my mind is running wild. But the direction he was going could seriously hurt the company and the huge bonuses the executives would get for the introduction of this new product."

"Why do you feel it necessary to come here and tell us this?" Alex asked.

"Until today, I wasn't going to say anything."

"What happened today to change your mind?" Leslie asked.

"I learned that you and Leslie are going to Charleston next week on a business trip."

"Yes, that's true," Leslie said.

I have been with the company for twelve years and have never been asked to go on a business trip. And here, only after a few weeks, Leslie has been asked to go to Charleston. I just don't want anything to happen to you two, like what happened to Peter. What better place than the mountains of West Virginia for something to happen. I think the recent $50,000 deposit might be for you and Leslie. I also talked to Barb and found out that she also made plane reservations for Tony for next week to go to Charleston. Am I being overdramatic?"

"It shows that you are human and have concerns for others. We thank you for that. But I think you are overreacting," Alex said.

"I made copies of the documents for you. Check them over and make your own decision. Just be careful. I better go." Brianna handed the envelope to Alex.

Brianna got up and headed to the door. Brianna opened the door to leave. She turned back to them. "Maybe you're right, too many gangster movies." And she was gone.

"What do you think, Alex?"

"I don't know. But Brianna seems concerned."

Alex moved to the window and watched Brianna walk down the street on her way back to the subway. She reached the corner by the deli and stepped off the curb. Suddenly, out of nowhere, a car roared down the street and hit her head-on and continued without even stopping.

Alex stood there wide-eyed, staring at the body lying in the street and not moving. People started running over. He saw several people on their cell phones.

"What's wrong, Alex?"

Leslie moved to the window and looked down the street to see what Alex was staring at.

"Oh no!" she cried out. "Brianna?" She grabbed Alex. Alex stood there motionless, staring out the window, holding on to Leslie yet not aware that he was.

More people entered the street. In the distance, he could hear sirens. But there was no movement from the body lying in the street.

Leslie looked down again, and they both saw him. There, standing in the back of the crowd, hidden in the shadows, a lone figure . . . Tony Neuman, Mr. Blue Shirt, a smile on his face.

CHAPTER 33

"Alex, do you see Tony? What's going on?"

"Yes, I see him standing there watching. But if he is standing there, who was driving the car?" Alex asked. "I have a bad feeling about this."

"Did he follow us here? Did he have anything to do with what just happened?

"I don't know, Leslie, but we can't take any chances."

They continued to watch while the police pushed the people back and started taping off the area of the accident. Leslie turned away from the window. Alex walked to her and took her in his arms. She was shaking. He had to force himself to be strong for her sake.

"Cindy! What about Cindy. We have to warn her," Leslie said, pulling away from Alex.

"I was thinking the same thing."

Alex took out his cell phone and called Cindy. After four rings, she picked up.

"Hello?"

"Hi, Cindy, this is Alex. I hope I didn't interrupt anything."

"Not at all. I just had my hands in dishwater up to my elbows. What can I do for you?"

Alex tried to keep his voice calm so as not to alarm her. But he also knew that she was a very strong woman and could handle this.

"I was just wondering if Leslie and I could stop by. We have a few things we want to discuss with you, unless, of course, it is too late?" Even if she said it was too late, he was going to insist.

"No, that's okay. I'll be here."

"Cindy, can I ask a favor of you?"

"Sure, what do you need? After all, I remember asking you to do something for me."

"Don't go out and don't let anyone in. I'll explain when we get there."

"That sounds serious. Is something up?"

"It is too much for me to explain over the phone. I'd rather do it in person. I'm at Leslie's place now. We'll grab a cab and get there as soon as we can. Please just do what I ask."

"Okay, Alex, see you both soon."

Alex hung up the phone and turned to Leslie. "We need to leave now. I want you to go pack a bag. You're staying at my place for a couple of days. I don't want you here alone. And I won't take no for an answer."

Leslie looked at Alex with an "I don't understand why" look and then turned and went to her bedroom. Alex could hear her opening and closing dresser drawers.

Leslie walked back into the room with a suitcase in hand.

"You said you had copies of the documents you took from the files. We need to take those too."

Leslie put down the suitcase and went out the front door. Alex followed her and stood in the doorway. He saw her talking to the neighbor across the hall. The woman had white hair, a pair of steel-rimmed glasses resting on the end of her nose as she looked over the top. She appeared to be in her sixties. She turned and went into her apartment. A few seconds later, she reappeared with an envelope and handed it to Leslie. "Thank you for holding on to this for me."

"Anytime, dear. Is that your boyfriend? He looks very nice."

"Yes, he is." Leslie turned and walked past Alex, handing him the envelopes. "Here they are, safe and sound. And they were not in my apartment as I said."

"Do you have everything you need for a couple of days? We won't be coming back here for a while."

"Yes, I've got what I need."

"Is there a back door out of here? I don't want Tony to see us leave."

"Yes, we can get out through the basement. It has an exit on a side street."

Alex picked up the envelope and put it in his knapsack next to the documents Brianna brought. "Let's go."

Alex picked up the suitcase and held the door open; and Leslie walked past him, leading the way down to the basement, through the laundry room, and out the door to a courtyard that was below street level. They went up a set of stairs, through a tall black iron gate covered with barbed wire, to the street. Alex looked up and down the street and, seeing that no one was around, headed to the far corner, made a left, and went to the next block.

He hailed a cab, and they got in quickly.

"I don't think anyone saw us." He gave the cabdriver the address, asking him to drive five to six blocks before circling back to catch the access to the bridge to the city.

Leslie grabbed Alex's hand, and they rode in silence, ever vigilant of cars around them. Not a word was said until they got close to Cindy's apartment. "Drop us off at the next corner on the right side," Alex instructed.

They were two blocks from Cindy's place. He wanted to walk the rest of the way to see if they were being followed. They rounded the first corner, and Alex quickly pulled Leslie into the doorway, hidden by the shadows. They waited to see if anyone turned the corner. When they were sure they were not being followed, they continued on down the street. At the next corner, he did the same thing. Turning the corner, they quickly went into a drugstore, watching out the window from behind the shelves.

No one came around the corner. They watched a little longer. Alex grabbed Leslie's hand. "Let's go. Everything looks fine."

Alex took out his cell phone and called Cindy. "We are around the corner. We will be right there."

They walked to Cindy's apartment. The doorman told them to go up. Cindy was standing in the doorway.

Alex engaged the deadbolt on the door and joined Cindy in the living room.

"You two look anxious. Are you okay?" Cindy asked.

"We have more information," Alex said. "A person who works with Leslie stopped by this evening and brought us some documents that she had taken from Sterling. I haven't had a chance to look at them yet." With that, Alex removed the envelopes from his knapsack and placed them on the dining table. He noticed Cindy's eyes staring at the envelopes.

"Did they kill Peter?"

"There is a good possibility that they did. Maybe there's something in these documents that will tell us for sure."

Cindy continued to stare at the envelope on the table. They all sat down at the table. Alex picked up the envelope and pulled out the documents. He turned to Cindy.

"Are you okay? Leslie, could you get her some water please?"

Leslie moved to the kitchen, found a glass, filled it with water, and brought it to Cindy.

"Brianna showed up tonight at Leslie's place while I was there. It was a surprise because she is not a friendly person at work. Brianna works with Leslie and is the assistant to the VP of Finance."

"That's true, Cindy. At work we call her the 'mean queen.' She doesn't talk to anyone and puts on a superior façade as if she runs the office and we all work for her. She probably hasn't said more than ten words to me since I started. And when she did talk to me, it was more of a command than a conversation. I was surprised that she even knew where I lived, let alone showing up at my door."

"What did she want?"

"What I took away from her meeting was that she was there to warn us," Alex said.

"Warn you?"

Alex pointed to the documents. "She brought these documents."

"She said that the envelope contained e-mails and letters from Peter that he was concerned about the new product Sterling is getting ready to launch. Basically the same concerns that Alex has been having," Leslie said, trying to bring Cindy up to date.

Cindy looked up at Alex. "Something else happened that you are not telling me. What is it?"

Alex looked at Leslie, not knowing if he should tell the rest. She nodded to go ahead.

"After giving us the documents, Brianna left, warning us to be careful. We watched her leave and walk down the street. As she reached the corner, a car came down the street, hit her, and sped away without stopping."

"What?"

"I think she was hit on purpose. We saw the guy who has been following you standing back watching what happened," Alex said. "We found out tonight that he was hired as a private consultant for Mr. Gianti. Also, he was not in the office the week you were in Canada on vacation."

"So Sterling is responsible for what happened to Peter and now Brianna?"

"Yes, I think they are responsible for both."

"I never really believed that Peter could have been murdered until now. I always hoped I was wrong. I didn't think anyone could do that to someone," Cindy said softly, as if talking to her herself.

"Don't underestimate anyone when it comes to money," Alex said.

Tears formed in her eyes. Leslie reached over and put her hand on top of Cindy's, trying to comfort her as best she could. Alex sat there, not knowing what to say. A moment passed. Now was not the time to look at the other documents.

"Let's see what else those bastards are capable of," Cindy said as if a command. There was now hate in her eyes.

Alex picked up the first document. It was a note written by Peter to Gene Matthews. He started to read out loud.

To: Gene Mathews
From: Peter Hudson

Re: 57126

I have been looking at the data from the results of 57126 and find that it has great potential as an insecticide. It appears to control all insects that affect our food crops, thus giving plants a chance to grow. At the same time it acts like a growth incentive for the plant to increase yield, not only more yield but at an earlier date, thus potentially allowing multiple plantings in a single year.

However, as good as this product is for crops, I feel it could have a detrimental effect on humans and should be further studied before released. The product has the potential of being converted to a pyrethrum based product. I surmise that a reaction with the mosquito saliva could change the product to pyrethrum poison. Pyrethrums are used in most household pesticides and insect repellants.

In low dosages however, the poison is not harmful to humans. It is also used for the treatment of head and body lice. Normally we get this product in low dosages on the skin which is a natural barrier, thus protecting us.

However, if the mosquito converts 57126 to a pyrethrum poison in its saliva, it would be injected directly into the blood stream when the mosquito bites.

A single or a few bites from the mosquito may have no effect. But what about multiple bites, or bites over an extended period of time. We need to find out if the body stores the chemical and if it accumulates over time. What is the effect on different age groups; i.e. children, adults, the elderly? Or on people with compromised immune systems?

I recommend that we postpone the introduction of this product until we have more information and the answers to these questions. I will continue to investigate the effects of this product to humans when used under field conditions.

Peter Hudson

"Peter essentially had the same concerns we have," Alex added. "He came to his conclusion based on the similarity in the chemical structure of the two compounds. The product needs more testing. He was just expressing his concerns and trying to protect the company's image. The same thing anyone would have done in his position. It is exactly what I was trying to do."

"It doesn't sound bad enough to have someone killed though," Leslie added.

"Let's see what else is in the envelope."

There were two other documents. Alex picked up the first one. It was a handwritten note written by Leslie's boss, Mr. Clark. It was not addressed to anyone.

> *Peter Hudson could be a real problem with the introduction of this product. The pyrethrum is not an issue. We can handle that with disclaimers. It is the other factor that could stop the product, damage the company financially, and prevent our large bonuses. Something has to be done to delay him from finding the real issue with this product until after it has been introduced and established in the marketplace. At that point we can do damage control if necessary. We have to keep expounding on the benefits. We may have to handle Peter the same way we did Dawn.*

"Who is Dawn?" Alex asked.

"Dawn was the person who had my job before me," Leslie said.

"Is she still with the company?" Cindy asked.

"She just stopped coming to work one day. No one has been able to get hold of her since she left. Her phone has been disconnected and e-mails sent back. Everyone assumed she just moved on."

"You said she worked for your boss before you, Leslie?" Alex asked.

Leslie was thinking out loud. "Do you think she found out something while working with Mr. Clark? Something that could hurt the company and they found out that she knew. And maybe she passed this information on to Peter? Could they be responsible for her disappearance too?"

Alex thought for a while. "It looks that way, Leslie. Remember the three deposits of $50,000 to the Miami bank? Could that be hit money to pay someone to get rid of Dawn, Peter, and now Brianna?"

"So their solution was to get rid of Peter and hire you to take the job. They counted on the fact that by the time you figured it out, it would be too late. They didn't know how tenacious you are. So now they are in a bind," Leslie thought out loud.

"Remember, there is a lot of money involved in this product."

"What hit money?" Cindy asked.

Alex pulled out the last document and handed it to Cindy. It was a letter from the Bank of Miami confirming three $50,000 transfers to a company called Schafter Inc.

"How could we find out who Schafter is?" Alex asked.

"Let me see the letter, Alex," Leslie said. Alex gave her the letter. "I can find out with one phone call."

"Cindy, do you have a neighbor who might let us use their phone so I can make a call?" Leslie asked. "I want to make sure it is on a safe phone."

"Yes, Mrs. Sester from across the hall would let us use her phone. It is a landline. She never got a cell phone. She has been very helpful since Peter's death and treats me like a daughter."

"It is nice to have someone like that in your life," Leslie said with a smile.

"Let's go see if she is still up," Cindy said, heading to the door.

Mrs. Sester was more than happy to let them use her phone. She enjoyed the company. Leslie took the phone first while Cindy and Alex talked to Mrs. Sester at the kitchen table over a piece of homemade cake.

"Hi, Daddy, it is me. I don't have time to talk right now, but I need to find some information for a friend. I hope that maybe you can help. It is about a payment made to Schafter Inc. from the Bank of Miami. I need to find out who Schafter Inc. is. It is very important for me." Leslie didn't tell her dad why she needed the information.

There was a pause. Leslie's dad was responding to her questions. Leslie gave him whatever information she could get from the letter.

"I need it as soon as possible, tonight if you can or first thing in the morning."

Another pause.

"This is really serious, Daddy, anything you can do tonight would be appreciated. I just need the name on the account, and anything else you can find without raising suspicion. No, there is nothing illegal about this. Remember I used to work for you."

Another pause.

"Thanks, Daddy. I'll talk to you tonight or tomorrow and promise to come up one weekend soon. I have someone I want you to meet." Leslie went into the kitchen. "You would be surprised how much information a bank president can get from another bank president."

"Excuse me while I make some calls myself." Alex left to use the phone while Cindy and Leslie entertained Mrs. Sester in the kitchen.

Fifteen minutes later, Alex returned. "Again, thank you, Mrs. Sester, for the use of your phone and the cake. It reminded me of home. We really appreciate it. I wish we could stay, but we need to go now."

They returned to Cindy's apartment.

"Okay. Let's review what we know or suspect. The product, 57126, is a good product but dangerous to the environment. Not only does the product change to a pyrethrum in the mosquito, but it depletes the oxygen supply. On the plus side, it will increase the world's food source. But long term, it has the potential to eliminate all animal life on earth."

"The executives are willing to take the risk because of the influx of money to the company as well as to their own personal bank accounts. They want to let the next generation worry about the long-term effects."

"So that is the premise of what we feel is happening. Do you both agree?"

Both Leslie and Cindy agreed.

"So let's list the people we think are involved or are part of the plot to keep the effects of 57126 a secret," Alex said.

Cindy got a piece of paper and pencil to take notes.

"Definitely Mr. Gianti, Mr. Clark, and Dr. Phillips," Alex replied.

"And of course Tony Neuman," Leslie added.

"We don't know how much Tony knows about the product itself, but we know he plays a major part in the cover-up," Alex stated.

"What about your boss, Alex? Do you think he is part of this?"

"My feeling is he doesn't know what is going on but is just an information gatherer for the others."

"I would also add Mr. Milton to the list with a question mark by his name. I know he was in some of the meetings, but no idea of his involvement," Leslie added.

"We also think that Dawn and Peter were killed as a result of what they uncovered or suspected. And Brianna is a victim, but we don't know her condition at this point. We heard the ambulance. She may have survived the hit and run."

"Can anyone think of anyone else?"

"Could Rob have been in on this as well? He has been in meetings with Mr. Gianti and Tony," Leslie added.

"Seems strange that they would have someone at his level in the company be involved in a scheme of this magnitude. What does he have to gain?" Alex replied.

"I'd hate to see the 'all-American boy' mixed up in this mess," Leslie added.

"Because we don't know who to trust at this point, let's not leave him out. You agree?" Alex asked.

No one said anything.

"Okay, add him to the list."

"There is one more person," Alex said. "We need to add the person driving the car that hit Brianna."

"What do we do now?" Cindy asked.

"First of all, I don't think any of us are safe in the city tonight, especially with what happened to Brianna. Cindy, go pack a bag. You will need about a week's worth of clothes. Casual and comfortable. We are getting out of town," Alex commanded.

CHAPTER 34

Rob exited the elevator on the sixty-first floor, coffee in hand. "New Jersey railroad had another glitch today. Train stuck in the tunnel. Everyone was complaining about being late for work. One of the headaches you have to face when you use mass transit."

"That is why I live in the city," Barb responded. "Brianna won't be here today, and Leslie left a voice message that she was sick and wouldn't be in. Only other person here is Mr. Gianti. Looks like it will be just the three of us today."

"Demon lady is not going to be here?"

"You haven't heard? She was in an accident yesterday and is in the hospital."

Rob looked surprised. "What happened?"

"I heard it on the news this morning as I was getting ready for work. Apparently she was hit by a car crossing the street and is in critical condition. The driver never stopped. Mr. Gianti had me send some flowers to the hospital this morning. He was very upset, more than I expected him to be. It seems like someone is hit by a hit and run every day in this city."

Barb thought she saw a look of fear on Rob's face. She watched as he walked back to his work area with his shoulders hunched over and his head down. Apparently Brianna's accident hit him hard.

Rob moved quickly to his desk, sliding in his cube, hoping not to be seen, his coffee still in hand. He turned on his computer and logged in. As he did each morning, he checked the morning news from New York on a local Web site. He wanted to see if there was any news about Brianna. But a different headline caught his attention.

STERLING EXECUTIVE KILLED IN FREAK ACCIDENT

Rob continued to read the news article below the heading.

A car was found in the Hudson River today. It apparently had gone over the edge of the New Jersey Palisades and into the river last night. No indication if the driver had either fallen asleep or lost control of the car on the many turns there. Sources tell us that the car was rented to Dr. Alex Gregory, who works for Sterling Chemicals. There is no information at this time if there were any other passengers in the car. No bodies have been found. Both New Jersey and New York police have been searching the river banks. This is the second employee from Sterling who was involved in an accident today. Earlier Brianna Welch was struck by a hit and run in Brooklyn. She was taken to Mt. Sinai Hospital. There is no information on her condition at this time.

Tony Neuman rushed past Barb and through the glass partition toward Mr. Gianti's office.

"Get your ass in here and shut the door behind you!" came an angry voice from within the office. He was looking sternly at the guy sitting across from him who was trying to hide in the large chair, his head bent forward, looking at the ground.

"So what went wrong? I don't pay you $50,000 to leave a person alive on the street. You guaranteed there would be no problems."

"She is unconscious and in a coma in the hospital. There is a good chance she may not recover. Let's just wait and see. I'll take care of it."

"You better. It deserves me right for getting someone who has never done this before. You guaranteed that there would be no problems. I hope the car can't be traced."

"The car can't be traced back to us. I 'borrowed' it for this accident."

"Let's check the twenty-four-hour news channel in my conference room and see if there is any update. They always have the latest information."

They went to the conference room and turned on the TV, hoping that there would be news about Brianna and that it would be good news. Good news for them at least.

The news commentator was talking about a fire in Brooklyn. They sat glaring intently at the TV screen. The announcer ended that story and continued on.

"We have an update on the accident that happened in the Hudson River last night. A rental car was found in the river early this morning. The automobile had gone over the end of the Palisades and crashed into the Hudson River. No survivors have been found. The police from New York and New Jersey are combing the riverbanks for signs of any bodies. But as of now, no one has been found. The car was rented to a Dr. Alex Gregory, who works for Sterling Chemicals. The rental agency reported that they saw three people in the car, a man and two women. We have tried to contact Sterling Chemicals to see if they would provide us with any other information, but all we got was a 'no comments' response. We will bring any update as we receive them."

Mr. Gianti looked at the guy sitting across the conference table from him. "Well, that's good news, saves me $50,000."

The news broadcaster continued on.

"Another employee of Sterling Chemicals who was struck by a hit-and-run driver last night in Brooklyn passed away early this morning without waking up. Her name was Brianna Welch. No leads on the driver of that vehicle. The police are investigating and treating it as a hit and run. If you have any information regarding this accident, please call the number listed on the bottom of your screen. Our condolences go out to the members of all the families. Sterling Chemicals is the manufacturer of food products, processing techniques, and chemicals to help increase the crop production worldwide. Now in other news . . ."

Mr. Gianti turned off the television. "Well, you lucked out this time and saved the company and me money. Now back to work."

"What can I get you?" the waitress asked as she stood in front of the booth in the restaurant.

"Coffee for starters would be great. Thank you."

The restaurant was almost empty, and only a few cars in the parking lot. A man walked into the diner and yelled to the waitress. "Hey, Beth, do you know who owns the pink Oldsmobile out front?"

"The guy in the booth." He pointed to Alex.

"Hey, bud, you left your lights on."

Alex turned around and looked into the parking lot. Sure enough, the headlights of the car were indeed still on. He had forgotten that older cars did not automatically turn off the headlights. He got up and went out to take care of the situation.

The coffee came, and Cindy and Leslie both took a sip. Alex returned and slipped into the booth next to Leslie. Hanging from the wall behind the counter of the restaurant was a television turned on to a news channel. Alex looked up to catch the news. Just then a new story came on about employees of Sterling Chemicals involved in an accident.

"I'm just so sorry about Brianna. I was praying that she would survive. She turned out to be a wonderful person after all," Leslie said.

"She was a great help to us, Leslie," Alex said.

Just then a video on the TV showed a black car being pulled out of the Hudson River.

"I guess we will never be found in the river," Alex said.

"What a good idea to stage that accident, Alex. But did you have to change for such an old car, and bright pink on top of it?" Leslie said with a laugh.

"Good to have one for now that is not registered. I'm glad Butch let me use it. Let's hope the next part of our plan works so we can get back to our normal lives."

Just then Leslie's phone rang. "Hi, Daddy. So do you have any information for me?" There was silence while she listened. All of a sudden her eyes went wide. "Thanks, Daddy. Love you. I'll see you in a few days." She turned to Alex.

"You will never guess whose name is on the Schafter account in the Miami bank."

Three days later and across the city on Eighth and Forty-first, a deliveryman entered the large building and asked for Mr. Walter Bratch at the reception desk.

"You can leave the package here," the receptionist said.

"I'm sorry, but I have strict instructions to leave the package with Mr. Bratch personally."

"His office is on the eighteenth floor. Just go up and ask for him."

The courier exited on the eighteenth floor and was directed to an office in the back corner of the floor. A nameplate next to the door read,

WALTER BRATCH
Editor In Chief

"I have a package marked urgent to be delivered to Walter Bratch," the courier said to the person sitting behind the large desk. "I was instructed to get an ID to verify that I have the right person and not to give it to anyone else."

Mr. Bratch pulled out his company badge and driver's license, showed it to the deliveryman, and then took the package.

As the deliveryman left the building, he turned around and looked at the large sign over the door.

NEW YORK TIMES NEWSPAPER

At the same time that package was being delivered to the New York Times, an identical package was being delivered to the New York City Police Department on Eighty-second Street.

Both packages contained copies of all the documents that Alex had, including his interpretation. The documents implicated Mr. Curtis Clark and Mr. Tony Gianti in the murder of Dawn Manning, Peter Hudson, and Brianna Welch in a murder-for-hire plot. It named Rachael Phillips and Tony Neuman as conspirators to hide company information that would be detrimental to the environment and also coconspirators in the death of Dawn, Peter, and Brianna.

There was also a letter from the Miami bank and the name of the person on the Schafter account, a person who was paid $150,000 to orchestrate the murder of Dawn, Peter, and Brianna. The name on that account was Rob Schimel, an assistant to a senior executive at Sterling Chemicals. The 'all-American boy next door' had a dark side. He was probably the driver of the car that killed Brianna and instrumental in the deaths of Dawn, Peter, and Brianna.

And last was Mr. Tony Neuman, a private consultant somehow involved in the murder-for-hire scheme.

Three people were killed to help a company out of financial ruin and give the huge bonuses to senior management, without any concern for the environment or the effect on all human life.

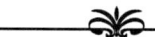

SPECIAL THANKS

I would like to give special thanks to Cynthia Chew and Rita Ng for their help in proofing this manuscript several times. Without their help and input, this book may never have reached publication.